10-07-15
$35.00

D1452466

WHERE A GOOD WIND BLOWS

This Large Print Book carries the
Seal of Approval of N.A.V.H.

WHERE A GOOD WIND BLOWS

PHIL MILLS, JR.

THORNDIKE PRESS

A part of Gale, Cengage Learning

GALE
CENGAGE Learning·

Farmington Hills, Mich • San Francisco • New York • Waterville, Maine
Meriden, Conn • Mason, Ohio • Chicago

GALE
CENGAGE Learning

LIBRARY OF CONGRESS CATALOGING-IN-PUBLICATION DATA

Mills, Phil, Jr.
    Where a good wind blows / Phil Mills Jr.
        pages cm — (Thorndike press large print western)
    ISBN 978-1-4104-8235-8 (hardback) — ISBN 1-4104-8235-9 (hardcover)
    1. Ranch life—Nebraska—Fiction. 2. Large type books. I. Title.
PS3613.I5697W47 2015
813'.6—dc23   2015018882

Published in 2015 by arrangement with Cherry Weiner Literary Agency

Printed in Mexico
1 2 3 4 5 6 7 19 18 17 16 15

ACKNOWLEDGEMENTS

Any effort to put thoughts to paper in some measure of logical and readable order must nearly always involve someone else. Such is the case with "Where A Good Wind Blows".

Thank you Cowboy Mike Searles for your encouragement, editing skills and friendship.

Thank you Melody Groves for reading my manuscript and making important suggestions.

Thank you Kelly Phillips for your excellent editing skills.

Thank you Major Mitchell and Shalako Press for your great support.

Thank you Karen Borrelli and Todd Aune for the great cover artwork.

Thank you Lynn Pisar for your support and encouragement.

Thank you to various members of my family who took the time to read early drafts and offer constructive comments.

Thank you to my wife, Linda, who was forced to listen as I read various chapters and excerpts, always followed by my asking "what do you think?"

Finally, for all those men and women who even today continue to shape our image of the American West and those who still dare to dream of wide open spaces, vast prairies and rugged mountains, I thank you and may a "Good Wind Always Blow".

This book is dedicated to my family and friends without whose support and encouragement this project might never have been completed.

Phil Mills, Jr.

CHAPTER 1
EVIL COMES CALLING

Angry, shifting firelight fought for space in the early morning blackness. Bright flames burned away the darkness, driving away the deepest of shadows and all pretense of night.

Fire bathed the scene with a soft orange glow. Ever-shifting flames provided the brush strokes on a canvas of destruction. Smoke with its choking smell made real what otherwise seemed like a nightmare, surreal and abstract.

A rising crescendo of crackling sounds and crumbling timbers climbed into the night silencing even the mournful coyote. A mixture of orange-hot embers rose on ever-present winds to die away, disappearing in the fringe that still defined night. Dark yellow shadows and long black silhouettes reflected against still unblemished ranch structures.

Buildings that had stood against time and nature on this vast Wyoming prairie now felt the heat of death. And, on this lonely, isolated outpost of humankind, the demons of hell came calling. They rode in on horseback.

Breaking glass and gunfire shattered the otherwise silent darkness. And, the night echoed with the sporadic sound of men yelling and shooting. Bullets tore into the ranch house walls, sending torn and splintered wood in all directions.

Glass jars stored on kitchen shelves exploded into a thousand tiny pieces and their contents spilled across the floor.

Rolling from his bed onto a hard plank floor, the old man instinctively sought cover next to his bed frame. Pinned down and for the moment unable to reach his own rifle, the man felt helpless against the barrage of gunfire. Fear, had it been an option, was overwhelmed by the man's rising anger.

Outside in the black darkness that comes just before dawn, he could hear men shouting. They taunted him with the courage of men nourished by whiskey and numbers. He was out numbered and out gunned. These men wanted him dead.

Rifles roared again and once more the onslaught was followed by laughter. This wasn't the laughter of picnics. No, this was sick laughter. This was a prelude to evil. For deep in the dark shadows of night, the clarions of death sought to claim a victim.

Frightened horses with eyes wide and blood streaked, with nostrils flared, snorted and reared. They lunged and shied, yearning to be away from this melee of torture and pending death. Two bolted into the night leaving their riders lying in the dust. Others pulled in terror against the corral fences and hitching posts to which they were tied.

"Get out here!" one of the gunmen yelled. "Get out here now!"

"Let's burn the old man out!" another man shouted.

An old chicken shed, long unused, was nearly burned. The fire's bright orange glow projected eerie shadows on the old man's bedroom wall. The firelight also flickered across the dusty ground outside. An ever-changing mix of light and shadows made it hard to see anything clearly.

These men weren't friends and neighbors. They were an eclectic mix of outlaws, drifters and hired guns. And, they were determined to earn their money and have some fun doing it.

The old man heard the crackling and hissing sounds of the chicken house burning. He had hauled those timbers down from the mountains years before. Now they were being reduced to ashes. Stray embers were caught in the wind. Their orange glow died away in the darkness as they rose into the night and were carried away.

"Damn them," mumbled the old man.

"Why don't you come and get me?" he shouted back.

John Meadows had homesteaded this ranch 22 years earlier. And, despite his 50 plus years he retained the same strong will and independent spirit that had made him successful over those years. However, it was that same defiance and stubbornness which now threatened to be his undoing.

Meadows was not, even by the most generous of descriptions, a big man. But, despite his lack of imposing stature he was wiry and tough as nails. Unknowing strangers like those facing him might see his thin shoulders and slight build and consider him frail and old . . . but they would be wrong.

Sure, the strength and endurance of youth had long passed. And, yes, his calloused hands were drawn and dark from years of manual labor under an unforgiving prairie sun. His skin was also dry and weathered from years working in the incessant wind. But this man was far from weak.

The old man was by God's design a

tough, hardened rancher. He lived to avoid trouble, but if it came calling he would not back down. Retreat was not an option; compromise, a rare consideration.

He walked with a slight limp, the result of a horse falling on him in his youth. Now the injured knee was aching from the awkward position in which he found himself on the floor. Unless he could change positions, the pain would only get worse.

The old man's defiant shouts were answered by still more gunfire, which ripped the checkered curtains from his bedroom windows and destroyed more items throughout the house. Once the latest barrage had subsided he felt something wet behind his left shoulder. The wetness moved down his back and along his left side. Suddenly, he was fearful he'd been shot.

Meadows grabbed the edge of the bed and tried to stand. Then he discovered the broken porcelain water pitcher kept on his nightstand. Water soaked everything in sight, including his back. He slumped back onto the floor.

"Damn them all!" he muttered again.

If I get out of this . . . , he considered, but his thoughts soon trailed away.

Meadows finally managed to crawl around the end of his bed and found his rifle. He also pulled on his boots. Then staying on the floor, he worked his way to the window.

There was considerable disagreement among the attackers on what they should do next. Most of the men wanted to burn him out. Others wanted to rush the house. Only a few wanted to wait the old man out, and Meadows knew eventually the majority would rule. Time was running out. His position had become precarious.

The fire created enough light to illuminate an area close to the house. That allowed the old man to see some of his ever-moving attackers. Now he finally managed to shoot back. The problem of course, was this merely defined his exact location in the house.

"Go around back. Come in behind him," someone shouted. "We'll drive him out."

Over the years, ranching in the Wyoming Territory had been tough and he'd seen considerable change. Meadows had survived drought, blizzards, locusts, rustlers and the Indian wars. His wife, Martha, was buried on a nearby hillside. Alone, he had raised a free-spirited daughter who now taught school and lived with his sister's family in Nebraska. Little had surprised him through those years, but somehow this was different.

Recently, a newcomer had moved into

Chugwater and upon his arrival had made it clear he was the man in charge. He left no doubt about his intentions. And area ranchers felt helpless, many for the first time in their lives, because they were unable to fight back. The ruthless stranger used paid thugs and outlaws to carry out his plans.

Murders were on the increase. Cattle rustling had become the norm. Already several area ranchers had been forced off their land at gunpoint. The "big boss" liked to start with intimidation. But, if for some reason that method failed, he sent his men to force outright removal . . . usually in the dark of night.

The few hands the old man could afford had already been run off or had switched allegiance. Only Meadows' long-time cook, his daughter's "pretend" grandfather, Juan Gonzalez, had remained out of loyalty.

Meadows had questioned what was happening. But, he was told to "shut up or face the consequences." However, backing down was not his nature. Warnings only made him ask more questions. Attempts to rally neighbors and townspeople had fallen on deaf ears. Everyone was frightened.

The warnings were serious and he knew it, even if he couldn't keep quiet. Lately he had begun sleeping fully clothed with a rifle nearby. Tonight they came to move him out.

"Maybe I should have listened," he mumbled.

There was a momentary lull in the shooting and he heard an explosion. It came from the direction of the cookhouse. He assumed it was on fire as well. Then he heard a woman scream.

"Oh my God! They've got Rosita!"

Rosita Gonzalez, the wife of the rancher's long-time cook, was more than 60 years old. She was crippled in one leg and nearly blind with cataracts in both eyes. Her hands and joints were ravaged with arthritis. The woman was being dragged across an open area between the house and the horse corrals.

Her husband also was dragged from their hiding place in the cookhouse. But unlike his wife, he was tied to a corral post where the men began torturing him with gunshots into his lower legs and feet. They tried to make him dance even though tied. He could no longer stand and was held up only by the ropes that bound him to the corral fence.

The man cried out in pain. His dark, aged face was twisted and strained. The pain was overwhelming. However, death would be slow in coming.

Meadows pulled away from the window and slumped against the wall, sick to his stomach. The putrid taste of vomit rose to his throat and fought for escape. Meadows swallowed hard. His friends were being tortured. He looked toward the ceiling and spoke softly.

"Lord, you and me . . . well we haven't had many talks since Martha died. Guess you know that. But, I'm begging you now. Come save Juan and Rosita from this torture. I ask not for me. You know my transgressions. But, these are good people. Please don't make them suffer . . . not on my account."

Meadows' prayer was cut short when the woman screamed again.

The woman was trying to ignore her own pain and discomfort. However, with each shot into her husband's mutilated body she cried out. It was as if the bullets were tearing a path through her own ravaged body, burning into her soul.

She felt the exploring hands of the men who held her. They began tearing at her clothing. Their foul, whiskey-laced breath sickened her and she felt revulsion and contempt. She fought down the urge to throw up.

"Stop!" shouted Meadows as he emerged

17

from the front door onto the porch. "Here I am! I'm the one you want! I beg you. No more pain for these people. They've done nothing. It's me you want."

The gunmen dropped the woman in the dust and turned their attention toward Meadows, who was now stumbling down the front steps. Somehow, the woman got to her feet and found the strength to reach her dying husband. Her hands were wet with his blood as she caressed his face.

"You have me now!" shouted a defiant Meadows. "Leave these people alone. They don't deserve this."

"We'll give the orders here," said a tall gunman with long black hair and a growth of whiskers stretching back over several days. In the semi-darkness, the man displayed no admirable qualities except for an ability to shout down the others. The Colts on both hips gave him a sense of authority and confidence.

"Winston wants you gone by sunrise. Get him a horse," he shouted at nobody in particular. "And find his hat."

"Let's hang him," shouted one gunman.

"Yea, we want to watch him twitch and dangle," said another with a sick laugh.

Their suggestions were ignored.

His hands were tied tightly, nearly cutting

off the flow of blood to his fingertips. Put astride a frightened horse, he was to be taken away from the ranch by two unhappy gunmen. His fate was unclear but any reasonable person could predict his future.

"Be sure he doesn't come back!" said the dark-haired man. "Winston won't be happy if he does."

"We hear ya Smitty," one of the riders answered.

The three men rode from the ranch complex as dawn was breaking. The prairie was a vast carpet of green, spring grass. The air was cool and dry.

A gentle morning breeze caught the scent of late spring sage and prairie flowers and cast their smells over the landscape. The sunrise, unaware of one man's perilous fate, rose with spectacular brightness, filling a bright, blue sky with light, hope and the promise of a new unblemished day, still filled with opportunity. It was as if God had spread a green carpet before them and warmed them with never-yielding promise.

Behind them, Meadows heard a shot, a woman's scream followed by a second shot. Then there was total silence. Not even the meadowlarks sang. The old man knew Juan and Rosita were dead, and he grieved in silence.

A cloud forced its way between sun and landscape, casting darkness over the trio of riders and covering the tiny group with a dark shadow of pending death. No one spoke.

Meadows turned in his saddle from time to time to look back. Smoke from the ranch complex mixed with clouds of the morning sky. Winston's men hadn't torched the main ranch buildings. But in that the rancher found little solace.

He thought of his daughter and prayed quietly for her future. In his mind's eye, he could see her as a child chasing butterflies across the prairie, her laughter carrying on the wind. He remembered the wonder in her eyes as she watched a newborn foal struggle to stand, wanting to go help him. And, he smiled as he recalled how she would torment the young hands with her natural good looks, only to out-ride and out-shoot many of them. She'd just laugh and say, "Daddy, you should have seen 'em."

As for himself, he accepted his future as part of some sealed and preordained fate, surrendering to a sequence of events which he could no longer control.

About noon, the group pulled up and stopped. Meadows figured his time was up. Nobody would find his body out here. He expected to be shot at any moment, and then left dead or dying. The two gunmen dismounted and ordered the old man to climb down as well.

"Can't get off with my hands tied to the saddle horn," Meadows pointed out.

While one of the men stretched his legs and relieved himself some distance away, the second man untied Meadows and then stepped back.

"Now get down," he ordered, his right hand resting on a still-holstered pistol.

In that brief opening, Meadows kicked his horse hard in the flanks and shouted. He wheeled the horse toward the surprised gunman, brushing past him with such force and ferocity that it knocked the gunman down. The animal bolted into a dead run. Leaning over the saddle to present a low target, Meadows urged his horse to fly.

He turned west and asked the horse for more effort. The two angry men had remounted and were in hot pursuit. And even though he could no longer see them, Meadows knew they were still behind him.

Meadows urged his horse on, and then on again, driving him in a race for his life. He took in deep breaths of clean prairie air and he could feel it slide by his face.

Then he felt something tear through the

flesh of his lower back, ripping his skin apart. Something buried itself deep in his muscles. There was a burning sensation and he could feel wetness against his skin. There was a sharp pain, and he knew it was a bullet lodged deep in his back.

Meadows struggled to stay upright in the saddle. He felt himself swaying and growing dizzy. The ground swirled under him, inviting him to fall.

The horizon became a display of yellows, pinks and oranges . . . swirling into a mix of blacks and purples, then a mixture of reds and greens. A giant yellow ball hung mocking him, growing hot on his back. Meadowlarks taunted him. Antelopes laughed. His horse danced to sounds only he could hear.

Meadows felt a pounding in his ears and then in his weakened state, he began having visions. There was a parade from his youth, then a preacher shouting out a sermon. And, he saw his young wife running toward him with long flowing hair and outstretched arms. He could hear her calling him home for supper.

There was a little yellow-haired girl chasing an old hen bound for Sunday dinner. She shrieked with laughter as the chicken scrambled just out of reach yet running toward some preordained end.

Then that same yellow ball from before began to burn his now unfocused eyes. He was lost. His mind soared skyward. All consciousness was gone.

CHAPTER 2
COWBOY TO THE RESCUE

A meadowlark rose from a small clump of prairie grass and caught the wind under its wings. Once lifted skyward, the bird was carried away toward some unknown destination. The same wind brushed across Jake Summers' face and for the moment he closed his eyes.

Man and horse had topped a narrow, grass-covered ridge where Jake drew up to survey the long green valley below. This was open range country. The land rolled away in wave upon wave of short grass prairie.

On the opposite side of the valley a few isolated pine trees clung to several rocky outcroppings. And at the far end nearly five miles away, a small mountain-fed stream rippled over an ancient bed of stone and rock. A few cottonwood trees stood as sentinels along its banks.

Jake looked over the panoramic vista before him and saw nothing unusual. He scanned the eastern horizon before turning his attention to the snow-covered mountains to the west. The young man took full measure of the land before him.

His horse shifted its weight under him and he was reminded of his duties as foreman of the Box T. While other hands were spending the day topping off young colts, fixing worn equipment or preparing for the upcoming hay season, Jake had assigned himself the job of riding out to survey the area.

Cows of Longhorn descent, along with a few late-season calves, grazed in the distance and drifted south toward water. There was no sense of urgency. Most of the calves were three to four months old and they ran to and fro in the late spring grass. The cattle were more than a mile away.

The sky was a clear, bright blue. The air was cool, but comfortable. Only a few puffy while clouds filled the distant sky casting isolated shadows across the valley floor. Jake daydreamed and soaked in the moment. The sun felt warm against his back and he took time to roll a smoke. His horse stood quiet under him with its eyes nearly closed, content to wait. A swish of its tail now and then to acknowledge a pesky horsefly was his only movement.

Jake often chose such moments to reflect

and evaluate his own life. He was a thought-ful, yet complex young man of 26 years. And, at such times he liked to probe into life's more philosophical underpinnings in relation to this vast, lonely land.

"It's almost more than the mind can grasp," he mumbled while holding his left hand to shield his eyes from the sun. "What we have here old boy is a paradox. How can land so beautiful, land so carefully painted by God's own paintbrush, in turn at times be so harsh, so lonely and so empty?

"How can land as immense and grand as to surpass all definition, at the same time reduce a man to a speck of insignificance? How can lands of wondrous rolling prairies and massive snow-topped mountains, be full of so much loneliness? It makes you shud-der from the emptiness."

Jake was not a philosopher by nature, or at least no more than most men his age. He was merely a man in awe of life's infinite beauty and goodness, yet troubled at times by its equally harsh cruelty. He found it hard to accept the two extremes.

Efforts to roll a second smoke proved futile. A rising wind blew his tobacco away leaving only a thin parchment of empty paper held by calloused fingers. He also was left for the moment with unanswered questions. He sighed, put his tobacco makings away, and took another look around.

This time out of the corner of his eye he noticed a running cow. She stopped now and then to look back, and then she ran again only to stop once more. She held her head high and anxious.

"Boy, looks like she's trying to lure something in her direction."

Then he saw a flash of gray/black. It looked like a large dog and the cowhand recognized trouble.

"Lobos! Wolves! Bet she's got a calf hidden down there somewhere and she's trying to draw them away," he said out loud, speaking as if his horse understood.

With the cattle so far away, he realized the urgency of the situation. Jake spurred his horse to a run and he felt the wind press against his face.

They skimmed over the rough ground. The cow horse grabbed large chunks of ground with each hurried stride and passed over them as if flying. Horse and rider plunged over the embankment, and half sliding and half running, they reached the valley floor. The horse never hesitated as it responded to Jake's urge to run.

Jake heard the cow's bawling torment long before he reached her. The cause of her distress was evident. Alone, she faced three hungry wolves smelling her newborn calf and other elements of the birthing process. She had hid the still wobbly calf in some clumps of prairie grass and rocks, and so far he had not been discovered. However, her attempts at drawing the wolves away had failed.

They had picked up the scent of the birthing process and were quick to respond. Now they worked together to take advantage.

An older-looking wolf with one droopy ear, a nasty scar along its left shoulder and splotches of white hair circled behind the cow and made darting runs at her legs. The cow kicked wildly while trying to spin toward her attacker. The wolf's age and experience kept him just out-of-reach of the cow's deadly feet.

A second much younger animal made a futile rush for her neck, hoping to find a straggle hold. A lack of experience and the cow's constant movement made his efforts difficult, if not impossible. When one of the cow's long horns nearly impaled the young wolf, his own blood flowed from a wound along his right side.

The third wolf circled and circled waiting for an opportunity to join the struggle. A quick lunge was answered by the cow's left hind hoof making solid contact with the wolf's side. With a yowl and a limp, he retreated if only for the moment.

The cow's need to defend herself was compounded by her obvious concern for her baby. Motherhood gave her a profound inner strength and although worn out from giving birth she was prepared to fight. Only death would stop her and the wolves sensed any such meal would be hard won.

Jake topped a low ridge and spotted the fight. And while he couldn't yet see any calf, the cow showed the obvious physical signs that one existed.

It was not unusual for newborns this late in the spring. With bulls running with the cows year-round, anything was possible. The fact the cow was here alone, away from the main herd, led Jake to believe his intuition was correct. He figured her reason for not simply running away would be found close by.

Jake pulled his rifle from its scabbard and took careful aim. However, the cow's actions and the nervous movement of his own horse prevented a clean shot. The fight was fast and furious, but it was clear the cow was becoming exhausted, and worn down. Her reflexes were slowing.

Dust hung on the air and mixed with the

smell of blood and pending death. There was a chilling blend of bellowing cow and snarling growls. Blood from several bite marks showed red on the cow's light brown hide. The wolves snarled with their noses wrinkled, the skin pulled back tight along both sides of their mouths, and their fangs gleaming with saliva.

The older wolf sensed the time had arrived to close the deal. He leapt for the cow's briefly exposed throat. Jake's rifle boomed. And, the old wolf died before hitting the ground in a twisted mass of hair and bones.

The cow bawled at the two remaining attackers and with one last attempt at drawing them away, she ran.

The third animal ignored her, sensing an easier meal would be found nearby. He also gave Jake an easy second shot, and died because of it.

The remaining young wolf had at first picked up the chase . . . but hearing the shot and the yowling, painful death cry of his companion, broke off. Then spotting Jake on horseback, he took off to find easier prey.

Jake made a quick search of the area and found the bull calf, a mixed breed with Longhorn features. It was unharmed, no worse for the experience. The newborn was much too young to realize how close to death it had come. Soon enough it would know for all the wildflowers and spring butterflies, this also was an equally harsh and cruel land.

After dismounting, Jake reached down to pick up the calf. He felt its soft brown hide and found his reflection in the young animal's large brown eyes. Then as he put his arms around the calf, he felt a warm and inquiring tongue brush against his face.

"Easy little one," he said softly. "Let's find momma."

With the calf draped over his saddle, he rode toward the main herd. It didn't take long before he spotted the worried mother watching him from a safe distance. He dismounted and put the calf on the ground.

With wobbly legs the calf bawled for its mother and with head high she came running. Jake watched as the calf sought nourishment and his mother smelled him for some identification.

The cowhand smiled, remounted and turned toward home, urging his horse into an easy lope. Shadows showed it was early afternoon, but there was much to be done before nightfall.

CHAPTER 3
A STRANGER COMES CALLING

The rider drew up 30 yards or so opposite Jake's right hand and stared blankly out from under a greasy, sweat-stained hat. He was unshaven. His clothes were covered with dust. Horse and rider blended as one under a blanket of gray dirt and dried sweat.

Both man and horse were tired, exhausted. The man's sorrel gelding stood with head down, worn out. The horse clearly had been ridden long and hard. The stranger was nearly done in as well. Still, Jake was wary.

"Even a tired snake can bite," he muttered to himself.

Curious why the stranger was on Box T land, Jake wanted some answers. Gently touching his spurs to the flanks of his own horse, he slowly moved forward.

Like two dogs meeting for the first time, their approach was born and bathed in suspicion. Both men were cautious of each other. Both had unanswered questions.

There was a feeling of tension on the hot afternoon air. Caution captured the moment and held fast.

It was Jake who broke the silence first. And for a brief moment, the air of uncertainty was eased.

"Afternoon stranger."

The man who looked to be about 50 seemed to nod slightly and tried to force a tired, inaudible response.

"Headed for Eagle River?" asked Jake.

From between two parched and cracked lips, the stranger tried unsuccessfully to force an audible response onto the morning air. The result was little more than a grunt.

This "no answer" response made Jake pull up. Now only about 15 yards or so away, he studied the man in detail, settling on his worn clothing and aged, wrinkled skin. His skin bore the darkened shades of a man whose waking hours had been spent under a relentless sun. His hands showed marks of hard usage, broken bones and arthritic knuckles. The face was covered with unshaven gray stubble, making him appear much older than he probably was.

Something wasn't right, but Jake couldn't get a handle on it.

"Looks like you've had a hard ride, old timer."

From the direction the old man had come, it was more than 40 miles across dry, short-grass prairie and rolling mountain foothills to the nearest town. This was open range in every direction. The country was home to maverick steers, pronghorn antelope, mule deer, coyotes, meadowlarks, and a few thousand more of God's seldom-noticed creatures. It was ranching country. Except for a few drifting and displaced Indians, humans were seldom seen. Even long-time buffalo hunters had left the land behind, gone the way of the shaggy beasts themselves.

Few men traveled so far from known water sources across this section of unfamiliar grassland. Coming from that direction had not been easy. More than likely, the man was lost . . . very lost. Most travelers stayed to commonly used roads further south and west.

As Jake again moved forward he noticed for the first time, the man's eyes, nearly glazed over from exhaustion, blank without color, as if drained of all blood and emotion. More than tired, this man was just plain hurting.

Then without warning, the old man slumped forward and then fell from his horse. He landed hard and the horse stepped sideways, turning in a half circle . . . too exhausted to fully shy away.

Now for the first time, Jake saw there was dried blood, horse sweat and lather mixed together down the horse's right flank. The man was hurt badly and only years of practiced horsemanship had unconsciously kept him in the saddle.

In an instant, Jake was on the ground, moving quickly to the old man's side.

The man gasped for air. He tried to speak. But all he could manage was a quick breath as he uttered "Sam," and fell into unconsciousness.

Realizing the old man was in bad shape, Jake, with some effort, managed to get him into the shade of some nearby rocks. Then retrieving his canteen, he gave the man enough water to moisten his dry throat and lips. The man stirred to life enough to want more water.

"Easy old timer. There'll be plenty more later. For now let's go easy."

The man either understood or simply gave up. He slumped back against the hard ground and said nothing. The water obviously wasn't enough to satisfy the man's needs. But, those needs would have to wait. The man needed a doctor's help, and soon.

Jake stood and looked at the horizon

around him. He really didn't expect to see anyone, but felt better having looked.

Large, puffy white clouds filled a pale blue sky and green prairie grasses rolled toward the horizon. Only due west and south did snow-laden mountaintops pierce the early summer sky and put a finite boundary on his sights. Except for a few birds, his view was void of all visible life.

Along a nearby stream of meager size, the early June air was filling with white, cottony fibers. From a stand of cottonwood trees, the windy currents captured the "cotton" along with its tiny brown seeds and carried them to new homes downstream. Now and then with a brief change in the wind, a few fibers found their way into Jake's otherwise unobstructed vision.

The only sound was the ever-present wind, a few noisy birds and the cottonwood leaves brushing together in a gentle, rustling motion. A dry, hacking cough by the old man brought Jake's thoughts back to the stranger.

Jake studied his wrinkled features and calloused hands.

"Just who are you? Are you some working rancher, or simply an old puncher whose luck has run out?"

His clothes were hard to read . . . an old,

36

brown leather vest over an ordinary faded red plaid, cotton, and long-sleeved shirt. His hat was dirty and gray, with a sweat-stained band. It was twisted along the front edge where its owner had often pulled it down tight against the wind. The man was obviously right-handed. Jake could surmise little else.

After making an adequate and sturdy travois from the deadfall of the cottonwood trees, Jake tied it to the man's horse. Then, he gently put the old man aboard.

"If Indians can use these timbers for the roof beams in their adobes, they ought to hold you old-timer."

The going would be slow, hard and long. Jake knew it would be well after nightfall before they could reach the Box T headquarters. He hoped the old man could hang on that long. After several hours of giving the man sips of water and carefully riding around rough terrain, Jake spotted lights shining from the windows of the Box T ranch buildings.

Situated in a quiet canyon down and away from a more dry and hostile environment, the ranch headquarters was an oasis of sorts. Discovered and settled more than 20 years earlier by the Thompson family of Pennsylvania, it had provided shelter and comfort for many a wayward traveler and cowhand over the years.

The ranch complex faced east toward the morning sun and was surrounded on three sides by stands of pine trees that climbed steadily westward, toward the snow-covered peaks of the Laramie Mountain Range.

The rolling foothills of the mountains stretched out before the Thompson front porch like a rumpled carpet toward a distant prairie horizon. Here the water was good, the air clean and the temperatures somewhat cooler than down on the prairie further east. And, here not far from the headwaters of the Laramie River, Jake brought the stranger.

Juan Martinez, a night horse-herd wrangler, was the first to spot them. He quickly rode back to the cookhouse and began ringing the dinner bell. His urgency and the time of day sent a message of potential trouble.

A couple of old cow dogs reacted to the sudden activity and began barking. The noise disturbed an old yellow tomcat trying to catch a mouse in the barn. Card games were put on hold. General gossip, with its normal amount of bragging, was stopped for the moment. The ranch hands of the Box T came running.

"What's the problem Jake?" yelled one of the men as he emerged from the bunkhouse barefoot, but carrying his boots.

"Found an old man. He's been shot," answered Jake. "Help me get him into the bunkhouse. Somebody fetch Jose. Tell him to bring his doctoring bag."

Jose Ramirez had become the de facto doctor on the Box T. With the little town of Eagle River several hours away and with many years of ranching experience, the old Mexican had seen just about every ailment. Mostly that meant setting bones and providing tonics to ease tired, sore muscles.

"What's going on Jake?" came a voice from the darkness.

Easing from the black of night into the lantern light came an older, dignified gentleman with long white hair and matching mustache and beard. His strong stride belied his more than 50 years of ranching. While his white hair and beard were obvious reminders of his 72 years, they were also outward signs of a life filled with pain and disappointment. This was William Henderson Thompson, owner of the Box T.

"Boss, I found this gent up on Laramie Mesa about mid afternoon."

"What's wrong with him?" the elder man asked.

"He's been shot and he's unconscious."

The Box T owner quietly and gently looked the stranger over by lantern light.

"Take him to the house," he ordered some men standing close by. "Jake, send someone to Eagle River and get old Doc Simmons.

"And . . . ," Thompson stopped in mid sentence. "Tell the hand you send to make sure the doctor gets here sober. Otherwise, he won't be worth a plug nickel for anything. Might as well cut on the stranger myself if that doctor isn't sober. Tell your rider to keep quiet in town. Get the doctor and get back. Something isn't right here.

"Jose, go ahead to the house and alert Maria we've got someone hurt bad down here. Tell her to prepare a room for him."

The ranch owner barked out instructions with military skill and confidence. He had been leading men for most of his adult life . . . much of it under duress. During the Civil War, his Union Calvary unit had fought with valor and courage at Gettysburg and points further south under Grant.

Jake greatly respected the man. Thompson had hired him five years earlier and only a year earlier had made him ranch foreman. He had become a father figure for the young cowhand.

"Jake . . . let's follow along. Fill me in on

how you found this man."

When they arrived at the house, Maria Lopez already had a room ready. She had taken the news of a hurt stranger in stride. She had learned through the years to expect the unexpected and be ready for it.

She was Thompson's housekeeper, but Jake often sensed deeper feelings between the older ranch owner and his attractive, young housekeeper . . . especially since the death of Thompson's wife of more than 30 years.

The loss of his wife, Elizabeth, four years earlier had left Thompson lonely and depressed. They had no children. And for Thompson, the drive and the ambition which made him a successful rancher had gradually faded since the death of his precious "Beth".

Still, with a good crew and a talented, young foreman in Jake Summers, the ranch had grown and prospered. Around the men, he seemed happy and often offered a smile and a word of encouragement. However, something was missing in his life. Only around Maria and Jake did he seem to find room in his life for a smile, and even a laugh now and then.

Maria gladly had accepted a greater role in running the Thompson household. She now also managed the cook's activities, planned meals and scheduled the few social activities held on the ranch. Nothing was ever said. Each was afraid, perhaps, to reach beyond a certain comfort level they'd now found with each other.

Jose followed the men into the bedroom with his bag of medicines. Maria ushered everyone else but Thompson and Jake out of the room.

With Maria's help, Jose cleaned the man's wound and did what he could to make him comfortable until the doctor arrived. Jose had determined that removal of the bullet or bullets were beyond his experience level. They decided to wait until morning and the arrival of a doctor.

As Jake walked back to the bunkhouse, he was filled with more questions than answers. The old man's sudden and unexpected arrival had brought a warning of sorts into this normally quiet valley.

The card games and smokes had resumed, but talk among the men was quiet and reserved. Everyone suspected the old man's appearance would lead to trouble.

"The old man going to make it?" asked one as Jake entered the bunkhouse.

The room was filled with the soft, golden glow of lantern light and the swirling, gray fog of tobacco smoke.

"Don't know yet. Sent for the doctor."

"Any idea who he is?" asked Charlie Richards, a good friend of Jake's.

"Not really. It's a mystery to me."

Jake took his time gathering up the makings of a cigarette. After he struck a match and took a deep draw of tobacco, he started explaining to everyone how he had found the man and what had happened.

Jake looked around the room. Each man was listening.

"Seems awfully strange. We best be on our toes the next few days. Watch for anything out of the ordinary."

The men quietly returned to their activities. However, while the card games continued, it was talk about the old man that held their attention.

Jake sat on his own bunk and pulled out a well-worn shirt, some thread and a couple of buttons. As he tried to mend a shirt by lantern light and replace a few missing buttons, he found the lack of answers only created more frustration. The result was more than one pricked and bloodied finger.

"Good thing the doctor is coming," joked Tom Scott, as he watched his friend's poor attempt at tailoring.

Jake didn't respond.

Then without looking up, he told the group, "Let's put out them lanterns boys, we've got work tomorrow."

CHAPTER 4
WHISKEY SOAKED BISCUITS

A solitary rusty-red rooster announced the arrival of morning. His message was quickly lost among the rising sounds of snorting, anxious horses held in the main corral. The morning air was cool and the animals celebrated the richness of the hour.

Daylight gradually broke over the eastern horizon, creating a thin line of light separating earth and sky. Now and then, a dog barked at some unseen varmint. A smell of spring burnished the air and mixed with the smell of strong coffee.

Each hand sought to take in great gulps of cool morning air and let it pass into his lungs while savoring each delightful and lingering scent.

Morning found the stranger delirious with fever and exhaustion. His personal effects provided few clues to his name and background. It was as if he had gone away without an identity. Even his horse, a dull

45

sorrel without any natural or manmade markings of note, provided few clues. None of the cowhands recognized the brand.

The arrival of the sober (if not nasty and ill-tempered) doctor gave hope to all that the old man might have a slim chance at survival. Not that the doctor really cared. He hated all things in this vast land and didn't hesitate to share his thoughts on the subject.

Yet, for more than 15 years, "Old Doc Simmons" had successfully plied his healing trade . . . complaining the entire time. It was said that once a new baby heard the doctor's sour disposition, it would start crying without being slapped.

The doctor examined his new patient carefully.

"Get me some hot water and stand back!"

In less than an hour, he had dug out a bullet from the man's side. "Shot from behind. Shot in the back," he remarked. "Lucky to be alive. Inch or two either direction. . . ." He didn't finish.

"Anybody know who he is?" the doctor finally asked, not really caring to know. When Maria and Jose failed to answer, he simply continued his examination. He didn't ask again.

"He's lost a lot of blood. But, I've got

some medicine for his fever and pain. He should come around in a day or two . . . if he comes around. Maybe he will . . . maybe he won't. Does it really matter?"

The old doctor looked around the room and decided his audience was less than receptive to his views on life. So he continued, "If he wakes up . . . which I doubt . . . he'll need bed rest and plenty of fluids."

The doctor then asked for a good stiff drink and some breakfast.

"Who found the old man?" the doctor asked between bites of whiskey-soaked biscuits. He really didn't want an answer. He was simply making small talk while he ate and drank his fill. Nobody bothered to answer his question. He didn't notice.

"I'll swing by in a few days and check on the old guy. Meanwhile, he dies, you bury him quick. Won't do to have a corpse lying around in this heat. And watch for strangers nosing around," the doctor continued. "Somebody doesn't want that old man around. They might not like hearing he's still alive."

Jake and the other men had been up before daybreak, eating biscuits and bacon washed down with strong black coffee. The foreman gave the day's instructions to the wranglers and then headed for the big house.

Sunlight was just breaking full and bright over the prairie. The day's emergence reflected light off the mountaintop snows on the west side of the valley down to the tree line. Jake stopped briefly to take in the full measure of nature's beauty. Morning shadows still hovered over the west side of the eastern foothills.

"Another beautiful early summer day," he thought to himself as he walked along. "What more could a man want?"

Dust stirred by milling horses in the corral mingled with the rays of early morning sunlight, creating a haze over the ranch complex.

With the first roundup of the season over, Jake and the other hands had settled into a routine of rest and repair. They had returned from the railhead at Chadron over in Nebraska two weeks earlier. Still, there was always something that needed doing, whether it was breaking colts, shoeing horses or any number of other things.

With the cattle shipped east, it was a time to regroup and get ready for the next roundup, which was still a few weeks away. It was a time for relaxation mixed with repairs and refitting. It was also a time for pondering and reflection for Jake Summers. Even at 26 years old, he sensed his own mortality.

Jake was a tall, lanky puncher with a shy but mischievous gleam in his blue eyes. A slight, but ever-present grin seemed to always cover his face and would break into a full-blown smile with little or no provocation. A few freckles dotted his weathered face and blended at the temples with a head of dark brown hair. He was slow to anger and spoke with a slow South Texas drawl.

Thompson had often told his young foreman he should consider settling down with his own place. He had even offered to help get him started. His offer was repeated upon Jake's return from Nebraska.

The Box T owner wanted to sell him a section of prime grazing land south of the main ranch complex. Situated along the Laramie River, the water was good and the location perfect for the start of a small ranch.

Still, any ideas Jake had about ranching came and went. Although young in years, he was old by cowhand standards and he knew it.

Prodded by a growing sense of change, Jake couldn't shake the feeling that time was running out. Every day he saw more and more homesteaders filling the valleys and mountain foothills. Many were choosing to settle along the Laramie, the Sweetwater and other rivers, even along many mountain-fed smaller streams. And as they claimed their parcels of prairie, the open range gradually was being divided and settled. Access to good water was getting harder. Some were even putting up fences.

"Sure," Thompson had told Jake. "It will take a few more years, but the great ranches of the open range will soon be gone. The land is being gobbled up one homestead at a time."

"This will always be grazing country," Jake said. "Without water, nothing but grass will grow."

"Will be a real shame," Thompson continued. "But, many will try various forms of irrigation. They will try to farm and grow crops. Those that adapt and accept change will make it through. Those that defy change will have a hard go of it. And . . . well . . . in the end they will still lose."

With the rising sun, Jake's thoughts turned back to the sudden appearance of the old man and the problems his arrival might cause.

Other ranch hands from surrounding

spreads often stopped off for the night. There was always some serious card playing as they returned from points east and their own roundups. The night before was no exception. As they moved on, it would only be a matter of time before word about the old man would be spread.

"It's those damn homesteaders," said Bill Henry while watching several Box T hands enter the main corral to catch their day mounts. Henry worked for the Double 7 Ranch about 30 miles south. "Hell, they're probably the ones who shot the old man."

Other Box T hands, waiting their turn in the corral, stood with lariats in hand and merely nodded in agreement. They said nothing. Jake only watched and listened.

"They're bringing in their crops and their fences," Henry continued, knowing he had a somewhat receptive audience. "Hell, don't they know it's too dry out here for cropping . . . unless they irrigate . . . then they'll take our water."

"Sure will," echoed a second Double 7 hand. "They must think this is Ohio or Illinois."

Henry interrupted his friend, "Who's to say when things get a little tough, they might go pick up a few strays here and there to feed their young'uns. Next thing they are rustling our stock to pay their seed bills."

Rumor had it that a couple smaller herds southwest of the Box T had been raided enroute to the railhead at Ogallala, also in Nebraska. Those ranchers had lost much of their stock to rustlers. A few good hands also had been killed. Homesteaders were being blamed.

Jake's thoughts on the subject were interrupted by the sound of the doctor's horse leaving from in front of the house. The doctor gave him a quick glance and was gone. Jake made his way to the house.

"How's your patient?" he asked Maria, who was sweeping off the front steps.

"We should know soon," she answered with the same cheerful smile she seemed to carry everywhere.

"Want some coffee Mr. Jake?"

This was pretty much the same routine every morning. Get the men started on their day and then meet with Thompson over coffee. Often these kitchen meetings were short. Thompson had learned to trust Jake's judgment on how the ranch should be managed.

These morning meetings often centered on Jake and his future plans. It was as if Thompson sensed his own mortality as well and wanted things squared between them.

"Jake, given any more thought about the stranger you brought in last night?" Thompson asked as he walked into the kitchen.

"Can't quite figure it," Jake answered. "There aren't many trails or roads up in that country. Maybe he ran into some of the rustlers we've been hearing about lately."

"Could be . . ." Thompson spoke softly as his right hand stroked his nearly white beard.

"When I was in town last week, old man Smith said he was missing some steers up on Cloud Cover Mesa. That's several miles from where you found the old man. But, maybe there is some sort of connection. I just don't know," he said quietly.

"Thought I'd ride back up to where I found him and take a second look around. See what I can find," Jake said.

"Good idea, but be careful. And, while you're up that way swing by Salt Creek Canyon and check on those whiteface cows and calves we've got grazing up there."

"I will."

"Jake . . . ," Thompson stopped him. "Take one of the men with you. Might run into trouble."

"I'll be okay. Besides I've got them checking the hay fields and mending harness today."

"Whatever you say," he answered.

Jake got up, found his hat, said goodbye to Maria and headed for the corrals to get his horse. The big bay gelding nickered at him as he approached.

He rode north, back tracking along the route along which he had pulled the travois a day earlier. The air was clean, clear and cool. The day was still young, with its potential as yet still undefined. Jake saw no signs of anything out of the ordinary.

Jake followed a series of grassy swales then rode east, and away from the river. Mountain foothills loomed on the western horizon behind him. Jake planned to stay off the ridge tops where he might easily be seen from a distance.

Thompson owned 100 red, whiteface Hereford heifers shipped in from back east. They were being grazed in a secluded mountain pasture away from the rougher range stock. It was part of his long-term plan to upgrade the overall quality of his herds. He also wanted to try some bulls from Scotland.

Rumors of cattle rustling in the area coupled with the sudden appearance of the wounded old man had put everyone at the Box T on alert. And, while nothing appeared unusual, he rode with caution. All of his senses were awake. No sound went un-noticed. Riding due east Jake felt the wind against his back. It was a good morning to be in the saddle. One of the ranch cow dogs followed along at some distance.

Jake and the dog had become friends of sorts after the Box T foreman had rescued him from being stomped to death by an angry steer. The dog was great at working cattle, but in this case the steer had turned on him, catching him off guard. The cowboy had gently picked him up and nursed him back to health. Now, the dog he called "Lucky" sometimes followed him . . . sometimes not. Today, he was there.

The dog liked to chase rabbits and birds but never caught either one. The fun was in the chase, not in the catching. He would often disappear for long periods before re-appearing somewhere along the trail up ahead. He stayed close, if not in sight.

Jake liked the dog's company and had taken to feeding him table scraps. Lucky had in turn become a loyal, if sometimes distant, friend.

Suddenly, the dog froze, acting as though he were a prize hunting dog. The ears on Jake's horse also sprang forward, alert to something ahead but not sure what. Jake recognized the signs of potential trouble.

He dismounted, ground-tied his horse and walked quickly, but quietly, to where the dog was standing. At first he saw nothing, and then about 50 yards from where he had left his horse and down a grassy draw, he spotted five men. They had a fire going. They also were using a running iron on Thompson's prized whiteface heifers.

"Lucky . . . we got us a problem," whispered Jake. "Got to stop them. Go for help and they'll be clean out of the country by the time I get back. No . . . me and you gotta do this alone."

Then with a smile on his face, he looked at the dog and said, "Them against us boy. Doesn't seem hardly fair for those hombres."

Jake found a better position and brought the apparent ringleader of the group into his rifle sights. Then he shouted for all to hear, "Men reach for the sky or die slapping leather." His message was followed by two quick shots meant entirely for effect. Then he changed positions.

Each of the rustlers reached for a sidearm with no signs either real or implied they meant to give up without a fight.

Jake's third shot hit the apparent ringleader in the chest and he fell dead. A fourth shot hit a second rustler with a branding iron still in one hand and a long barrel pistol in the other. He also fell, mortally wounded.

A third man, who had been helping hold down the heifer, stood up and tried to run for cover. Instead, he tripped over a rope holding the animal. He fell and was now pinned down behind the still-tied heifer. He pulled his pistol and began firing in the direction where he believed Jake was hiding.

A fourth man on horseback had a rope stretched from his saddle horn to the heifer's neck. He first tried to dismount but Jake shot him in the shoulder. Somehow, he remained astride his horse.

The man still managed to untie the rope around his saddle horn. He was now free to escape. Wheeling his frightened horse around, he spurred it into a run. Meanwhile, blood oozed from his wound and stained his shirt.

Upon hearing the first and second shots, the fifth man had run to his horse, mounted and now was riding for his life. Jake had no choice but let him ride. The third gunman hidden behind the heifer was keeping him pinned down with sporadic gunfire.

By using the heifer as a shield, the rustler was firing at will. Jake was afraid of hitting the animal which was still tied down. She struggled, but could not get up. The gunman tried to keep her calm despite the shooting. She represented his only cover.

Then he heard a noise to his right and he turned quickly to see a dog . . . a snarling, angry dog with teeth and fangs bared moving slowing toward him. The man pulled back and took aim at the dog, but in that instant he became exposed to Jake's rifle and died for the mistake. In falling, he squeezed off a shot that ricocheted harmlessly off the ground.

"Good job, Lucky!" Jake told the dog as he gave him a hearty pat on the head and shoulders. "Guess that makes us about even."

Jake took time to bury the three rustlers. He knew it would slow down his pursuit, but it was also the decent and humane thing to do.

Even if they were thieves, they deserve to be buried, he thought. *Then we'll follow them other two.*

A quick count of the heifers and Jake was satisfied they were all okay. He wanted to follow the trail of the two other rustlers and he had no trouble finding their tracks. *Shod horses. They shouldn't be too hard to follow.*

Now and then he found signs of blood

from the wounded rustler. They rode east down off the higher mountain country and out toward the rolling foothills. And not surprisingly, they passed near where he had found the old man.

Near the site where the old man had fallen from his horse, Jake found two more sets of tracks and footprints. Two men had watched, hidden from view while he had met and helped the stranger the day before.

Both men apparently had watched Jake and the stranger for some time. He found two empty tomato cans and a can of unopened peaches. There were other tell-tale signs of boredom. However, today the horizon was clear of everything but a few noisy birds and some large, puffy white clouds that now and again hid the sun from the land below.

He breathed a deep sigh of relief. If the men he was following were the same men who shot the old man, he might also have been within gun range the day before and not known it. It made him shudder.

Jake mounted his horse and slowly, cautiously continued to follow as the two sets of rustler tracks continued east, where they joined a larger group of at least 10 horses. Whoever these men were, they had apparently found friends and had turned for home.

"Lucky, maybe me and you. . . ."

A gunshot stole the serenity. And, its sound turned a calm and nearly idyllic morning into a chaotic reality. Jake felt his skin grow cold with excitement as adrenalin forced every nerve to attention.

Must take cover . . . , he thought in a split second.

The first shot had caught Jake unaware of anyone's presence. He had been concentrating on the horse tracks. He felt pain from the second shot a split second before hearing its sound. The bullet hit him in the upper part of his left arm near his shoulder. A third shot grazed the side of his head. He was spun from the saddle and was sent earthward. Death was nearby and closing fast.

The wounds and hard ground sent a round of pain throughout his entire body. His horse jumped to one side and once free of its rider, began to run.

The fall momentarily stunned the cowboy. And while he had been tossed a few dozen times over the years by nasty mustangs, this was different. The ground seemed harder when introduced without warning. His head hurt. His eyesight was foggy. There was blood. There was pain. Lying in a heap on a hard, unforgiving ground, he needed cover and soon.

Jake realized he needed to find shelter. Pain or no pain he was a sitting target out in the open.

As mind fog gave way to clarity, he sought immediate answers to unknown questions. His now damaged body refused to move. Only after he received a surge of adrenalin did his legs find strength enough to carry his body toward a stand of cottonwood trees and deadfall.

His left arm was hurting and wet with blood. Blood oozed from his head wound and ran into one eye. Dirt mixed with the wetness of his blood and momentarily slowed the bleeding. His entire body cried out in pain. Still, Jake managed to get up and make a few staggering steps toward cover. It wasn't much in the way of cover but it would have to do.

Jake barely reached it as a second round of shots tore splinters from the branches and limbs around him. With his right hand free to use his pistol, he dug in behind a rotting log for the battle he knew was coming.

He could hear voices, including his own, above the roar in his head. *Must not lose consciousness.*

Then he heard a rifle shot followed by the yelp of a dog. Jake feared the worst.

"Get the mutt?" shouted one of the gunmen with a sickly glee in his voice.

"Hell no, just scared the damn thing. But, I sent him packing. He won't be back."

"How 'bout the puncher?" one high-pitched voice called out.

The second man answered with a sickly laugh. "Caught him square. Knocked him right out of the saddle."

"Whoopee!" shouted the first gunman. "Is he dead?"

"Don't know . . . but I aim to find out."

Jake watched from his makeshift shelter as two men slowly emerged from behind some rocks to seek out their prey. However, he also was becoming light headed and his vision was blurred by blood and dirt in one eye.

Stupid. Stupid. Stupid, thought Jake. *How could I be stupid enough to ride right into an ambush like that?*

"Where's he at?" asked the owner of the first voice. He was a small, greasy, unshaven man with a slight limp. He had yellow teeth and an unkempt appearance. "Thought you shot him?"

"I did you idiot. I know I did," said the

second man. He was much taller but no less unkempt and dirty. Only a greasy vest and matching black, dirty hat distinguished him from the first man. That was until Jake saw a nasty, ragged scar running down the left side of his face from just above the left eye to below the left jaw.

Jake squeezed off a pistol shot that missed both men.

"Take cover," yelled the taller man.

"He's still alive," the smaller man shouted.

"You idiot," the first man yelled. "You think them trees are shooting at us."

The mid-afternoon sun began to take its toll on the two assailants. They complained back and forth about the heat and the lack of shade. They also realized the rest of their friends were headed back to Chugwater without them.

Meanwhile, Jake, weak from the loss of blood and his cramped hideout, began to fear he would pass out at any moment.

"Let's get out of here," whined the smaller man. "Winston ain't paying us enough to sit out here and get shot at and maybe get kilt. I'm burning up."

"Shut up, you no account coward," said the man with the scar. "You circle around behind those rocks and come in behind him. I'll go left and maybe we can catch him in crossfire. Now get going!"

Jake saw the movement. He rose to one knee and squeezed off two shots before falling unconscious from the loss of blood, exhaustion and the heat.

Scar had circled left and jumped over some underbrush. He fell and it saved his life. Jake's two shots which would have hit him chest-high instead exploded into a tree trunk behind where only moments earlier he had been running.

He jumped to his feet and ran back toward his original hiding place. Like in many fights, if the issue had been pressed, victory was at hand. Instead, he pulled back to reconsider his position.

Arriving back at his original hiding place, he found his companion had never left. Still cowering behind some rocks, the smaller man had merely pretended to enter the fray.

"I ought to shoot you myself," Scar shouted. "Let's get out of here."

CHAPTER 5
COMES THE WIND AND FIRE

Dust was everywhere settling in one uncovered crevice then another. The soil was dry. Any root system that might have otherwise held it together had failed. The dirt was no longer subject to the laws of gravity. Free of bondage and unchained it could not be held. Mixing easily with the unceasing wind, the fine, dry powder blew skyward, adrift on the currents, before settling back ever so gently on the exhausted person of Sarah Alicia Meadows.

Breathing was difficult, as if the insatiable heat wasn't enough to endure. Soil laden clouds born of the land were pushed skyward by even the slightest of breezes.

Only where the prairie grasses managed to cling stubbornly with deep driven roots did the land lie still. But, where wheel and plow tore those roots away, the soil rose in a choking fog of dust and dirt.

Regular stops to water the horses from

nearly dry streams gave Sarah an opportunity to try and wash the dust from her face. It also helped cool her but provided no long-term relief.

Homesteaders, thought Sarah with disdain. She understood their coming, but found it hard to accept the plows with which they so skillfully destroyed the prairies and native grasses. *We're gradually losing the open range to plows and fences.*

While she taught their children, she also had tried to instill a certain sense of responsibility about the importance of protecting the land. She was a rancher's daughter and she disliked the plow and all it represented.

Out her window she could see more and more grass as yet untouched and unfenced. A sea of big bluestem grass, rolling and undulating as far as the eye could see. Now and then a sod home broke the horizon marking where some determined farmer fought the land and elements for a foothold and livelihood.

The stagecoach rumbled westward, chasing daylight and losing the race. Darkness would envelope them long before the lantern light of Hale's Crossing would draw them in like a moth to flame. And, even in the darkness there would be no relief from the stifling heat and powdery dust. It would be a long, dirty night.

Sarah woke before dawn and started to put on clean clothing before deciding, *what's the point?* It had been a short night full of strange sounds, barking dogs and men laughing. Sleep, what little had come, had been hard and very short. Her eyes stayed closed little better than the poorly locked door to her room.

She thought of little but the soul-draining fatigue deep in her muscles and bones. Sarah simply wanted to get home and put this travel ordeal behind her . . . and soon! Enduring this ordeal was not the problem; she was tough. She wasn't some soft city girl from back east. She was the daughter of a Wyoming rancher. Still, she longed for easier times and journey's end.

The musty, dirty-smelling stage station began to give way to better smells of strong coffee, bacon and biscuits. It was only then she realized just how hungry she was.

She made quick work of dressing, gathered her things and left the small room.

"Morning missy," came a voice from in back of a large table-filled room. And, as her eyes became accustomed to the dim light she saw a large man wearing a grease and food-stained apron frying bacon on a cook stove.

"Hello," she mumbled.

The room was empty of anyone else. But, she knew from the sounds outside that others were up and about. It appeared from the scattered dirty dishes and half empty coffee cups, the others had already eaten.

"Am I the last one up?" she asked.

"That you are missy," the cook answered. "You had better et quick or those gents might up and leave you here. Course that wouldn't be so bad. I could do for some female company."

His comments were followed by a grin that revealed a set of tobacco and whiskey-stained teeth.

Hungry or not, Sarah felt a combination of revulsion and contempt. She hurriedly used cold coffee to wash down a slice of greasy, half-fried bacon, which was sandwiched between two slabs of tough, over-cooked sourdough biscuit. She considered the option of throwing up. But, she decided the food had tasted bad enough going down; it could only taste worse coming back.

The company of dogs and surly horse handlers would be better than this man and his poor excuse for breakfast.

As she passed through the station door into early morning darkness, she heard from somewhere behind her, "come again missy, should you get lonely." That was followed by an ugly laugh and the sound of a frying pan hitting the floor and curses. She shuddered, but not from the early morning chill.

The stage moved out from the isolated station at first light. The air was cool and a morning chill seemed to settle into Sarah's tired muscles.

The team of horses moved out briskly with little encouragement.

They obviously had more sleep than I did, she thought to herself.

From the coach window, she could see the light of morning behind them long before the sun broke free from the distant horizon. First came shades of oranges and reds, and then the sun itself emerged and began its race across the sky. Along with its ascent came a return of the oppressive heat from yesterday. The heat stole the chill and began to burn away at her thoughts.

Sarah gazed from the coach window and let her mind wander. Outside was a vast sea of grass. Grass extended as far as she could see on both sides. Not a tree was in sight.

Fatigue creates its own state-of-mind, a mental and physical stupor of sorts. Drained of all energy, the body, but more importantly the mind, shuts down by degrees until little active discernable thought is left. It was into this realm that Sarah wandered.

She sat awake, but in a glazed state of consciousness. Moments stretched into minutes, even hours and there was little known awareness of all around her. Recall of the passing moments was all but impossible. Yet the eyes were open . . . the brain active.

The prairie swept away as the coach rolled westward. Like a vast carpet of greens, golds and browns, this land had been nourished for years by thousands if not millions of grazing buffalo. But, mostly it was kept clear by periodic prairie fires. The sky was a muddy, hazy blue . . . neither clear nor cloudy . . . simply there. This was a land of simple beauty, as yet virgin to the plow, free of fences . . . no end in sight.

Only yesterday the coach had started from Kearney. At first the stage had followed recently constructed roads surrounded by crops and homesteader farms. Then finally the horses plunged head first into this wondrous grassland. All traces of civilization were quickly lost as the coach became swallowed and seemingly lost in a vastness only God could appreciate in its massiveness.

For this young schoolteacher from Buffalo County in the Nebraska Territory, the journey was both frightening and equally thrilling.

Uncle Lewis had said his goodbyes quickly with a tone of sorrow in his raspy voice. Aunt Ruby had been more thoughtful in her even-tempered farewell.

"We'll miss you," she had said while filling a platter with ham and eggs. "And, you tell that no account brother of mine he had better have a good reason for bringing you home."

Her father must have had a good reason. His letter written almost three months earlier had been short and vague on details.

"My dear daughter, I write you out of necessity. My health has not been good lately and I'm afraid some of my new neighbors are inclined to take advantage of my weakened state. Please come home at your earliest convenience and help me see to things. I know your children shall miss you greatly, but come if you can. With a father's great love." John Meadows

Sarah had moved in with her aunt and uncle four years earlier. They had expressed the need for schoolteachers in the small

Nebraska community of mostly farmers and ranchers. It was an area where new one-room schoolhouses were being constructed at a rate of one a month.

Their request had come at a good time for John Meadows. His free-spirited daughter, whose mother had passed away at her birth, had been raised among tough and wild cowhands and ranchers. On several occasions, he had tried hiring women to care for his young daughter but few stayed long. She was a handful.

Meadows had decided to join several others and end their westward trek by staying in the Wyoming Territory. Meadows built a sod home near his wife's grave. Here they would stay. It was home for Sarah.

She had learned to ride a horse almost before she could walk. And, her marksmanship with a rifle had bested many of the local wranglers. These were qualities more fitting a son than a pretty young daughter that troubled her father.

"You might tone down that spirit of yours if you ever want a husband," her father had said more than once. "Put on a dress and act like a lady," he would gently add.

John Meadows was extremely proud of his only child. "But, she could use a little female refinement," he would often say to himself.

So when Ruby wrote about the need for a schoolteacher in Buffalo County, he nudged Sarah eastward into the care of his more refined sister and her store-keep husband.

Sarah had welcomed the change of scenery. It was a chance to prove herself away from the influences of day-to-day ranch life. And, while it had been hard to see her go, her father knew it would be best.

Sarah Meadows had left a thin, gangly young tomboy and was returning a beautiful young woman. But, deep down in her ranching roots she still was as tough as nails and twice as determined. The same "never give in or back down spirit" that so strongly defined her father, was equally pronounced in his daughter . . . refined or not!

"Softness and tenderness will someday win you a passel of young suitors," her father once said. "However, toughness will win you their respect and keep you alive out here."

The four years of teaching had not gone without incident . . . but slowly the refinement came. Ruby had written her brother in the winter to say just how beautiful a young woman his daughter had become. And, there was no shortage of suitors from among aspiring young lawyers, bankers and farmers looking for another hand.

The coach hit a larger than normal hole in the roadway and Sarah was bounced back to the reality of the moment. The terrain was changing ever so slightly.

"How many more hills to cross?" she wondered aloud.

Then she smelled the smoke.

"What the . . . ?" she wondered out loud. A quick look and she knew. . . . "Prairie fire!"

There was a rising roar on the air created by a hideous mix of fire and wind. And although the flames were still some distance away, the darkness caught them and threatened to engulf them in its perilous fury.

The stagecoach had already turned, leaving the road behind, now searching, and seeking to escape the flames that must surely follow the miles of smoke stretching across the distant horizon.

"Hold on lady," shouted the driver as he whipped the team into a frantic run.

"We'll never out run it," she hollered.

Sarah knew that trying to out-run a prairie fire could be fatal. Not trying would be equally fatal.

Pushed by high winds, she knew a prairie fire could burn up to seven miles in just an hour, or about 10 feet of dry grassland per second.

The lack of spring rains had left the short-grass prairie grasses dry and highly combustible. Fall and winter when the grasses were dormant were the more common seasons for fire. This spring was different.

It mattered little to Sarah in this race with death that such fires actually renewed the very prairie she loved so much. Roots of the grasses now in flames would not be harmed and would soon emerge in tender new growth. Dead growth was being cleared away by the same flames the stage raced to avoid.

With the prevailing wind pushing the flames southward at an incredible speed, Sarah knew that unless they reached a river or some other protection soon they were doomed.

Huge fireballs were hurtling past them, igniting the grassland ahead of them and around them. Wild animals raced along side the coach, also seeking shelter.

There had been efforts to produce rain in the area. Sarah remembered how in Kearney local citizens had tried to secure the services of an Irishman by the name of Frank Melbourne to come make it rain.

Others had tried by using explosives, kites, balloons and other gadgets to make it rain. Nothing had worked; now the land burned in a fireball around them.

The horses' nostrils caught the smoky air and drove it deep into fragile lungs. They sensed the urgency of the moment and leaned into their harness with eyes wide and nostrils flared. The short, dry grass gave way in front of them creating a new pathway with each stride, pushed onward by a lashing whip.

Sarah covered her nose with a handkerchief and took short, shallow breaths of smoke-flavored air. The fire was moving very quickly, even faster than she suspected. "Why didn't we see it sooner?" she wondered out loud.

Off to the northwest, a wall of thick smoke obscured the sky and it was moving toward them. As they ran a race they could not possibly win, Sarah knew their only hope was to reach the Platte River somewhere out ahead of them. Turning back was not an option.

Failure to reach the river would mean a tortuous death by fire, heat or suffocation from smoke. The fire was gaining. Even inside the coach Sarah could feel the heat, tremendous heat. The horses had run to near exhaustion. They were pushed onward now out of sheer fear and panic. Even they could not sustain such a pace much longer.

Smoke filled the coach and by looking out the window Sarah could see the orange flames devouring the dry prairie grass in great gulps. Blowing embers touched her face and it was as if they were alone in a cloud of smoke. The horizon was gone. They were all but lost.

Then at that darkest moment, they suddenly plunged downward over some unseen embankment. The driver fought the team to keep the coach upright. The horses and driver never slowed as they drove into the shallow Platte River and started for the middle.

"Out of the coach," screamed the driver. "Into the water! Protect your head and hair from flying embers and sparks."

He was hurriedly trying to unhitch the lunging horses. They fought to be further away from the madness.

"Get away from the coach in case it flames," shouted Sarah.

Instead the driver pulled a bucket from the coach and began filling it with water. He started throwing water on the coach's wooden frame. Once, twice, then three times flying embers landed then caught setting the coach on fire. Just as quickly the driver suffocated the small flames with his buckets of water.

Meanwhile Sarah had lain down in the shallow river and from time to time lowered her head into its waters. All around her various species of wildlife, from rabbits to mule deer, shared its wetness. She prayed the fire would stall and not jump the river.

She, like the animals around her, was terrified. Yet, she was amazed at the numbers of animals continuing to plunge into the river around her. Many with their hair singed, others with flesh burned.

There was a sickening mix of smoke and the smell of burnt hair and flesh on the air. Her morning meal found its way back into her throat. The resulting nausea and vomit only added to the growing stench and rapid decline of the water's quality. Burning embers of grass landed on the water and sizzled. Puffs of steam rose to join the cloudy mix of smoke rolling and rolling over them.

Sarah watched as the old man fought to keep the coach from burning. He totally ignored the burns on his own body and the swirling smoke-filled air. Inhaling great amounts of smoke from his exertion, he would stop from time to time and drop into the water to resoak his own clothing with a measure of protective wetness.

The team of horses had reached the far side of the river, yet stood nervously in its wetness. One tried to bolt but harness and the other three animals held him back. Neither trying to climb out on the far side of the river, nor turning back toward the inferno, they stood and waited. They were frozen by their own indecision and lack of human leadership. They trembled in fear.

What the Platte lacked in depth it made up for in width broken up by numerous sand and gravel bars. So far the fire had not crossed that width, happy for the moment to catch and burn small patches of vegetation on the gravel bars.

As the fire began to subside, its height and fury spent, the stage driver sought one of those islands for rest. Sweat flowed freely, exhaustion crippling, he sat and cursed. Sarah stood, and with legs slowed by waist deep water, moved toward him.

"You okay?" she shouted. "That was close! You okay? The worst seems to be over."

He merely gazed at her through tired eyes; still glowing from a blackened, sweat smeared face. Then suddenly, he clutched his chest with a big, blackened hand. He gasped one last breath of smoke-filled air and was dead. His heart failed, pumping no more, as his life came to an end on a gravel bar lost in a prairie sea.

"Mister?" repeated Sarah as she finally reached his side.

"Mister!" she shouted to no avail.

The gravity of his death swept over her like the smoke of recent minutes. A shear massive loneliness, an almost unbearable burden of uncertainty, tore at her physical and mental well-being. She wanted to cry, but didn't.

Sarah fought the gravity of her situation. She was alone in a river, unsure how far from the nearest town or settlement, with a dead driver, a team of frightened horses still unsure of whether they would take flight or stand their ground, and no earthly idea which direction to head for help.

The freshly burned prairie to the north would still be too hot to travel over. Her only choice, if she could hitch the team, would be the south side of the river.

Maybe, just maybe, I can find one of those old roads used by the pioneers heading west years ago, she thought.

It took considerable time and effort, but she managed to bury the driver where he'd fallen on the gravel bar. She managed to dig a shallow hole for the large man and then covered his body with rocks. She knew with the first heavy rain and a rise in the river his body could be uncovered. Still, she had done the best she could and after saying a few comforting words over the grave she returned to her own situation.

After hitching the still-nervous team, Sarah climbed aboard the stage to try her hand at driving. "I used to drive teams when I was younger. I can do this," she asserted out loud.

"Yaw . . . get up there," she shouted as the team and coach began to roll from their water refuge and up the far riverbank. Within minutes the team was moving at a slow but steady pace over the grass-covered ground.

Back across the river in the distance, she could see a vast blackened prairie still smoldering from the fire. Where the density and type of vegetation was heavy, those areas were still burning. As far as she could see, it was a wasteland. Ahead of her was a great unknown, vast land of rolling hills and so far no discernable roadway of any kind.

CHAPTER 6
SLEEPING WITH FLEAS

The day had been hot enough. Now smoke hung heavy and stifling on the unusually still air. The wind that had only just recently carried flame and death across the prairie now laid quiet, innocent.

Sarah sought an inner strength and courage to face what lay ahead on this vast, treeless prairie. She was worn out, exhausted and in considerable physical pain. But even though her faith was being tested severely, she never wavered.

"The Lord will provide and guide me. I know He will," she spoke softly.

Then she found them. They were hidden at first and hard to see; the tracks of wagons driven long and deep in the hard soil. Wagon wheel ruts carved deep by the passing of thousands of pioneers in years past as they pushed for Oregon. Some of the same tracks her own family had followed in their trip west years earlier.

"Even Chugwater," she noted.

Exactly what route the tracks would take she was not totally sure, but she knew they led west.

Covered with blackened, now dried soot, her hair dirty and matted to her head, her clothing filthy and torn, her school teacher hands now sore and scratched, her muscles aching, her legs bruised and cramping, Sarah Meadows turned the team toward home somewhere out ahead.

The team settled into an easy pull. They also were worn out. For a while the old wagon ruts were easy to follow, but now and then, they disappeared, all but overcome by Buffalo grass. Then just as suddenly, they would reappear.

Sarah worried about losing the trail and drifting off lost. She fought the urge to sleep. Her only hope, and she knew it, was to stay with the wagon trail, while at the same time keeping the river off to her right.

There were no other landmarks, not a tree or mountain in sight for more than 40 miles in all directions. There was only a sea of rolling grass swaying in the ever-present wind.

"I've got a worn out team and no clue where I'm at," she said out loud. "And, in a few hours it will be dark."

Off to the south, she could see a few buffalo, the remains of the once great herds of the plains, grazing, unaware of their own heritage and their own eventual fate.

Then toward dusk she found people, a family of homesteaders, appearing out of nowhere. Ira Williams' Soddy rose up before her as if some aberration, dreamlike. The sod home blended into the landscape. Here the old man had literally set down roots by taking advantage of the Homestead Act of 1862. Now he worked from before sunup until after nightfall trying to eke out a living.

A boy of about 13, alerted by the family's barking dog, was the first to see the blackened coach and its ash-covered driver. He dropped a pail of still warm cow's milk and stood wide-eyed and speechless.

"Pa! Pa!" he shouted as he ran for their dugout home leaving a recently milked Jersey cow to fend for herself. "Come quick!"

Chickens scattered as the boy ran among them trying to reach the small sod house.

In her exhaustion and fatigue, Sarah questioned her own eyesight. The deep shadows of early evening, coupled with the setting sun in her eyes created a backdrop of sharp contrasts. She blinked and wiped one hand across her dirty face.

The one-room house faced south and the roof was grown over with buffalo grass. Sarah noticed where someone had tried growing flowers along the eaves, but the effort had failed in the hot dry weather. Those that survived mixed with a few bleached elk horns thrown on the sod roof. Two windows covered with oiled paper allowed the only light to reach the small interior.

Two old, matching sorrel mules stood tied to a makeshift corral fence. They didn't move despite the excitement around them.

Had the old trail passed a hundred yards or so further north, she might have passed the homestead altogether and been swallowed up in the grassland beyond. She shuddered at the thought.

Why do so many families try to live out here? she asked herself.

Sarah knew first-hand the poverty and hardships these homesteaders faced on a daily basis. Her young students had taught her as much. Many had poor food, which often ran short, a lack of clean water, inadequate clothing and no access to medicine or doctors.

Yet these families, in the face of prairie fires, drought, grasshoppers and other natural disasters, had an unwavering religious faith and belief in the doctrine of hard work. She had learned to respect their determination, even if she disagreed with how they plowed the sod and tore up the earth for their crops.

Sarah drew up the team to survey the situation. However, she had stopped too late to avoid detection by dog and boy. Now the entire family appeared to stare at her in the haze of late afternoon.

As Sarah urged the tired team toward the group, Williams walked out to meet her. She drew up again and waited.

The man wore suspenders over a dirty, gray cotton shirt. His long beard and hair needed washing but Sarah thought he was otherwise well trimmed. The boy, who also wore suspenders and pants much too short for his height, followed close behind anxious and nervous. A frail-looking woman stood in the Soddy door with two little girls peeking from behind her long skirt.

"Hail there," shouted the man after coming to within 30 yards or so.

Sarah lifted one arm in a weak gesture of greeting, but said nothing.

"Are you alone?" the man continued as he strode closer. He carried an old squirrel rifle. It was hardly the type to ward off an attack or raid of any substance . . . even from a worn out young woman.

"Look pa! It's a woman," said the excited boy.

"Yes, I see it is."

"Pa . . . be careful," he exclaimed. "She could be some kind of she-devil from the fires of hell!"

"Be still boy," the older man said sternly. "Looks like she came through that fire we could see east of here last night."

Sarah finally responded.

"We nearly died. The driver lost his life. The team ran so hard. There were so many animals. The flames. The smoke. The. . . ."

"Easy young lady. Slow down. You're okay now. What did you say about the driver? Where were you headed?"

"The driver is dead. I buried him," Sarah said. "He saved my life . . . then he, well he died. He just fell over dead."

"Young lady, looks like you could use some help. Climb down and come into our home. We don't get many visitors. You're sure enough welcome," he said calmly.

At the man's urging, but with obvious reluctance, his wife took control of the situation. The woman found her some clean clothing and allowed her to wash and clean up from head to toe before eating.

Williams unhitched the team, gave the

horses some grain and turned them out with his own horses to graze through the night.

The exhausted Sarah was in no shape, mentally or physically, to argue.

The sod home was dimly lit with only a couple of grease lamps, a candle and one kerosene lantern. The lantern was considered a luxury given the high cost of kerosene. It reminded Sarah of her youth living in a similar dugout with her father.

The Williams family found a corner in the small dugout for her to sleep. The boy gave up his rope bed for the night and Sarah lay on a mattress filled with straw. A handmade cotton quilt with a pomegranate pattern was taken from a worn trunk to provide her with a clean covering. A muslin sheet was hung to provide her with a degree of privacy.

Exhaustion overcame her. Not even a thousand fleas could stave off the sleep her body so desperately sought. She found sleep as if in death itself.

Morning came unannounced and late. Even the family rooster had remained uncommonly silent; perhaps sensing the family's guest needed rest. Her host family had let her sleep. When she finally woke she discovered everyone was already busy with his or her daily chores.

Sarah looked around the sparsely

furnished sod home. There was a rough-hewn table, four handmade chairs, a couple of trunks in one corner, some shelves supported by old boxes, three rope beds with straw mattresses and a wash stand with a dusty-white porcelain pitcher and matching bowl. On one wall covered with newspapers was a wreath of dried wildflowers.

Although the sun hadn't yet cleared the eastern horizon, Williams had his team of mules plowing sod in a distant field. The two young girls were gathering eggs, and the boy was again milking the old cow.

The man's wife had said little since Sarah's arrival. Now she fried two fresh eggs over a fire of cow chips and twisted straw so Sarah would have some breakfast. She hadn't bothered to ask if Sarah was hungry.

The woman looked frail and thin. Her hands were calloused and bore the scars of considerable manual labor. Her brown hair was long and dirty, with streaks of early gray. She wore a threadbare gingham dress. She appeared to be about 40 years old, but Sarah guessed she was much younger.

"I'm mighty grateful," Sarah spoke first trying to break the silence between them.

"Ain't nothing," the woman answered.

"It's a whole lot of something, I can tell you that!" Sarah said. "I was nearly lost out there . . . then you folks were there for me."

"You eat up. I got your smoky clothes soaking."

Sarah noticed a dull, forlorn haze in the woman's eyes bordering on a cloudy stare. It was if she had already given in to death in this earthen chamber, maybe even willing the same. Any youthful sparkle or laughter she might have brought to this prairie outpost was long gone.

Women in this land often succumbed to the ever-present wind and prairie grasses. Sarah had heard stories how many had gone insane after years of dirt floors, insects, mice and unbearable loneliness. Even with the walls sealed with old newspapers and with a sheet hung overhead to keep dirt from falling on them nothing could hold back the wind and the torture it wrought on the mind and soul.

"I can't take it anymore," the woman suddenly volunteered.

"Yes," Sarah answered. "What do you mean?"

The woman stood in the doorway and gazed outside, morning sunlight shining on her tired face and tear-moistened eyes.

"We came west with such big dreams. I didn't want to leave my folks in Ohio . . . but I came anyway. It's so dirty. And, God forgive me . . . that damn wind never settles. Even when I hang our wash outside to dry that wind blows dirt from the fields! . . . " she hesitated.

"I understand," Sarah said quietly. "Believe me I do."

"There's always an angry thunderstorm, or the bitter squeal of a winter blizzard. Everyday the wind is always there," she cried softly, struggling for some type of understanding.

Sarah understood. Many times her Uncle Lewis would relate stories he'd been told of men and women driven insane by the constant never-ending blow. They couldn't accept it and were driven mad.

"Back in Ohio, we had music. We had flowers. We even had shade trees . . . massive oaks . . . and oh my . . . we had nice clean clothes and stoves that burned coal . . . not cow dung! Most of all I remember there were gentle evening breezes and ice cream socials . . . not this incessant howl of the devil always screaming, taunting us with his hot breath in summer and God's icy indifference in winter . . . trapping us behind these dreadful walls for days on end.

"My God, I can't take it anymore. I'm losing my mind!"

Sarah approached the woman quietly;

unsure of what to say.

"It will be okay. My father always says 'even as the wind blows up one storm, it always blows that same storm away. A good wind always follows the bad moments in our lives and brings a blue sky and sunshine'. Even as it seems the world is against us, God is always with us."

The woman gave Sarah a pleading look and asked, "Doesn't it ever stop?"

"If it did, we'd all fall down," Sarah answered with a grin, trying unsuccessfully to lighten the moment.

The woman didn't get the humor and continued to stare blankly through tired eyes, trying to see a better place deep in her mind.

"Ever wonder the places the wind has been or the things the wind has seen?" Sarah asked. "I often do. That raindrop that touched my nose . . . was it picked up from some distant ocean and blown over the mountains just for me? That breeze from this morning . . . did it once rustle the hair of some little boy in far off China?

"Sometimes there is peace in knowing we aren't so different from other folks," Sarah continued. "The wind that touches our lives has no doubt touched others before us. The things that bother you and me probably are troubling other folks as well. Maybe you need to get out and meet your neighbors. You might be surprised how much just talking to other folks can help."

"I don't know," the woman spoke softly, as she wiped tears from her cheeks.

"Your husband said he would take me into Gothenburg in a couple days. You should go along. It would do you some good to see other folks. What do you think?" Sarah asked.

"I can't."

"Why not?"

"The young'uns . . . we have chores."

Sarah interrupted, "Drop them off with one of your neighbors . . . heck that boy of yours can even take that old cow along so she's milked regular."

That evening a nearly full moon cast a bright light over the landscape, and a gentle cool breeze pushed away the day's heat. Night sounds joined together to serenade the Williams family and their guest while they ate a meal of rabbit soup and sourdough biscuits.

Elizabeth Williams wore a new dress, a gift of appreciation from Sarah, and she smiled for the first time in days. Her husband was amazed. *Just because I said she should go into town with us?* He scratched his head.

93

"Is ma sick?" Sarah overheard the boy ask his father.

"Hush boy!" the man answered. "Can't figure womenfolk."

Sarah slapped at a mosquito and crushed two. Not even some pesky insects could ruin this night. A falling star streaked across the dark night sky and she smiled.

CHAPTER 7
FRIENDS HELPING FRIENDS

Card games and good-natured banter among all the hands gave way to concern and worry upon the return of Jake's horse. Tom Scott, a long-time friend, had been watching and waiting. He was the first to see the bay gelding as he came running up to the main corral with bridle askew and empty saddle.

The horse whinnied at the other horses and stopped at a wooden water trough to drink his fill. Tom approached slowly, not wanting to spook the obviously nervous animal. The horse provided no clue as to Jake's fate.

Everyone knew it would be futile to mount a search in the darkness. Jake could be anywhere.

By morning, there was widespread speculation about the foreman's health, especially in light of the stranger's sudden appearance the day before. Thompson

95

ordered all those who could ride to start searching.

"Tom, you follow the travois path north up to where Jake found the old man. He was headed that way this morning. Take Charlie Richards with you. Check the mountain meadow where the new heifers are being kept. Jake was going to check on them. He may be up there. And check those small meadows just below the timberline.

"The rest of you men fan out northeast and northwest."

Tom was two years older than Jake. But, they had worked together for about 10 years after meeting on a ranch in the Judith Basin Country of Montana. Jake had only been 16 at the time. Only 18 years old himself, Tom had taken the tall, skinny, freckle-faced young man under his own young wing.

Jake Summers had left his parents, two sisters and their south Texas home at 14. And by doing odd jobs, he managed to work his way north. He eventually caught on with Harry Haythornwaite's (later known as Haythorn) last trail drive out of Texas headed north to Ogallala, Nebraska. When Haythorn decided to remain in Ogallala and settle down, Jake headed for Montana.

"My job was to watch the remunda and ride drag," he had often explained. "It was a dirty, dusty mess. I never swallowed so much dirt in my life, and for just $30 a month. At night we would often use a rope corral to hold the horses close," he recalled. "Most were too tired to bolt anyhow."

Jake had said, "Pushing cattle wasn't easy. Little food . . . we were always hungry. Beef . . . that's all we had at times. And, we only made about 10 miles a day, maybe 15. Many a time our horses would have sore backs. It wasn't a whole lot of fun watching the south end of northbound cattle from sunup to sundown.

"Sometimes that herd would be strung out two or three miles in a long line. We only had 12 punchers. It was hard keeping track over such a distance," Jake had explained.

"And stray cattle . . . we picked up strays with sore feet all along the trail from Texas to Northern Kansas. Expect we left a few behind ourselves for the next bunch of drovers," he once told Tom. "We always ate some of the strays left by the other outfits ahead of us. Then we left our own sore-footed cattle behind for the next herd behind us.

"The boss paid us a dollar bonus for each new stray we managed to find and could add to the herd. On one particular trip, the old man had more cattle at the end of the

drive than he started with . . . even when
our losses were figured in. Strays just kept
getting into our herd," he chuckled. "Guess
they were just lonesome.

"We started from Texas with a mixed herd
of steers, heifers and cows and by the time
we reached Nebraska they were really a
mixed up bunch."

Jake shook his head at the memories.

"How'd you boys handle them babies
born on the trail?" Tom asked.

"They couldn't keep up. I heard tell some
drovers just put a bullet in them and left
them behind. But not us, we had a system.
Our trail boss got him an idea from the
Goodnight outfit. We'd pick up them
young'uns and put them in a wagon during
the day. But since momma cows know their
babies by smell, we had to keep them
separated. Wouldn't do to let them get the
scents mixed up.

"Word was that Goodnight had his punchers put each calf in a sack with a number
during the day. At night he turned them
calves out with the cows. Come morning it
was back in the sack. Not sure whether that
was true or not, but our boss figured if it
worked for Goodnight and his crew it might
work for us.

"Not sure it was worth the effort, but we

did it anyway," Jake laughed. "Left Fort Worth trailing Longhorns . . . arrived in Ogallala nurse-maid to a wagonload of baby calves."

Tom Scott and Charlie Richards had followed much the same path north into Montana where they met up with Jake Summers. Tom had grown up around cattle in west Texas and it was only natural that he would eventually help take a herd north.

Charlie Richards could trace his family back to former Louisiana slaves. He enjoyed working cattle. It was better than picking cotton on a hot, humid day. He also learned, like many other black men of his generation, there was work to be found on the great ranches of the west.

Somehow all three managed to travel north doing odd jobs until they reached Montana and met each other. All three had later gone south together to join Thompson's Box T crew. And each had decided to stay.

With Tom's guidance Jake had learned quickly and had a knack for ranching. Together, they had been a tough and often times rowdy duo. They often discussed working their own spreads someday. However, after Jake became foreman of the Box T, neither Jake nor Tom discussed ranching on his own. Both had settled into a routine.

Tom respected his friend and was proud of his success. He had natural leadership qualities, but for the most part was quiet. Jake had always given Tom credit for all he knew about ranching. There was a mutual respect between the two of them.

Now, Tom had to find his long-time friend.

Jake awoke to total darkness and realized his adversaries must have given up the fight, or they had left him for dead. He needed help and soon. Jake felt something wet on his face. Disoriented he tried to move his arm to brush the wetness away. He could barely move, but his hand found Lucky's warm coat. The dog was licking his face.

"Hey boy," he called out weakly.

The dog responded with a low whimper.

"Guess I got us into a mess here. I was just sure they got you."

After a few moments, as if waiting for the dog to comment on their predicament, Jake asked, "You okay?"

Jake found it almost impossible to see in the darkness, but it was obvious from the dog's reaction he was okay. The rustler's shot had only resulted in a flesh wound.

After the two outlaws left, the dog had found Jake unconscious. A few licks on his hand and face failed to revive the man so the dog had settled in next to his friend, but remained alert and awake.

Fatigue and a loss of blood overtook Jake once more and he fell asleep as he felt the dog lay down beside him. The warmth of a friend lying so close was comforting.

When Jake woke a second time, it was still dark. He realized it would be hard, if not impossible, to find him if he stayed hidden. So despite the pain and the risk of his assailants returning, he had to get into open ground. He could only see out of one eye, but by crawling, standing, walking, falling and crawling some more, he managed to reach a spot along side the trail where he might be found. The dog could only follow.

Jake once more found a quiet solitude and peace behind his closed eyes. And despite the distant music of coyotes howling, he drifted off to sleep.

Tom and Charlie found him just after daybreak. The dog heard them coming and ran to meet them. He eagerly led them back to where Jake lay asleep. They got him back to the ranch house where Maria and Jose went to work.

"This is becoming an everyday thing," Maria said.

"He's going to be fine," she assured an

anxious and worried Thompson. "Go tell Tom and the men, he's okay. He lost some blood which has made him weak, but other than a wound in the arm and a bad headache, he's okay. May hurt him to wear a hat for a day or two though."

By morning, Maria's prediction of a headache proved correct. With a throbbing headache and with his body aching from the previous day's events, Jake was fatigued beyond memory. He fought mentally to comprehend what had happened but found his brain could only absorb so much. Understanding, if it were to come, would be left for some middle-of-the-night revelation.

Jake ached in places he never knew could hurt. His neck and shoulders were sore from landing with such force on the ground. His head throbbed. Scraped skin and bruises marked his lean frame. Still, he tried leaving Maria's careful attention for a return to work and his ranch duties. However, she would have nothing of it.

"Get back in that bed," she admonished. "I'll be the one to decide when you're ready to get up! Besides that old man you found has been asking for you. He wants to meet you . . . in one piece."

"But . . . ," Jake stammered.

"You heard me, young man," Maria continued.

Then with her good-natured smile, she asked, "Am I going to be forced to tie you down?"

"No," he answered quietly as he lay down again.

One thing was crystal clear, he thought. *Death paid me a visit and failed to get me this time. But, this is a wake-up call. Life is too short, too unpredictable.*

Within a couple of days, Jake was up and about. Although he weakened easily, he was restless and wanted to resume his ranch duties. Tom had been appointed temporary foreman in his absence.

"That friend of yours is doing such a good job in your place maybe I need me two foremen," joked Thompson.

"Yeah, well," was all the response a restless Jake could muster.

The time off had given Jake a chance to visit with the other Box T patient. The old man he had rescued was gradually coming around and feeling restless himself.

Jake learned the man's name was John Meadows. He was a rancher from over near Chugwater.

"They came and took my ranch," Meadows told Jake and Thompson. "They put me on a horse and forced me off my own ranch. I had no choice. Some of Winston's goons shot me. I'm going back. You can count on that. I'll be damned if I'll ever give in to Winston and his bunch of cutthroats . . . at least not peaceably."

Jake smiled at the man's bluster. He respected the old man's grit and determination. But, the man's effective fighting days had long passed.

"What exactly happened, and who is this Winston?" Thompson asked.

"A few months ago, a man by the name of Harold Wayne Winston moved into our part of the territory. Originally from back east somewhere, but more recently down in Colorado. He bought a small ranch and we all welcomed him as a new neighbor. Wasn't long we figured out he wanted a bigger stake of the country. He started buying out other ranchers. At first that was okay. But when some were forced to sell or else, things got ugly."

Meadows continued, "He brought in thugs and hired guns to provide persuasion. A couple ranchers, good men, died under suspicious circumstances. Others had their cattle run off and their homes burned.

"I refused to leave," Meadows said. "And for awhile they left me alone, and then my foreman was killed. Then some of my cattle turned up missing. My horses were run off. Finally, they did me in as well."

Thompson rubbed his chin and was thoughtful in his reaction.

"Sounds like a mess," said Jake.

"Those two men who ambushed you. I recognize your description. That big one is called Scar. He's a mean one. They work for Winston. Other one sounds like Willie Temple, cowardly cur dog. He follows Scar around . . . like his shadow. Neither one of them any good . . . like a couple of egg-sucking dogs," Meadows said.

Thompson looked at the old man, then at Jake. He was formulating a plan-of-action. For the first time in several years, the ranch owner actually had a sparkle in his eyes. There was a battle to be fought, a war to be won.

"Jake, I want you and Tom to ride over to Chugwater and get a lay of the situation. Don't take any chances and don't fight any battles. Just get an idea of what's happening then send word to us with details. When Meadows and I get word from you, we'll gather up some of the men and drift on over to pay Mr. Winston a visit," he added.

"No hero stuff. Keep a low profile."

As Jake started toward the door he turned

and gestured toward Meadows. "Sir, I'm curious. Just who is Sam? You mentioned that name a couple times when I found you."

The old man chuckled then said, "Sarah Alicia Meadows, young man. Sarah Alicia Meadows. She's my daughter. Lives with my sister out in Nebraska and teaches school."

"Thanks, I was just wondering," Jake said.

CHAPTER 8
JOURNEY INTO THE UNKNOWN

The black darkness of early morning sought sanctuary deep in the cervices of every brick and timber. It was deep into the St. Louis night . . . moving ever so gently toward dawn. Only dockworkers along the Missouri River moved with any sense of awareness or urgency. Sunrise would find the boat they were loading moving up-river steaming westward.

Molly Collins intended to be onboard. In her pocket she carried a ticket and a letter, a proposal of sorts from a man she had never met. He was a rancher near a strange sounding placed called Chugwater, somewhere out in Wyoming.

This was her chance for freedom. It also meant a new and hopefully better life. So what if she had picked him from an advertisement in the *Matrimonial News* like a new pair of shoes. The life he promised had to be better than what she had now.

She just had to make sure she didn't miss that boat.

Molly worked her way down the cobblestone streets toward the river. They were wet from an early morning shower and she knew from experience it would be easy to slip and fall. She stayed in the shadows hoping to avoid being noticed by the few passers-by at that early hour.

An alley cat of mixed breed and color raced across the street in front of her and barely missed the hooves of a horse pulling a milk wagon. His howl and scream of discontent were without merit, for he went untouched and none of his remaining lives was used.

"At least he wasn't a black cat," she muttered out loud. "I don't need any bad luck right now."

A drunk, wet from the rain and nursing a whiskey bottle with its few remaining precious drops of liquid, called out to her from his prone position under the steps of a brick boardinghouse.

"Gotta drink lady?" he called after her. "Help an old man out. How 'bout a drink?"

The rain fell again and she felt its wetness soaking through her clothing. She hurried on toward the river.

Not far now, she thought to herself.

Her long red hair clung to her scalp. She felt the wetness running cold along her neck and downward along the skin of her back. She shivered. Her valise was soaked along with its contents. Like one of the many river rats she watched scurry along the docks and climb the big, heavy ropes, she felt wet and scared.

Marcus Dunn, the rancher with whom she had been corresponding for almost three months, had sent her money to make the trip west . . . plenty of money. She was to take the train from St. Louis to Cheyenne. Then she was to take the stage to Chugwater. He would meet her there.

Instead, she chose to save money by taking a riverboat hauling passengers and cargo up the Missouri River. She planned to leave the river in Omaha or Sioux City and then take the train west. With the money saved, she purchased some new "more suitable" clothing in which to meet her future husband.

Molly Collins was only 17 years old and by most every standard used to measure such things was considered attractive. She also was much older and mature than her years. It had been her misfortune to have a mother who worked the streets at night. Nobody knew who her father was. Her father could have been any number of male callers her mother had entertained 17 years or so earlier.

Her upbringing had hardened her to life in the back alleys, bars and dark side of South St. Louis. She had never been out of the city for more than a few miles her entire life. Her world consisted of a few city blocks.

Men were a part of her life. Trusting them was another matter. For Molly, trust was harder won and tougher given. Few men had ever taken time to try earning her trust. Fewer still had actually earned it. Now she was preparing to trust someone she had never met.

And, while she had thus far avoided taking up the work of her mother, it had not been easy. Men were drawn to her . . . all kinds of men. Her mother chastised her for being so "uppity." She had often told Molly, "It ain't such a bad life if you're careful of the mean ones and avoid disease."

For almost five years, she had worked cleaning rooms in the boarding house where her mother plied her trade. It was hard and dirty work. Cleanliness ranked somewhere below a good Saturday night drunk for most of the residents.

Molly wanted more.

A kindly, old bartender named Isaac at

the Roughneck Bar and Gaming House had helped teach her the basics of reading and writing. He had been a teacher back in Ohio in some past life. Fortune, or the lack thereof, had dropped him into the city's slums and outhouses. He gladly had filled the role of father to the young Molly for much of her life . . . often encouraging her to "break out" and "be somebody."

Now she was escaping. She had shared her plans with no one. A riverboat captain with whom she had shared a few drinks had promised her safe passage up river. Now she sought a Missouri River Packet call the "Mary Stephens" and the freedom it represented.

Once she'd climbed the narrow gangplank and was settled on board, she thought, *this might actually work out.*

The rain slacked off and dawn began its foggy, humid awakening east across the river over Illinois farming country. Sweat would soon replace rain as the moisture on her forehead. And by sunrise, the buildings of her childhood were left to memory. The river entered Missouri and the rising prairie beyond. It would wind west and northwest like a snake from the Mississippi River at St. Louis for more than 2,500 miles into Montana Territory.

The boat, which was a stern wheel wooden hull packet, was loaded with farming equipment, saddles, harness, foodstuffs, newsprint, bolts of fabric, and rolls of barb wire. It carried the necessities of an ever-expanding West. There were other passengers but most kept to themselves. Wives made a point of steering their husbands away from Molly.

Near Westport, Missouri, the Captain slowed the boat to visit with some men fishing near the mouth of a smaller stream that fed into the main river. He bartered some beans for a mess of fresh frog legs which were fried to great delight for him and a few select passengers. Molly was among them. A few of the legs had not been properly cleaned and tried leaping from the frying pan.

Later in the evening, Molly could hear bullfrogs croaking along the riverbanks and she wondered if they weren't crying out for "lost cousins".

But, they were tasty, she admitted to herself.

The next morning Molly stood on the forward deck and watched the river ahead. It was as if she expected some grand revelation to endorse her decision to leave. She used a small umbrella to protect against the unrelenting sun. However, the humidity and insects, especially the mosquitoes, were another matter.

She watched birds of all types and colors fly to and fro over the river. Insects dipped and dove at the water's surface. Smaller streams and muddy-bank creeks fed the river from time to time. However, it was the sun and heat that stole what energy she had and forced her inside from time to time. It was a hot, humid, boring trip.

"Not like the city," the captain had said the morning of their fourth day. "You'll get used to it. And just wait until you see them snow-covered mountains and the vast prairies without a single tree. My . . . they are grand!"

Late one afternoon, a spring storm gathered on the western horizon out over Kansas and then swept over them in a brief spate of anger. A high wind signaled the storm's arrival and anything not tied down was sent flying into the muddy river water and beyond. Along the riverbanks trees bent low under the storms driving force.

"Better take cover," shouted the boat's captain to all within earshot. "This could be a mean one."

Molly found shelter under a tarp-covered pile of goods and crates on the forward deck. There was no time to go below. Two young boys about 13 years old quickly joined her.

Together the trio rode out the brief storm, each struggling to fit in the small makeshift shelter. Each seemed content to share a common desire to stay dry, although the boys couldn't help but stare at Molly and her red hair.

The storm passed quickly, leaving the boat wet and the deck slippery. The boys' mother came looking for them and was not happy upon learning they had shared time and space with Molly. She grabbed one by the ear lobe and began to reprimand them both.

Toward the east a cloud formation towered thousands of feet into the late afternoon sky. Spellbound by the sheer volume of its mass, Molly watched as the clouds reflected the sun's setting rays into a myriad of colors. This mountain of clouds rose up heavy, massive as if to crush all life below.

Different shades of yellow mixed with cream and taupe near the top. And, as the sun fell toward darkness it bathed the structure's upper regions with warm, subtle oranges, yellows and beiges.

However, nearer the ground, this magnificent mix of clouds darkened into eclectic shades of blues, grays and purples. No longer warmed by the sun, the same thunderstorm, which had passed over them earlier, now tore at the cloud's underpinnings. Streaks of lightning ripped through the clouds signaling the storm's eastward path. More than one Missouri farmer would feel its wrath of heavy rain and hail long into the night.

Molly stared in awe and felt a chill.

Morning brought a return to sunshine and humidity, and subsequent days brought more of the same. The trip was for the most part uneventful.

One day just north of Leavenworth, Kansas, a young boy fell overboard. She watched him reach playfully at a diving bird, then fall over the rail into the swirling river below. Molly screamed, then gasped for the same air the boy sought in dying. He drowned before he could be pulled from the fast-moving current.

There were brief stops at small river towns. Places like Franklin, Lexington, Leavenworth and Atchison. Towns where wagon wheels, barrels of flour and even some cloth were welcomed.

Passengers came and went. Molly kept to herself and stayed on board. For the most part, it was a time of boredom and anxious anticipation.

Molly folded the letter for the hundredth time then gazed at the trees along both sides of the river.

Molly Dunn . . . I like the sound of it, she thought.

Now and then, the swamped wreckage of other vessels could be seen along the riverbank and in the river itself. Submerged tree trunks and shallow sand bars were the main obstacles, but with dry weather further west, the river was abnormally low and most hazards were clearly visible.

She leaned over the railing and watched the water flow by. The riverboat wasn't making very good time and that worried her. Still, there was the ever-present possibility of running aground on a sandbar. The result was a more cautious approach to navigating the river. Molly was suffering from a combination of boredom and anxiety.

After watching the skyline change little each day from the deck of the boat, she was ready for solid ground. The captain had promised her that the floating part of her journey was nearly at an end.

Once the boat had been tied up to the docks in Omaha, Molly said her goodbyes and got off. The train station was easy to find and before long she was on board the

Union Pacific and headed due west. Cheyenne and her future were somewhere over the distant horizon.

CHAPTER 9
AN AWAKENING SPIRIT

A sign worn from years of neglect marked the Cheyenne-Deadwood stage station. The building was old with its best years long gone. The coming of the railroad had changed things, now reaching most of the same places as the stagecoach. And despite the decline in riders, the station held onto the past and waited for the end.

Men and women came and went. There were passing glances and little talk among those whose lives were so briefly entwined. Each person had his own story to tell, few had anyone to listen. This Wyoming station wasn't the place for telling or sharing.

There was a drummer from Chicago, three prospectors headed for Deadwood, and a woman grieving for a lost child who died of yellow fever. There was a banker from Denver and two cowboys looking for trouble. There was an old man, long past his prime, going to visit family in Douglas.

There was a rancher headed for a stockman's meeting and a disheveled preacher clutching a satchel and a Bible.

Sarah was soon among them. With the ordeals of recent days behind her, she found the station and purchased a ticket for Chugwater. It would be a long, bouncing, uncomfortable ride across the open grassland. And, honestly she had had about enough of stagecoaches, given her recent encounter with the prairie fire.

Just outside, sitting on an old wooden bench slick from years of use, she spotted a young woman with long red hair. Her pale complexion from years of being indoors gave her a frail, almost unhealthy appearance. The woman seemed tired, pensive, and deep in thought.

Probably just needs some sunshine and fresh air, thought Sarah.

"Waiting for the stage?" she asked cautiously.

"Yes . . . yes I am," Molly answered, looking up surprised someone might actually be talking to her.

"Which direction you headed?" Sarah asked with a sweeping gesture of her left hand.

"I'm going to a place called Chugwater somewhere north of here."

"Really? Me too! My father has a ranch near Chugwater."

There was a brief pause then Sarah spoke again.

"My name is Sarah Meadows."

Molly returned Sarah's smile.

"It's nice to meet you. I'm Molly Collins."

The two women struck up a conversation. Then after a period of time and despite their widely different backgrounds, a mutual admiration was born.

Both women were worn out. Yet, their new friendship gave way to a renewed energy and excitement. However, once they boarded the Cheyenne-Black Hills stage their small talk gave way to long periods of silence.

The coach rolled north surrounded by the never-ending grassland. The mood inside the coach gave way to quiet, nervous anticipation. Both were close to journey's end now.

Molly broke the silence.

"Are the Indians still hostile out here? I mean should we worry?"

"When my family moved here this area was full of Indians," explained Sarah. "However, most of the hostilities were north of our place, up in the Tongue and Powder River Country. We would sometimes see them. But, they never bothered us.

"Once the great herds of cattle started moving into the area, up from Texas, it became cattle country. The great grasslands just filled up clear up to Mule Creek Junction and beyond. It was an exciting time and still is with so many big ranches.

"Then, of course, there is our little spread," she laughed.

Sarah watched from the window for familiar landscapes. She had sent a telegram to her father from Cheyenne and eagerly awaited their reunion.

Four years, she thought. *I wonder how much he's changed. I wonder how much I've changed. Will he see any change in me?*

Molly tried to sleep but her nerves would not permit rest. How many times had she second-guessed herself about this whole thing?

Now and then she took a worn piece of paper from a small handbag and looked it over before gazing out the window in silence. It was the advertisement that had caught her attention.

"A rancher of 30 years, 5 feet 8 inches, with a Wyoming cattle operation would like to correspond with a young lady or like widow of loving disposition, object matrimony."

She often reread his letters for she had

kept every one. They promised a better life in a vast, wonderful land. Curiosity gradually had given way to mutual attraction. That was followed by promises of love and means. Marcus Dunn was tired of bachelor life. She was just plain tired.

At first the notion of writing a strange man out West seemed crazy. But, she knew a couple of the "boarding house girls" who had advertised in the *Matrimonial News* in Kansas City and then successfully passed themselves off as "ladies of means" to lonely miners in California.

By the time their future husbands discovered their real past, they were simply happy to have female company, by whatever the means.

"Will he like me? Will I like him? What can you really tell about a person from his letters? Will I really be able to live in this vast land? Will it be lonely out here? My God, what have I done?" she mumbled to herself.

Sarah overheard and smiled. "You'll be fine. If your Mr. Dunn is mean or bad, you'll come stay with dad and me.

"In fact, if you have any doubts when you meet him, you can stay with me until you decide what to do," she volunteered.

They both laughed, and then lapsed back

into their own respective thoughts and doubts.

"When I find the right man or he finds me," said Sarah, breaking the silence. "I want us to be equals, like-thinking partners if you will. Don't misunderstand . . . I know how to keep house and cook. I can even shoot if necessary. And . . . well . . . I can even rope and brand calves if necessary. I will do it all willingly if that's my role. I'll take up the cause and ring the dinner bell without complaint.

"But," she continued, "My husband will be a man . . . someone I want . . . not just need. There are plenty of lonely cowpunchers out there who need a woman for all kinds of reasons short term. But, I want a man who wants an equal partner long term. I want a man who loves this land like I do."

"You think I'm settling?" Molly asked.

"No," Sarah hesitated, quickly realizing she may have said something to offend her new friend.

"I think . . . I think everyone has a different situation. We must each respond in our own way. I'm no Esther Morris or Susan B. Anthony but I do have some pretty strong opinions on things. I mean shouldn't men and women be equal partners? Don't you think it's time women had the right to vote in places besides Wyoming?"

"You sure aren't bashful! I'll agree with that," said Molly.

Then shaking her head, Molly continued, "You are one modern woman. Most days, I'm just concerned about having a place to sleep and finding my next meal. Any way . . . I know about Susan Anthony. . . . but who is Esther Morris?"

"Who is Esther Morris?" asked an incredulous Sarah.

"Why she started the drive for women's suffrage in the Wyoming Territory. That's why Wyoming women can vote today. We can even serve on juries. In most states, we still can't vote."

Sarah caught her breath and exclaimed, "Wyoming women got the right to vote in 1869 and we aim to keep it when this territory finally becomes a state."

"She is like Susan Anthony then," Molly said.

"Better," answered Sarah as the stagecoach swayed onward.

"No wonder you Wyoming women are so opinionated."

Sarah just smiled.

"I'm afraid I'm just looking for a good man and a good home," noted Molly. "I'll leave the politics to someone like you. Let

Marcus Dunn need me, want me, whatever . . . from his letters he seems to be a good man. I will make him a good wife and in return I'll have a permanent roof over my head, a warm fire in winter, decent food and a man with a good heart . . . and there will be no more hungry days, saloons, drunks, one-night stands and morning bruises. Now, that will be heaven."

The coach rumbled onward. Only the sound of the driver cracking his whip from time-to-time and his shouting at the horses broke the silence. Now and then a meadowlark could be heard above the sounds of metal and wood fighting each other as the stage rolled north.

After a few hours the driver stopped the stage to give the horses a chance to rest. He urged the two passengers to step out and stretch their legs.

"Don't go too fer," warned the driver. "I seed growed men get lost out here . . . wandering off . . . paying no mind where they was. Every blade of grass, every hill looks the same out here . . . but they all got a history, a story to tell."

While Sarah dug through her cases for a book to read, Molly walked alone, slowly, listening to the birds and the wind, always the wind. At the top of a nearby hill and with the stagecoach still in sight, she gazed toward far off horizons in every direction. The wind was stronger here and it seemed loud in her ears.

Such a vast land, she thought suddenly feeling very small and vulnerable. *We are in a vast ocean of grass and we're so tiny . . . so insignificant.*

She felt almost frightened by the great distances and she turned often to make sure the stagecoach was still within sight. Reassured that she wasn't totally alone, she watched as the never ceasing wind caught, pushed and shoved each blade of grass into wave upon wave of swaying motion. Still, each blade returned to its original position only to be pushed over again and again.

It never gives up, she thought.

"Amazing isn't it?" said Sarah as she joined Molly.

"I never tire of seeing it. My father always says 'this is where the good winds blow.' The wind, like God, is always there. It always brings us a new day, a fresh blue sky and a warm sun. It always blows the storms away and carries the bad in our lives to far away places."

Molly observed, "It's so beautiful in its vast, unending simplicity. Wind, sky and grass . . . add a few birds and I believe you have described the great Nebraska prairie."

"Actually, we're in Wyoming now," explained Sarah. "But out here, it's hard to tell where one stops and the other begins.

"However," she continued, "Things aren't quite as basic as you make them sound. There is something over each hill . . . more animals than you can count, Indians, buffalo, wildflowers, prairie dogs, antelope, coyotes and much more. But you are correct about one thing . . . sometimes the simple things are the most beautiful."

"Listen," Molly said quietly, "You can hear it!"

"What? Hear what?"

"The wind, the blades of grass brushing against each other, the birds singing, the land itself . . . but mostly the wind."

Sarah sighed, and said, "The wind . . . it's just a part of our lives. Its sound is the melody of life's daily anthem . . . even when blowing up a big dust storm or a big snowstorm. We live with it. It's part of us."

Molly looked and listened as if seeing and hearing for the first time the basic elements of the land itself. "It's so clean, so pure, and so basic. It is nothing like the back streets and slums of St. Louis."

Sarah took a few steps forward and turned toward the eastern horizon.

"I often believe we stand in the midst of God's greatest symphony . . . the wind rising in volume . . . then falling away . . . then rising again . . . over and over toward some inevitable crescendo . . . then near its peak it falls away once more . . . never quite complete . . . always teasing . . . nearly driving us mad with expectation," said Sarah.

"Few over a lifetime ever recognize that the simple beauty of life is in the notes . . . not necessarily in the song as a whole. We often wait for something better. Yet, we fail to hear the beautiful rise and fall of the notes that make up our daily lives."

Sarah stopped for a moment and looked at her friend so deep in thought. "Enough of this. We'd better get back. I'd hate for us to get left behind . . . even for a concert," she laughed.

"A lot of people come out here and see a vast empty expanse, a great rolling prairie void of life. They see the elephant," Sarah continued as they walked.

"Elephants . . . out here?"

"Come along, I'll explain," said Sarah.

"What they're really saying about themselves is 'I'm too busy. I have too much on my mind to see and hear all that's here. The voices within are just too loud. They don't see the beauty in life around them.

They don't hear the wonder of it all . . . like butterfly wings rising on the wind, or a coyote's lonely, mournful song in the dark of night."

Molly took a quick look around, sighed and then followed her friend toward the waiting coach. A soft breeze touched her cheeks and she shivered at the vastness around her, but at the same time she never felt more alive.

CHAPTER 10
LONELY IN A CROWDED ROOM

The cool, early-morning air felt good going down. Jake and Tom took long, deep breaths of the good, clean air and enjoyed the moment. They rode easy and quiet, in no hurry to learn their fate in Chugwater.

Jake felt he had a score to settle with two of Winston's no account gun hands. But, that would take care of itself in due time. He warned himself not to let his guard down and stick to their plans.

The two men passed near where Jake had been shot and moved on without stopping. Cottonwood trees gave way to pine, juniper and aspen.

When the sun stood directly overhead, the two men stopped to eat and rest their horses. Maria had packed some food and underneath some old and weathered pine trees they ate.

Rather than ride directly toward Chugwater, the two men had decided to circle east then ride into town from a direction unrelated to old man Meadows. It would take an extra day of riding, but they were in no hurry.

They briefly rode above the tree line where the cold and mountain winds prevented trees from growing. They followed old game trails and soon began working their way back down. They were descending toward a vast open prairie stretching as far as the eye could see.

A cool breeze weaved its way among the trees and underbrush as they descended. The breeze slid past each branch and nudged the leaves into motion. Now and again it pushed harder, forcing even the limbs to yield and move aside. The leaves rustled in the quiet, noiseless vacuum.

There is a message up here so close to God, thought Jake. *In the grand scheme of life, a man's roots normally run deep in the soil. But, up here . . . up here you ride close to heaven itself.*

Few men ever stray far from their birth place . . . often setting down roots close to home, Jake continued. *Yet, those that leave usually have a reason. Some get pushed out and still others choose to leave on their own,*

Jake had left. Now and then he wondered if he had been wrong to leave.

Left to his own devices, man most often will choose to stay close to his roots, his family bonds. Jake knew that. Most of his immediate family had stayed close. Most remained only a few miles from each other. However, Jake had decided to run. The bonds that held him to family and kin had been torn apart.

A sorrowful wind had brought death and despair to his family. Unlike the cool breeze through these mountain cottonwoods, the Summers family had suffered greatly from losses during the Civil War.

Jake's father died from unhealed wounds he received fighting at Gettysburg for the South. A carpetbagger killed his older brother, Jesse, down in Texas. And, his mother found comfort behind tearful eyes and the insanity that followed. Only his aged grandmother had tried to bind the wounds. But, even she was torn by pangs of guilt about her daughter's declining mental state. She was weakened for it.

Jake Summers was an only a teenage child of 14 . . . a restless teenager at that . . . when he left home. His grandmother could not hold him.

Lulled into a quiet melancholy by the rustling leaves and cool air, Jake drifted through his past and wondered at the fate of his family. Only the sound of horseshoes striking rocks broke through the silence. The thud of hooves on decaying leaves and the familiar creaking of saddle leather stirred him awake. Then he heard Tom speak.

"Jake, I been thinking," Tom was saying. "Jake, you listening or you daydreaming?"

"Be careful," Jake answered with a smile. "Don't think too much. Your brain ain't used to it."

The good-natured banter continued as the two men rode.

"I was wondering why you don't take Thompson up on his offer to start ranching?" asked Tom. "I mean he's willing to help and all."

"Think so?" asked Jake.

"Thompson has all but given you that section of ground down on the North Laramie," Tom continued. "That's a great little place. Get you about 200 heifers and some eager bulls and you'd be set."

"Well, maybe," Jake answered. "What about you? You after my job?"

Tom laughed but didn't answer.

The two men fell silent. Both lost in their own thoughts of future options and long-term plans. Deep down Jake knew his friend was correct. *The country is filling up. Maybe it's time to seize the opportunity.*

Jake and Tom rode south along a series of ridges rising to escape the prairie floor but still consumed by a massive blanket of grass. Now, the wind blew stronger from out of the north pushing them from behind.

Meadowlarks and the incessant, never-dying wind filled Jake's ears with singing while intermittently mixed with the muffled sound of his own horse's hooves striking the dry, hardened earth.

He was lost, not in a physical sense for he knew where he was in relation to the ranch complex. No. . . . He was lost in a maze of deep thoughts and self-evaluation.

Life was good. But, could it be better? he wondered.

Jake knew his youth was gone; he felt older now in so many ways. By many standards, he was already an old man. Now he sensed something was missing . . . something of substance and value. But, he was unclear and confused about what it was he sought or needed to be happier.

A startled bird rose from relative security among the grasses and threw itself upon the wind in front of him. His horse momentarily was startled and Jake was suddenly awakened anew to the purpose of his mission. Spurs touched flank and he picked up the pace.

That night, after supper, Jake lay in his bedroll and stared at the stars and a big, yellow full moon. The stars covered a deeply black canvas of night sky. He thought them so close as if touchable.

"Ever notice the sounds of night?" he asked Tom, not really expecting an answer. "There is no sweeter music than the notes of the night. There is a gentle blending of all those sounds while we seek sleep and the darkness descends over us. While black of night covers the land, filling every crevice and form, we rest on faith and experience that dawn will soon bring a new and possibly better day. And, we rest easy. What could be better than that?"

Off in the distance was some unnamed mountain lake. Moonbeams were reflecting off its surface and the water shimmered in the moon's light. Coyotes cried a mournful, lonely song. And, deep down the Box T foreman was overcome by a massive loneliness.

A lot of friends and acquaintances don't necessarily reduce the loneliness, he thought. *Even in a crowd, loneliness can grip your soul and tear at your heart. You can feel it in your shoulders and the ache reaches deep. Sometimes a person needs the reassurance of a kind word, a gentle touch or the presence of a caring friend. Deep in a man's soul, sometimes there's something missing even when there are lots of folks around,* thought Jake.

Loneliness is something hard to explain and even more difficult to describe. And surprisingly, it's often not even noticed by those most near . . . those to whom such prevailing and tortuous agony should be obvious. Lonely is often found in a crowded room.

Jake knew that feeling. It had come more and more often lately, often deep in the night when the inner voices cry loud their tortuous message. Driving home the pain, the aching, depressing pain most often felt in the blackness of night. Loneliness is not new to most cowpunchers in this vast land, he thought to himself. But, recently it was having a greater and greater pull on his soul.

In the distance, he heard a coyote cry and Jake felt his pain and came close to feeling the animal's tears.

Men don't cry, he thought. *Why not? We endure a pain that never seems to end in this vast and empty land. Cowhands are a lonely lot.*

Again, a coyote moaned and Jake shuddered. Only Tom's nearby snoring saved him from further agony. He glanced into the deep blackness surrounding the campfire. And in that moment thought he saw something in the dark shadows before realizing it was only his imagination moving against the current of common sense.

Come sweet morning and take my mind to a better place in the light of day, he thought as sleep came reluctantly over him. He slept.

An early morning breeze caught the stir of Tom's breakfast fire and sent a puff of camp smoke into Jake's still sleeping face. He gagged, coughed and quickly rose to a sitting position with a gasping attempt to reach clean air.

"What the . . . ," he exclaimed while waving his hands back and forth to break up the smoky cloud surrounding him.

"Can't you . . . ," he paused. "Get a fire going without choking a man to death? For heaven's sake!"

Tom smiled, and poured himself a cup of coffee. "Time you was up anyhow."

Morning took on a new face. There was a quiet sense of nervous expectation. The relaxed talk of the previous day was gone. They said little and both watched their surroundings for anything out-of-place.

Jake often checked their back trail, not really expecting to see any one . . . "but just in case."

Now and then their horses seemed uneasy about something. They often would see the markings high on a tree where a grizzly bear had stood on his hind legs and scratched his claws on the bark.

"Wouldn't want to meet that fellow anytime soon," noted Jake.

"Amen," said Tom.

Although Thompson had warned them to watch, report and wait, they knew to expect the unexpected. They intended to pose as drifting cowhands looking for work. That guise of course could blow up entirely if someone they knew spotted them.

After a day and a half of riding, they were in mixed grass country. They had passed through short grass country at the higher elevations. Hill after rolling hill gave way to the grasses and wildflowers of early summer. Trees were scarce now. Usually they were found along streams and creeks where prairie fires had failed to reach them and their thirsty roots could reach moisture.

Meadows had described the area as beautiful, but full of great emptiness. Jake found the same . . . in a vast sea of waving grass from horizon to horizon. It was a land of such vastness as to test all measure of believability and all measure of comprehension. It was an undulating, rolling sea of grass rising to meet heaven itself.

"Give me some snow-covered mountains," Tom said. "Along with some pretty grass-covered valleys."

Jake smiled. "There is a special beauty here as well."

As they drew up near the town of Chug-water, growth along the Laramie River became more evident. They had seen ranch houses along their route but nothing seemed out of the ordinary. The ride had been uneventful. Now it was time to go to work.

Jake decided to check the local saloon for information while Tom got them a room at the hotel. Both men needed a bath, a shave and some clean clothes.

"However," Jake noted, "We don't wanna look too pretty."

The saloon was nearly empty at mid-afternoon so Jake found no competition for space at the bar. The barkeeper was a rough sort, more adept at stopping fights than pouring drinks.

"Quiet town," said Jake with the hopes of drawing some reaction from the obviously bored barkeeper.

He got a grunt in response.

"Know anybody hiring?" Jake continued.

"What line of work you in?" the barkeeper

asked as he glanced at the gun hanging from Jake's right hip.

"Cattle mostly," he answered.

"Around here . . . ," the barkeeper looked him over, then around the room. "Well, around here working cattle can have all kinds of meaning. Guess it depends on your specialty."

The barkeeper slowly looked at the young man as he stepped down the bar to face Jake. Once satisfied Jake was just an out-of-work cowhand, he continued. "Late in the spring for hiring. Spring work mostly done . . . too early for fall. However . . . if you can handle . . ." he stopped mid-sentence.

Through the saloon doors walked a large red-faced man wearing a dark, dust-covered suit about two sizes too small. The man's face was covered with sweat and his shirt collar was soaked through. Jake figured the man to be about 60. An entourage of about five gun hands and several hangers on followed him.

Jake looked back at the barkeeper who had suddenly found work wiping glasses. He knew better than to reopen their previous line of talk . . . especially when this gent had an obvious level of self-importance.

"Drinks for everyone," shouted the red-faced man. "I'm in a celebrating mood today."

Winston, thought Jake.

After watching the group's activities and their reflection in a large mirror over the bar for about 15 minutes, Jake decided to find Tom.

His sidekick had gotten them a room then ventured to a nearby general store for much the same reason Jake had gone to the saloon . . . information. As Tom approached, he heard two men arguing.

"We've got to do something and soon," he heard one man say.

"We do and Winston will have us dead by nightfall," said the other.

"At this rate, you ain't going to have no customers left."

As Tom entered the store the men fell silent. The store clerk and apparent owner merely nodded an awareness of his presence and began dusting his shelves. The second man straightened his hat and left.

"Afternoon," said Tom.

"How can I help you?"

"Know anybody hiring?"

"No I don't, stranger," said the clerk. "And, if you want a piece of friendly advice I'd move on down the road. This ain't a real friendly town right now," he continued bluntly.

Tom probed deeper.

"Seems like good cattle country. Would imagine several ranches in the area. Somebody must need some kind of help."

The clerk glanced out the front window then with the tone of his voice rising, he said, "Man named Winston owns most of the spreads here these days . . . or at least claims he does. But, unless you know how to use that Colt on your hip, I'd keep riding."

Realizing he may have said too much, the storeowner went back to dusting.

Tom turned and left the store. He found Jake sitting in a rocking chair in front of the hotel.

"Real friendly town," he muttered with a sense of futility in his voice.

"People seem just plain scared," Jake noted. "Hotel clerk told me there have been several killings recently. Mostly ranchers. Local sheriff apparently is some old man unable to prove anything or too afraid to even try. Only last week a young rancher named Marcus Dunn was found hanging from the rafters in his barn. Sheriff ruled it a suicide. Makes you wonder how he got up there carrying a rope with his hands tied.

Winston's men moved in the next day . . . barely got him buried before they took over lock, stock and barrel."

The two Box T hands watched the stagecoach roll past the hotel and stop in front of the general store where a sign hung loose all but falling from disrepair. The driver climbed down and opened the coach door opposite where the two men sat.

"Chugwater, ladies," the driver announced. He said it so loud even the locals were reminded where they lived.

Down the street came a short man with delicate features and a wrinkled, frumpy black suit. He wore no hat but had to work at not losing his wire-rimmed glasses. He was half running and half walking and totally out of breath. He was waving some papers.

"Ladies, ladies," he was calling out. "Hold on. Hold on."

The men couldn't hear or see the women but it was obvious the man urgently wanted to talk with someone getting off the stage. They were amused at the man's labored appearance and effort.

"What is it?" Sarah asked as he came closer.

"Miss Meadows? Miss Collins?" he asked.

"I'm Sarah Meadows. And, this is my

friend, Molly Collins. How may we help you?"

Tom turned to Jake, "Wonder what's going on over there?"

Jake said nothing, but watched closely, although the stagecoach was blocking most of their view.

"Miss Meadows, I was unable to locate your father and give him the telegram you sent. I'm afraid he won't be here to meet you."

An extremely disappointed Sarah said, "What do you mean you couldn't locate him? He has a ranch just north of here."

"That's just my point," the little man continued while wiping sweat from his forehead. "He's not out there anymore."

"What?"

A bewildered Sarah grabbed the front wheel of the coach to steady herself. "What do you mean he's not out there?"

The man answered, "I don't know the details. . . . except he's gone. I suggest you ask around town. Maybe someone can give you some information." Then he turned to Molly.

"Now Miss Collins," he continued.

Molly had moved to comfort her friend.

"I'm afraid I have bad news for you as well."

Now it was Sarah's turn to provide comfort while still battling her own emotions.

"What is it?" Molly asked. Her nerves giving way to fear.

"Mr. Dunn, to whom you recently sent a telegram."

"Yes," she said as she stepped toward the little man. "What about him?"

"Heee. . . . heee," stammered the man.

"Yes, speak up man," she said. "Is he standing me up?"

"No madam. He's dead. He committed suicide . . . last week."

Whether it was the news, the heat, the long trip or all the above, the world suddenly caved in on Molly Collins. She fainted.

Sarah rushed to the aid of her new friend. The storekeeper, coach driver and other onlookers quickly joined her.

"Wonder what all the commotion is about?" Tom asked Jake.

"Not sure," he answered. "But, it appears at least one of those young ladies is sick or something."

"Maybe we should offer to help," said a grinning Tom.

Jake said nothing. He sat and watched.

CHAPTER 11
WINSTON HIRES
TWO PUNCHERS

A blistering midday sun heated the dust-filled air and made it hard to breathe. And while the two hands sat on the hotel porch in the shade, they could only assume activity around the stage was in some way related to the weather.

Passing horses stirred the dusty street and sent clouds of earthly powder into an already hazy day.

A couple of skinny boys passed by and whether by deliberate intent or slovenly habit, they shuffled their feet as if to create a furrow in the dry street bed. Behind them, dirt loosened by their passing lifted skyward and was carried into the mix of earth and air, tinged by the smell of horse manure.

Their nostrils recoiled in an overworked struggle to screen the flow of dirty air into heavy lungs, and Tom sneezed.

With their attention focused on the coach's arrival and its passengers, Jake and

Tom failed to notice the approach of three men from the opposite direction. By the time they realized they were no longer alone, it was too late to react.

"On your feet gents," came a gruff voice from behind them.

"What the . . . ?" Jake started to his feet.

"Easy stranger. Winston wants to see you now!"

The words brought both Box T hands back to reality. They quickly remembered why they were in Chugwater. As they turned to face these intruders, it was Jake who froze. Not more than six feet away stood a tall man with a scar running from just under his left ear down across the side of his face.

"Scar!" he thought with a sense of fear.

Jake recognized him immediately. He prayed he was covered with enough dust, dirt and whiskers to hide his own identity. It soon became evident that the gunman had no idea who he was addressing.

Behind him, like a faithful, loyal dog stood Willie Temple and another man who shared his poor attention to hygiene and cleanliness.

Tom, however, was the first to respond.

"Who is Winston?"

"You'll know soon enough. Come along. And, we ain't asking again," Scar's voice rising in anger at their slow response.

"You'll know. You'll know," Willie kept repeating as he bounced around like an overly active child. He kept giggling and Jake could see a portion of the man's last meal still stuck in his yellow, dirty teeth.

"Lead the way boys," said Jake.

"Boys? Did he call us boys?" muttered Willie.

"Shut up you idiot. Winston is waiting," scolded Scar.

As they entered the saloon Jake noticed it wasn't any busier than during his earlier visit. They found Winston sitting behind a table in a back corner. He didn't see the barkeeper from before.

Winston sat behind a table covered with a food and beer-stained tablecloth. A soiled towel was stuffed into his collar to prevent excess food from reaching his sweat-soaked shirt.

However, his sloppy eating habits only enhanced his chances of getting dirty. He talked with his mouth both open and full. And, the result was a constant shower of partially chewed food exiting the teeth and drool-filled opening in the front of his face.

On this particular morning, he was especially irritable. Things were not going well. Those around could only bear the brunt of his foul nature. Sweat found a permanent home on his forehead and he made no attempt to brush it away.

"Watch this," he stammered with a mouth full of biscuit crumbs falling across his massive stomach.

A cockroach making its way across the table in front of Winston had caught his eye. It was time for some fun and the cockroach was totally unaware that it was about to become the main participant. With a flick of his wrist, Winston plunged his fork into the unsuspecting roach pinning it to the wooden table. He then held it up for all to see.

"Anyone cross me . . . anyone mess with me!" he muttered.

Then just as quickly he rubbed the roach against the table edge effectively removing it from his eating utensil. Then he continued to eat. Any normal decency and etiquette in such a situation was totally lacking.

"Sit down gents," Winston told Jake and Tom who had remained silent during the man's performance. Jake assumed they had few other options.

"Understand you two are new to town? What are you doing here?"

"Who wants to know?" Jake responded

At that Willie took a step forward with his right hand on the butt of his pistol. "Why you . . ." His words trailed off as Winston raised a hand. Scar was also moving to grab his arm and hold him back.

Winston smiled. "My boys take exception when strangers don't show me respect. You'll learn."

Winston was worse than dishonest. He enjoyed the challenge of cheating others, the bigger the swindle the better. He had over the years cheated many an unsuspecting and naïve investor.

One such person was an absentee investor from Ireland who bought a ranch in Southern Colorado. He had hired Winston to manage his new ranch. However, Winston cheated the man out of more than $100,000. The man's friends would later say it was "like hiring a fox to guard the hen house."

Winston had claimed most of the man's cattle were lost to winter blizzards and such. In truth, they had been trailed to Dodge City and sold. The profits went into his private bank accounts. When the investor became suspicious, Winston relocated to Wyoming.

Suspect herd books were his specialty. He liked to call it "creative accounting".

In another instance, he sold the same cattle twice, then skipped town leaving both parties behind to argue their ownership of the animals.

Efforts to develop a similar scheme with Alexander Swan, president of the Swan Land and Cattle Company, fell through when Swan's Scottish employers fired him when they began to suspect his own herd books were incorrect.

Winston merely moved into Chugwater and set up shop for another scheme.

"Now boys, these two gents just got into town. They don't know the facts of life in Chugwater. They don't know how I do business. But, they'll learn."

Then turning to Jake and Tom, he said, "I want to know . . . and since you are new to town . . . this time I'll ask twice. But in the future, I'll ask once. Get my meaning? Now why are you in Chugwater?"

"Looking for work," Jake said. "Figured with so much grass around there must be ranches needing hands."

"Work . . . huh?" Winston repeated the word only half believing the cowhand in front of him.

"Where you boys from?"

"Montana," answered Jake. "Been punching cows up in the Judith Basin country. You ever hear tell of old Bob Thoroughman, up near Cascade in the Chesnut Valley?"

"Can't say as I have," Winston said.

"How 'bout the Cannon Brothers or the Bickett and Mills?"

Winston turned to his followers, "Any you boys hear tell of anybody like that . . . up in Montana?"

Nobody answered.

"Guess I'll need to take you boys at your word," said Winston turning his attention back to the two men sitting in front of him.

"Guess so," Jake mumbled.

Suddenly, Jake realized their horses still tied in front of the hotel carried the Box T brand. Someone familiar with the Thompson ranch and brand would know immediately these two strangers were not riding Montana horses. He took a quick look around hoping these hired gunmen wouldn't know one brand from another. But, they needed a change of horses and soon.

"Tell you what," Winston continued. "I've been expanding my holdings recently and could use a couple more punchers."

"Boss . . . ?" Scar interrupted.

Winston raised a hand to silence the gunman. "Never mind. We'll see if these boys know anything about cows."

Pointing to Jake he said, "Go out to the old Meadows place and tell Smitty I sent you to punch cows. He'll put you to work."

Then turning to Tom, "You go with Nelson here and take some supplies out to the Dunn Ranch. Then all of you meet up at the Meadows place. Smitty will know what to do with you.

"Now both of you get out of here."

Jake hated for the two of them to be separated but for the moment he figured it safe. A quick look at Tom told him to keep quiet and go along.

Winston was unsure about the hiring of the two young cowboys who had suddenly shown up in Chugwater. And, while it was not unusual for drifting hands to come and go, he sensed these two weren't the usual drifters. Still, he hired them out of need for more help.

"They'll deserve some watching," he told Scar and Willie after the two Box T hands had gone outside. "Make sure you two keep an eye on them, you hear?"

After a few moments, Winston returned to his eating and Scar chose the moment to ask a delicate question.

"Yes, what is it?" Winston asked.

"Well . . . the old lady on the Bar 5 won't leave," said Scar. "And, well . . . well the boys aren't too keen on running the old lady out. Her being a grandma type and all."

153

"What do you mean she won't leave? Run her out! We need that spread!"

Scar hesitated.

"Well . . . some of the boys . . . not me and Willie mind you . . . but some of the others are a little skittish about railroading the old lady. Well . . . they don't want to do it."

Winston bellowed, "Damn it Scar. You send Charlie Norton and a couple others out to that old lady's place this afternoon. I'm tired of messing with her. If she doesn't leave . . . tell them to burn her out. Now get going!"

As Scar stepped down into the street, he mumbled "someday me and that old man are going to have a . . ."

"Ain't we suppose to be watching them two new hands?" Willie interrupted.

"They can watch themselves for all I care," said Scar. "We gotta find Charlie Norton and send him after that old lady."

Jake and Tom stopped by the hotel to pick up their things and compared notes.

"By the way, we need to get us some new horses . . . at least for a few days," Jake pointed out.

"I don't understand," Tom said.

"The Box T brand on them horses of ours . . . somebody might recognize the brand and give us a way. Keep your eyes open for a switch of animals."

Jake had been riding for about an hour when he noticed a long thin column of gray smoke rising from the horizon off to his left. Curious, he turned his horse in that direction, touching his spurs to the flanks of his horse to step up the pace. He sensed a need for urgency.

From atop a long ridge he tried to survey the smoke-filled scene below him. There was a small ranch complex of neglected buildings and the barn was on fire. Jake dismounted and worked his way down the ridge and into a small stand of cottonwoods, trying to take a closer look without being seen.

Someone was in trouble . . . serious trouble.

What he found sent a chill up his back. Three men were yelling at an old woman tied to the horse corral fence. Her gray hair had a wild and unkempt look and her clothing was torn. He recognized men from town. They had been among the "hangers on" with Winston back in the saloon.

Although frightened, the woman didn't appear to be seriously harmed. There were some red marks on her face. Rawhide roping tightly bound her arms to the pole fence.

Jake moved closer by following a shallow stream that coursed its way along the side of the corral then the house before disappearing in a stand of short grass. A few cottonwood trees and the stream bank provided some degree of cover.

The men were so occupied with abusing the woman they never considered someone else might be nearby.

"Lady, don't make me shoot you," one man shouted.

"Charlie, let's just shoot the old lady and get back to town," said another.

The man called Charlie stepped up the woman and grabbed her by the hair. "Listen you old coot . . . sign this worthless place over to Winston and we'll be on our way. This dump ain't worth dying for. You understand me?"

"Go to hell," the woman shouted.

A slap across her aged and wrinkled face echoed across the clearing and made Jake flinch.

"Old lady, we gave you a chance. Now you'll die for your stupidity. Boys, let's go search the house, then torch it!"

As the three men crossed the clearing to the house, Jake seized the moment and climbed into the horse corral from the opposite direction. Using the woman's equally aged horse for cover he quickly came up behind her.

"Don't move," he whispered.

"Who's there?" the woman asked softly and with surprise.

"Lady," he spoke quietly, "I'm here to help you. Don't move sudden and don't let on I'm here."

She nodded in understanding but said nothing more.

One of Winston's men glanced back from the porch, but failed to notice more than the woman's horse moving around the corral. The woman was still tied. He sighed then entered the house after the others.

"Look for anything valuable," Charlie Norton called to the others.

There were sounds of things being broken in search of money and other valuables. Now and then one of the men would shout after finding something he thought valuable.

Jake cut the leather ties and told the woman, "we've got to find some cover."

She turned and faced him and motioned toward an old bunkhouse situated opposite the barn. Although stiff from being tied, the woman was wiry and tough as nails. She ran for cover without breaking stride.

Jake started over the corral fence. Wet boots from wading the stream and nearly fresh horse manure combined to make his boots extra slippery. He slipped and came down astride the top fence pole, and then fell off the fence onto the ground outside the corral.

He gasped for air as a sharp pain tore through his groin area. His brain failed to function and his entire mid-section cried out. Jake couldn't help but grab himself as he pulled his legs up to his chest in agony. With blurred eyes and pain beyond words, he lay on the ground and prayed for a quick death.

As his senses returned and the pain began to subside, he tried to standing . . . reaching out to grab the corral fence for support.

Two of Winston's men appeared on the porch with their treasures. One dropped his valuables into a bed of nearly dead flowers and reached for his pistol.

Already smoke was coming from inside the house. A crackling sound punctuated the afternoon air as a gray plume of smoke from the house mixed with smoke from the barn and climbed over the prairie. It mixed with tall, white cumulus clouds hovering overhead.

From a prone position, Jake found his own pistol and fired twice at the house, forcing the men back inside. Both shots were wide of their mark but served a defensive purpose, if only for a moment.

Suddenly, a couple of rifle shots from the bunkhouse tore splinters from the porch railing and provided additional cover. Jake ran for safety in the old bunkhouse.

The woman opened the door and let him inside.

"I'm obliged for your help," she shouted. "But you sure as hell ain't much of a shot."

Then under her breath, she mumbled, "For a young man you sure can't run either."

In a still high and pain induced voice, Jake tried to explain, "But, I . . . the fence . . . I!"

The woman wasn't listening.

"Here they come," she shouted. "Let's fill the air with lead."

Jake found a window, broke the glass and took careful aim.

Forced into the clearing with a burning house behind them, the horse corral on one side and the barn already crumbling in ash-covered destruction, the three men had few remaining options for cover.

One died at the base of the front steps from a rifle shot.

Jake shot the man named Charlie in the right shoulder. The man grabbed his wound with his left hand as a dark red liquid oozed through his fingers. Still, he managed to return fire while struggling to reach his horse.

The third man had not even pulled his gun, choosing instead to run straight for his tied horse along the far side of the corral. Mounted and turning for a run to safety, Jake's second shot brought him down in a crumpled mass.

The wounded Norton tried unsuccessfully to mount his horse, but the frightened animal wouldn't stand still. As the horse turned in panic it flung him aside while catching his foot in the stirrup. The animal ran, dragging the gunman with him out onto an unforgiving prairie . . . and death.

Jake stepped back from the window and found the woman looking at him. With the danger past, he noticed her hardened demeanor seemed to soften . . . if only a little. He admired her "tough as nails" approach even it lacked in femininity.

No wonder she was willing to live on this wind-swept ranch, he thought.

"I'm Elsie Gardner," she said. "Never seen you in these parts. Who might you be?"

"I'm Jake Summers."

"Young man, I was in a tight fix. You saved my old hide and I'm grateful."

"Glad I could help," he answered shyly. "Where are your men folk?"

"Ain't got none. Not anymore.

"What are you doing out here?" she asked.

Before Jake could explain, there was a roar from the house as the roof caved in on the main structure sending a shower of sparks into the afternoon sky.

"Winston has been trying to drive me off this place since he hit town. Maybe I should've listened."

"Now what?" Jake asked.

"I still own the place by God," some of the defiance from before resurfacing in her voice. "Guess I'll go stay with my brother in Cheyenne until I figure things out. I've buried a husband and three young'uns out there on that hill. I can't stay away. I'll be back, you can bet on that."

Jake helped her hook up the old horse from the corral to her wagon. She gathered a few possessions from the bunkhouse, a few jars of canned vegetables from the cellar and an old quilt hanging from the clothesline.

"Young man, you be careful. With a little luck maybe we'll cross trails again under more friendly circumstances one day. I owe you!"

"Well . . . you might be able to help."

"How young man?" she asked.

"I could use a new horse . . . just for a few days mind you. Mine is kinda tuckered out and well . . . would you mind if I rode one of yours and left mine here for a spell?"

"Pick one out from the corral. That sorrel gelding over there is a good cow horse and he's gentle."

"I'm much obliged ma'am. I'll come trade 'em back in a few days," explained Jake.

"Never mind. Take your time. Before you leave turn them loose up in that meadow yonder," said the woman as she pointed north. "There's water and plenty of grass. You'll find your animal up there when you're ready."

The prairie grasses and rolling hills gradually swallowed up her departure and she was gone.

Jake took one last look around the still smoldering place, glancing at the two new graves along the stream. He switched his saddle to the new horse and drove the remaining horses to the meadow the woman had pointed out. Then he started once more toward the Meadows Ranch.

Winston is dangerous, he told himself as he rode away. *Me and Tom better watch our back trail.*

Then atop the ridge, he stopped long

enough to straighten a small sign. "The Bar 5." He smiled, touched the brim of his hat, then nudged his horse into an easy lope.

CHAPTER 12
TOO HOT FOR FLYING

The Meadows Ranch sat in a quiet draw at the base of a small, unnamed group of mountains. The terrain rose sharply behind the ranch complex, but in front of the ranch house the prairie rolled out like a carpet as far as the eye could see.

Jake approached by following the road from town, then turning off to follow a series of grassy ridges that partially hid the main ranch complex on two sides.

Two old cow dogs spotted him as he topped a ridge above the ranch house. One was a black and white mix standing nearly back deep in a stock tank of water trying to stay cool. The other was a rusty brown mix that immediately began barking at Jake's sudden appearance and approach.

In a matter of moments, both dogs were trotting cautiously in his direction with water dripping, leaving small pot marks in the thirsty dust. The rust-colored dog barked with contempt at the stranger's approach. The black and white merely followed with a yip now and then. The first dog showed both teeth and slobber as his lips and nose pulled back taunt, fang teeth exposed. His hatred of Jake was immediate and without question . . . but also without substance.

Jake pulled up and waited. And, after a few moments the black and white pulled back, deciding the stranger was no threat . . . besides there was a cool water tank waiting. He had thought better of the idea and retreated. Now without his buddy alongside, the rust-colored dog reluctantly gave way. Still, he made a few parting barks over his shoulder as he gave ground.

After dismounting by a second nearly empty water tank, Jake dropped the reins so his tired and thirsty horse could drink. He walked across the dusty open ground between a bunkhouse and some horse corrals. There was an absence of movement by anything larger than an insect. Then he spotted an old man resting in the shadow of a broken-down wagon lying on its side.

"Too hot to work?" he asked the old man. It was more a statement of the obvious than an actual question.

The old man grunted an illegible response

from behind cracked, dry lips, force apart by an almost equally dry tongue. He then closed his eyes and found a cooler spot behind his eyelids.

A fly broke the dusty, heated silence buzzing from the old man's arm to his nose and back again before even it decided it was too hot and dry for flight. The old man and the fly had come to terms. There would be no swatting and in return no buzzing. In the harsh reality of the moment, if only for a moment, they had found common ground.

"Where's Smitty?" asked Jake, not really expecting an answer. He got none.

The heat and dry weather had reached its peak here on the dry side of the Laramie Mountains.

"This the Meadows Ranch?" he tried one more time without success.

Jake turned toward the cookhouse and bunkhouse with the intent of finding someone more informative. He spotted an old man he took to be the cook. The man had just thrown some garbage into a pit behind the cookhouse. However, before he could say anything the old man disappeared inside the building.

As Jake approached, all hell broke loose.

"Get out! Get out I said," shouted the old cook from inside the cookhouse. His rising voice and tirade was followed by the sound of falling pans and breaking glass. One more "get out" was followed by the sight of a black and white mongrel dog covered in flour escaping out the back door and into the day's sunshine.

With a quick and well-practiced left turn behind a trash pile, the dog narrowly missed being struck by a metal pan. The cook's relatively poor eyesight and reflexes befitting those of most worn-out cowhands turned cook saved the day. The dog stood with tongue hanging, almost grinning, as he watched the cook return to his work.

The mongrel's dash for safety briefly stirred the hot morning air and alarmed a thousand feasting black flies on the rotting and foul-smelling garbage. However, in a matter of moments normalcy returned and each of a thousand and two participants found solace in the day's routine.

"Afternoon," Jake called out.

The startled cook was caught by surprise and he reached for the pistol on his hip that he no longer carried. Turning quickly, he forgot his nemesis the dog and instead eyed the Box T foreman with a combination of contempt and instant anger.

"Looking for Smitty," Jake said.

"I'm not him," the cook said.

"Figured that much," answered Jake.

"He ain't here."

"Well . . . I kinda figured that much as well," Jake responded with a high degree of sarcasm. "Where can I find him?"

"Went over toward Winston's home place. Reckon he'll drift in for supper. Who wants to know?"

"Thanks, I'll wait," said Jake without answering the man's question. "Then again, maybe I'll look around some."

"Suit yourself," the surly cook mumbled as he went about his business, first glancing at the pile of fly-covered rubbish where he knew the dog was hiding.

Jake remounted and began an ever-widening circle of the ranch's building complex. He noted to himself, *this was obviously a thriving, successful ranch at one time . . . plenty of grass and water. Protection from winter winds and weather.*

The cook's mongrel friend followed. Jake became aware of his presence when a meadowlark rose in heated anger at being disturbed. The dog emerged, his mouth open as if grinning, tongue dangling to one side as if delighted at some practical joke he might have just played on the poor unspecting bird. Jake smiled back and shook his head.

"Come on," he stated. "Show me around the place."

They followed an old wash for a couple of miles southeast of the main ranch complex before turning due east. They topped a ridge and Jake reined up to take in the long undulating vista before him. Out ahead of him was the ranch building complex, but it lay unseen from this vantage point . . . hidden by wave upon wave of grass-covered hills.

Behind him, Jake could see a late spring storm was brewing. Cumulus clouds, the big, puffy, massive type, were building in the northwest against a beautiful blue sky. The clouds towered thousands of feet into the sky . . . white and fluffy with occasional tuffs of gray.

Even the sun had started its afternoon dive toward a hiding place behind the Rocky Mountain range to the west. It was coincidental that it was late afternoon and the sun made the same pilgrimage every day about the same time.

Although a wonder to watch, experience told Jake that some serious wind, thunder and lightning would pay them a visit by evening. He turned his horse toward their temporary home at a lope. There was now a sense of urgency about returning to the ranch before dark.

After about an hour he spotted two riders headed in his direction and he quickly identified one of the riders as Tom and the second man known as Nelson arriving from the Dunn spread. He waved and wheeled his horse in the direction of his friend.

Nelson continued on toward the ranch complex without saying anything to the Box T punchers.

"What did you find out Jake?" asked Tom as the two men were reunited.

"Not much . . . except they have a mean old cook and some noisy dogs. I see you found another horse."

"Picked out one from the Dunn bunch. He won't be needing it."

Tom continued, "One thing's for sure, Winston keeps a tight rein on things around here. Mostly out of fear. Folks get too nosey and they end up dead. Maybe we should head for home and report to the old man."

"Let's give it a day or so. Then you can go report what we've found," Jake said.

"One day, maybe two," repeated a nervous Tom. "Now let's go see if that surly cook of yours can fix a decent meal. I'm starving."

"Let's hope it's beef and not one of those dogs," Jake muttered.

CHAPTER 13
MANY QUESTIONS,
FEW ANSWERS

The hotel was furnished with an eclectic mix of Victorian style and Wyoming rustic. A well worn, brown leather couch hugged one wall in an otherwise bleak lobby. An ugly print of Dutch windmills and tulips hung in an overmatched frame above the clerk's poorly kept desk. A seldom-cleaned spittoon sat on the plank floor wet with poorly deposited tobacco. The lobby challenged the olfactory senses with an unpleasant mix of spent cigars and stale perfume.

An elderly man with black vest, starched but sweat-stained white shirt and broken spectacles greeted the women with a degree of enthusiasm bordering on contempt. A sarcastic "rooms upstairs" followed his "sign here" directions. Upset at being interrupted, he quickly returned to his dime novel. The two women were left to find their own way to the second floor.

Sarah finally got Molly into one room.

Then she settled into one for herself. Sweat clung to her forehead and her collar was wet. Every muscle ached from hours of riding in the coach. She was worn out, but couldn't rest.

Not there anymore, the words kept repeating themselves over and over in her mind just as the telegraph operator had said them. *What could have happened? Maybe the man was mistaken.*

She gazed through a dirty windowpane overlooking the town's main street. The dusty street was all but empty in the midday heat. Despite the disadvantage of having been gone so long, she tried to formulate a plan-of-action. None was forthcoming and she was frustrated.

"The answers certainly aren't in this room," she told herself. "I've got to get out and ask some questions."

She left her small room to make some inquiries. Sarah knew her father had not been the most social of area ranchers but she figured he had to buy supplies. That would mean regular trips to town.

"Somebody will know something," she mumbled to herself as the door to her room closed behind her.

Sarah first went to see Agnes McGee, a widow who had lived most of her adult life in Chugwater. The woman's husband had built the first General Store in town and just at the point of nearly making it work he died of pneumonia, leaving her almost penniless. She had survived, but it made a lasting impact on her mind and body.

"Lands sake!" she shouted upon finding Sarah standing at her front door.

"Hi . . . Ms. McGee."

"When did you get home Sam?" the woman asked.

"Just today."

"Heavens girl! You've sure grown up! You hungry? You thirsty? I got some hot coffee. Come in! Come in! Tell me about yourself."

Sarah entered the dimly lit parlor and found a seat near the woman's fireplace. The house smelled of mold, unwashed clothing and an old woman in bad need of a hot bath. Cleanliness had fallen to shortcuts and near misses. The results were less than pleasant. And, the old woman failed to see and smell the obvious.

"Ms. McGee? They say my father sold our ranch and left the country. I don't believe it."

"Lordy, Sammy girl, things are bad these days . . . since that no-account Winston showed up."

"I figure he's behind my father's disappearance . . . but how?" Sarah asked.

"Ain't even safe for a respectable woman to be out on the streets these days," the old woman railed. "Them goons of Winston's are always leering at you. You'd be better off staying inside teaching them young'uns of yours. I say 'to hell with them!' I go where I please," said the defiant old woman with fire in her eyes.

"My father . . . ?" Sarah interrupted.

"I'm sorry Sarah. I just don't know. Haven't seen him in six months or so . . . how is he?"

Sarah explained once more, "They say he sold out and left . . . no word to me at all."

"Does seem some peculiar. Maybe he went fishing. He liked to fish sometimes. Them was good days. My Julius liked to fish. Trout was in all the streams back then . . . even the shallow ones. Want more coffee? It's just wheat grounds. Can't afford none better."

"No thanks," answered Sarah. "You think Winston . . . ?"

"Now when my Julius was alive we had us some coffee . . . came from South America. Them sure was the good days," the woman continued with her mind wandering.

Seeing she was getting nowhere, Sarah rose to leave.

174

"Ms. McGee, thank you for your time. I must be going. You take care of yourself."

"Leaving so soon? Why you just got here!"

"Yes, I need to be going."

"You come again dear and soon. I'll bake us some ginger cookies. You can take some to that school of yours. And, you tell that no-account father of yours hello for me."

"Okay, I will," Sarah answered with a wave goodbye.

"Sammy," the woman called out after her. "You fry them trout in plenty of lard . . . you hear? That's best."

Two more hours of asking around town got her no closer to finding her father. Now Sarah was more frustrated and angry than she was disappointed and worried.

As she started up the hotel steps she spotted a carriage coming down the street in such a hurry bystanders had to jump out-of-the-way. And for Sarah there was a moment of recognition. "Elsie Gardner!"

"Whoa! Whoa!" shouted the old woman, as she pulled back hard and stopped in front of Sarah.

"My Lord girl . . . what are you doing here?"

Sarah stepped back into the street and grabbed the sweat-lathered horse by the bit while noticing the woman's uncombed gray hair and still-red face.

"Mrs. Gardner! What's wrong? What's happened?"

"Winston's goons. They've finally burned me out. They even tried to kill me . . . but I didn't sign their damned old papers. I still own the place."

"Are you okay?" asked Sarah, as a few other townspeople started to gather around. "Did they hurt you?"

"Only my pride child . . . only my pride. I'm okay, thanks to a stranger who showed up out of nowhere to help me," explained the older woman.

"A stranger . . . ?"

"Yep . . . a tall young man. Rode in out of the blue. Never seen him before."

"That's strange," Sarah noted.

"Said his name was Summers. I believe it was Jake Summers."

"Never heard of him."

"Me neither . . . but he sure enough saved this old woman's hide. I was about gone I can tell you . . . then he was there."

Sarah touched the woman's arm. "You sure you are okay?"

"I'm fine. But, your father . . ." she stopped short.

"What do you know? I can't find out anything," Sarah asked anxiously.

"Not much . . . but it doesn't look good. Most folks figure he's dead. Whatever has happened to him, you can bet Winston's behind it."

"I'm so worried. He's just disappeared," noted Sarah.

"Young lady I would high-tail it out of this country until things settle down. Come with me to Cheyenne . . . we'll figure something out."

"Thanks, but I can't. Not till I know what's happened for sure."

The old woman took Sarah's hand and looked in her eyes. "Promise me, you'll come to Cheyenne if things get rough . . . you hear? Promise me!"

"I understand," said Sarah. "Now let me help you to the stage station."

After helping her friend catch the stage, Sarah went to check on Molly and explain her frustration.

"There are people here who know more than they are telling," she told her friend once the hotel door was closed. "Winston even burned out Ms. Gardner . . . and she never hurt anyone."

Then Sarah realized she wasn't the only one in a dire predicament. The look on Molly's face was blank, without expression. Her young friend looked pale, weak and confused, obviously concerned about her own future.

"It doesn't make any sense," Molly started. "His letters were always so cheerful. He was always writing about his ranch and his plans . . . and us."

She began to cry.

Taking a tear-stained handkerchief from her red, swollen eyes, she continued. "Since when does a man do all that planning, then commit suicide?" she asked, not really expecting an answer. "What am I going to do?"

Sarah turned and walked across the room. She looked down into the tear-stained face of her lonely and scared friend.

"Sometimes our greatest achievement, our finest hour is born in the ashes of our lowest moments, our deepest despair. I have the utmost confidence you will find the strength and resolve to meet and overcome even these personal challenges. God is always by your side. You will make the correct decisions."

"I just don't know," said Molly.

"A person can endure far more than you might think. You have two basic options as I see it," continued Sarah. "One . . . gather up your things and go home to the past. Or two . . . set down roots here and summon up the courage and fortitude to face an uncertain future. Sometimes we feel best at that moment when we realize we have overcome great odds and obstacles to achieve the seemingly impossible. That moment of personal achievement can be very fulfilling and boost our confidence and self-worth immensely. But, the choice is yours to make.

"And . . . ," Sarah hesitated. "Quitting is easy but it also can be habit forming. Now and again, we must face the evil in our lives."

Sarah leaned over and gently put her hand on Molly's shoulder. "It's going to be okay. It really is. Put your faith in God. He will see you through."

Being a mail-order bride had been hard enough for Molly to accept. Now she wondered whether she should take on the role of widow. "I never actually met the man," she said. "We just corresponded by mail and telegram . . . yet I came to know him . . . maybe even care for him."

Sarah answered, "I suppose it could happen . . . but I don't see you playing the role of his widow. Maybe write a few letters to his family, put a few fresh flowers on his grave now and then . . . but you'll need to move on with your life.

"Somebody named Winston has become awfully powerful in this area recently. He supposedly bought my father out . . . and he's running your Mr. Dunn's ranch as well. Could be these things are all related. This afternoon I intend to ride out to the ranch and see what's up. You stay in town and ask a few questions."

She hurried down the board-covered walkway toward the livery stable. She would need a horse. She also figured Abe Knowlton, the livery owner, would be a good source of information on what had been going on in town.

Knowlton and her father had come west together 20 years earlier. Both had decided to remain in Chugwater rather than move on with the Oregon-bound wagon train.

While Meadows had become a successful rancher, Knowlton had chosen to work shoeing horses and repairing wagons, making branding irons and other equipment for area ranchers. He also had become successful. As the town and area ranches had grown, so had demand for his work.

The two men had never been good friends, but they did talk from time to time. Sarah figured he would have some information.

"Sorry young lady, I haven't seen your father in some time," he said nervously while watching the street behind her for any sign of Winston's men. "He came by maybe two . . . no three months ago for some advice about a lame horse. Haven't seen him since. Heard tell, he sold out to Winston and left the country. Least, that's what I heard . . . now I got work to do," as he turned away and started toward the barn.

Sarah called after him, "I need to rent a horse."

"I'll have one ready in about 30 minutes," he answered without turning around. He waved his big right hand in acknowledgement of her request but kept walking.

She decided to check out the General Store. As she approached, Sarah spotted Winston inside talking to the store's owner. A couple of gunmen stood nearby. Two others stood outside on the rough, plank walkway smoking cigarettes and swapping stories. She could feel their stares.

"When I get me enough of these ranches," Winston was saying. "I'm going to fence them all. Then I'll control all the grazing and water for miles around.

"Just need me a few more sections then I'll go to stringing barb wire from here to Hell and back," Winston exclaimed.

"It will be the ruination of the cattle business," said the storeowner. "What will happen to the other ranchers? Cattlemen need open range."

"The hell you say!" shouted Winston.

The storeowner continued to explain his point, "I'm just saying fencing off the range could lead to overgrazing and the day of the big roundups will be gone."

"I really don't give a tinker's damn about the other ranchers. I'm building me an empire here and by God nobody is going to stop me."

Winston turned toward the open door then back to the storeowner, "Now you going to order me some wire or not? Or maybe, I need to get into the store goods business myself."

"I'll order your wire," said the subdued merchant. "But, it's going to lead to range wars. Mark my words. The other ranchers ain't going to take it. Not at all."

"To hell with them," said Winston. "And listen, I don't want that cheap stuff. I want the one that has the barb locked into a double strand wire. Understand?"

"Yes, I understand."

"Good. Get it here as soon as possible. I want to start fencing the old Larsen place, then across to the Meadows Ranch."

Suddenly, the storeowner was aware of what he was hearing.

"How you going to do that?" he exclaimed. "You'll have to cross the Hutchinson spread and the Williams section. That's about 10 miles you don't own."

"Not yet, my friend! Not yet! But, you just watch. My men plan to start negotiations real soon if you get my meaning. Now get me that wire."

With his closing comments, Winston left. He gave Sarah a passing glance, touched the brim of his hat and stepped off the wooden walkway into the dusty street. He stopped only briefly to take a quick look back at Sarah before starting down the street. Scar and Willie were riding in his direction.

"Boss, we got some good news and a potential problem," said Scar still mounted on his horse.

"What kinda problem?" Winston demanded.

"Charlie Norton and. . . . !"

"What about Norton? He ran old lady Gardner off her place didn't he? I saw her get on the stage about an hour ago . . . headed for Cheyenne."

"That's the good news. But, Norton's dead and the two men with him can't be found. The old woman's house was burned to the ground . . . just like you said."

"How . . . ? When . . . ?" demanded Winston. "Who did it? Couldn't have been that old lady! What about them two drifters we just hired? Was you watching them like I said?"

Scar took a deep breath . . . looked at Willie Temple . . . then back at Winston.

"Well, I'm waiting!" Winston shouted.

"Couldn't have been them two punchers. We was watching them just like you told us," lied Scar as he looked anxiously at Willie for support. Both men realized the ramifications of admitting they hadn't been watching Jake and Tom.

"Well that old woman couldn't have done it . . . not alone. Something ain't right here," said Winston as he stormed off toward the saloon.

Sarah failed to hear the exchange between Winston and his men. However, she found the storeowner was in no mood to discuss her missing father either.

A trip to the bank also turned up nothing. She had learned nothing new about her father's disappearance. It seemed he had just vanished into thin air, but she was convinced Winston was somehow involved.

The livery owner had a sorrel mare saddled and ready when Sarah returned. He said nothing as he handed her the reins.

184

But as she prepared to mount up, he said, "That'll be two bits a day paid in advance."

Sarah countered, "What about a rifle? I need a rifle."

"That'll be another two bits."

She paid him for renting the horse and rifle then rode from town.

The landscape had changed little over the years. The wind blew hard against her face and she struggled to keep her hat in place. She marveled at the land around her and admitted she was glad to be home, despite the circumstances.

The longer she rode a nagging mix of concern and fear rose up inside her. It threatened to overwhelm her. A strong sense of loneliness crept over her.

As she neared the ranch complex, she realized she'd been daydreaming for most of the ride and had no real "plan of action". She had started out to see for herself that her father was really gone. Now as she rode close, questions gave way to nervous anxiety.

Better be careful, Sarah thought. *Would be easy to get yourself in a bind out here alone. . . . away from town . . . away from anyone you know.*

In the distance, she could see a couple of cowhands chasing a steer down a shallow ravine. She could hear a barking dog near the ranch buildings and there was someone shouting.

Sarah had often as a child used a "secret spot" high on a ridge above the ranch house. It was secluded, nearly impossible to see unless you were on top of it. Yet, it offered a panoramic view of the ranch complex and the pastures beyond. It was there she decided to go first.

She had often come here when she was young. Most often it was to be alone. It gave her a place and time to think, to dream. But, sometimes to just sit quietly and try talking to the mother she never knew.

Sarah had often wondered what life would have been like had her mother lived. But, it was a useless exercise. She knew it was impossible to undo the past. It was like counting each blade of grass or the stars at night. It only left her frustrated.

Her first look at her home in more than four years left her in anguish. Gone was the chicken house where she had gathered eggs each day. Blackened embers of the recently burned building were all that remained. The place looked worn and run down. The house needed paint and there were wagons sitting about in disrepair.

Then she noticed a lone rider making his way around the building complex as if he was looking for something. She wondered aloud, "One of Winston's men." A scruffy-looking, old cow dog followed.

The rider eventually disappeared from her line-of-sight but she sensed he was still close by. She figured it wasn't safe to leave her hiding place with so many riders about. The decision was made to wait.

After all, she thought, *I do know the trails from here to Chugwater . . . at least in daylight. Shouldn't be all that hard at night.*

About dusk she saw the same rider as he rode across some high ridges southwest of her hiding spot. Then she spotted two other riders. The first stopped and waited for the second man while the third man rode on toward the ranch buildings. They were well out of earshot of Sarah's hideout. After visiting for a few minutes, they rode toward the bunkhouse.

Darkness swept over the prairie like a blanket, leaving only starlight as lanterns to guide the way toward Chugwater. Into this black night, Sarah started back toward town. In the distance, she could see lightning as a storm was building on the horizon. She could only hope it would stay north.

Finding her horse where it had been tied out of sight proved to be the easy part. Things became much more difficult after she was horseback.

Four years away from home . . . and having just returned . . . her memory of where the road should be played tricks on her. A symphony of cicadas, night birds and yipping coyotes pushed her toward uncertainty, regret and fear.

Sarah had waited too long. Now the darkness obscured all landmarks and familiar trails. Cloud cover from the building storm quickly hid the stars and made it impossible to determine north from south. She was lost! She was also totally unprepared to spend a night on the open range.

The ranch, she thought. *I can find the ranch house. Surely they wouldn't turn me away and besides I might learn more about what's been happening. Still, I'm a stranger to whoever is down there . . . and after dark is not a good time for me to be meeting anyone.*

Angry and disgusted at herself for waiting so late, she continued in the direction of town . . . or at least the direction she thought town should be.

After riding for what seemed like hours, Sarah admitted she was lost. *I should have made town by now.*

Sarah found a few trees along a small creek and decided to stop for the night. The reasonably high creek bank would protect her from any wind and would provide a defensive position from where she might make a needed stand.

Stand . . . I must be crazy. I've gotten soft these past few years . . . and a whole lot stupid. However, nobody should be out tonight, she reasoned, *and if they are I won't let them surprise me.*

So with her back against the high creek bank, her toes only a few feet from the trickling creek and her horse tied to some nearby trees, she wrapped herself with the only extra clothing she had . . . a lightweight jacket. Although it was an early summer night, she knew it would get cold.

With that rationalization, she sought and found sleep.

Some time later, in the blackness that comes before dawn, she awoke with a frightened start. There was at first a rising roar she believed to be the wind perhaps a tornado. There was also thunder and lightning rotating in brief intervals.

She felt the painful sting of small hail striking her skin. As the hailstorm's intensity began to rise, she cowered among some rocks with her saddle over her head for limited protection.

In a matter of moments, the hail gave way to rain, but the ground was literally white with hailstones, highlighted by flashes of lightning. A cold, driving rain quickly melted some of them away but the damage to Sarah's battered psyche was done. She was alive but prayed for the dawn of day.

Then she heard a second roar . . . a rushing, wet roar, and she immediately knew . . . *flash flood*!

CHAPTER 14
RAINY NIGHTS AND
RUSTY NAILS

The man called Smitty ran things with a strong will and quick trigger finger. Run out of New Mexico for killing two men over a woman, he was more accustomed to late-night negotiations and cattle rustling than legitimate roundups and cattle breeding.

Few men actually liked Winston's answer for a foreman, but most tolerated his outbursts. Those that didn't usually died with their boots on. More than one puncher had met his maker over remarks made during a simple card game. Smitty didn't bluff. His sense of justice whether right or wrong was the final word.

"Where you boys been working," Smitty asked.

Jake gazed over a plate of cold biscuits, fried beefsteaks and beans and said, "Up north. We came down from Montana."

"Montana, eh? Where 'bouts?"

"Up in the Chesnut Valley country.

Worked for old Bob Thoroughman. Got tired of mixing cattle and sheep," Jake explained.

Tom added, "Can't stand those woolies."

That brought a murmur of agreement from around the rough, log-hewn cookhouse table. Obviously, the other men at the table preferred cattle as well.

"Sheep are coming," Jake muttered more to himself than anyone else. "They are coming even to this country."

"What did you say?" demanded a man known as Billy Longwell.

"Sheep. Like it or not they're coming," Jake answered, speaking louder. "After the winter of '86 more and more ranchers have turned to sheep."

"The hell you say!" Smitty snorted through an ugly mix of chewing tobacco remnants and biscuits. "Sounds to me we got us a wooly lover sitting right here amongst us boys."

"How 'bout it Summers? You like mutton?" asked One Eye with a laugh.

Jake realized the leanings of his now quiet audience. In many respects he felt the same, but he also recognized the realities of coming change.

"Not at all . . . but look around you. Ten years ago you couldn't find sheep in this country. Back in '70 there were less than 10,000 head in the entire territory. Hell, 10 years later there were 500,000 or more. Who knows how many there are today. That's all I'm saying."

Everyone was quiet for a few moments. They knew Jake was correct. Sheep were being brought into the territory in large numbers.

"Maybe it's time some of us started sending a message to some of these mutton lovers. Maybe it's time they were discouraged a little. Winston will never have sheep," Smitty said.

"Yea!" Longwell shouted.

One Eye added, "Maybe we should go visit some herders . . . set 'em straight."

"Encourage them to try cattle instead," laughed Smitty. "They might enjoy some good beefsteak."

Jake didn't say anything more. But, he wondered from their tied down guns and rough demeanor just what kind of cowboys these men might be.

Tom sat quietly.

Smitty eyed both of them with suspicion.

"Winston sent you, did he?"

"That's right," offered Tom.

"Well, guess that's good enough for me. Summers, you ride due north in the morning. Follow the Laramie up to Muddy Creek . . . you'll find 'em.

"We've got some new steers up there. Meet up with Charlie Polter. Tell him I sent you. Get a good count, look them over and report back to me by sundown. Tell Polter I'll be in touch. Tell him to sit tight.

"Scott, you ride with One Eye and Longwell into Chugwater. Tell Winston we expect another delivery of steers any day now. Tell him things went real smooth up on the Sweetwater."

Jake couldn't help himself. "Where'd you get steers this time of year? Roundup time has long since passed."

Smitty stood and asked, "What's it to you stranger?"

The foreman's hands rested gingerly on his pistols.

"Nothing. Nothing at all. One steer's same as another I guess."

"Better mind your own business. Do your job and keep your mouth shut. You just might end up with the sheepherders after all. You got a problem with that?"

"Nope."

The tension was thick. Jake realized he had pushed a little too far.

Tom, realizing his friend had been backed into a corner, tried to break the tension.

"How 'bout a friendly game of cards? Any you gents ready to lose some money?"

Smitty eyed Jake with a cold, questioning stare then let a smile cross his lips.

"Break out them cards," he roared. "We need to have some fun. Maybe teach these greenhorns a lesson in poker!"

Jake glanced at his smiling friend and then looked away.

Tom watched Jake and said, "Whose dealing? I feel real lucky tonight!"

After only a few hands, Tom found himself saying, "Don't go there!" Suddenly, a new tension filled the room.

Winston's men were more than obvious in their efforts to cheat. It was as if everyone expected everyone else do be doing it . . . except Tom of course. He was not impressed.

"If I didn't know some of you were cheating, I sure would suspect it," he said to those around the table.

"You directing that comment at anyone in particular?" asked Smitty as he gazed from behind his cards.

"Yeah! You meaning me?" asked a surly gunhand by the name of Chester Holt.

"Maybe he means me," said a second gunhand named T. J. Whitaker.

A bolt of lightning followed by a clap of

195

thunder broke the tension.

Immediately, Smitty was shouting instructions.

"Summers, you and Crocker, along with One Eye go check the corrals. Make sure everything is closed up good. Sounds like we got a mean storm coming. Check the barn doors as well. We'll settle this card game later.

"Scott, you go with them. Put my horse in the barn and make sure he's unsaddled, wiped down and fed," Smitty directed. He waited to see if Jake or Tom would resist his instructions. "I'll be up at the big house."

"Let's go," said Jake.

By the time those few chores were done, the storm had arrived. They were stranded in the barn. Both Jake and Tom watched its arrival from a partially open barn door. The barnyard was highlighted by streaks of lightning revealing mud puddles and a driving rain.

The barn was old. Smells of rotting boards and musty old hay shared a place in Jake's nostrils with the smells of horse sweat and manure.

Saddle blankets worn and dirty lay over stall gates drying from a day's usage. Saddles with sweat-stained cinches were thrown carelessly over anything sturdy enough to hold them.

Enough mice and rats to feed a dozen hungry cats shared a half-full oat bin. Only one old tomcat slowed by years, not desire, had kept their numbers at bay. Lately, rodents were winning the battle.

The barn floor consisted of soil compacted into near rock hardness by years of usage and all measure of traffic. It was devoid of any moisture save for occasional horse urine. Its smell reflected as much.

Old horseshoes, their usage long done, were cast carelessly about. Nail tips cut by some unknown farrier lay encircling an anvil of some size and weight.

It was into this ambience of sights and smells that Winston's men gathered while Mother Nature railed outside.

"What do you make of all that talk about new steers?" Tom asked Jake in a whisper.

With the other men standing in another doorway smoking cigarettes, Jake said, "Sounds like rustling to me, but from where? Winston already controls most of the area ranches.

"But," he continued, "Could be the reason they are so short of hands right now. The honest ones have left. The others, except for this sorry bunch around the ranch, must be out gathering new stock . . . one way or another."

The rain had begun slowly, leaving pot marks in the dusty soil. Gradually growing in intensity, the water formed small, muddy pools, which gave way to larger puddles before making miniature rivers across the open barnyard.

The sound of raindrops striking the metal barn roof was magnified inside. Millions of water droplets fell earthward only to have their rush to earth interrupted by the barn roof. Here they were slowed only briefly, collected and then carried in a rush over the edge in a waterfall of some magnitude.

Whispering became futile. Talking was hard enough. Rain striking metal made a sound too loud to overcome. But, old man Crocker tried.

This was the same man from whom Jake had tried to gain information earlier in the day. Now bolstered by a day of rest, he was ready to talk the night away. There would be no lull in conversation no matter how difficult. Rain hitting a metal roof was to be talked over, not enjoyed in silence. The old man, who was long past his prime, felt the night must be constantly filled with sound . . . human sound . . . most often the crackling nonsense of his own voice.

"Be a muddy mess by morning," he said

to nobody in particular.

"Betcha those grassy draws will be full of wet steers seeking shelter," he added.

"Maybe," answered One Eye. "Maybe not. They may have made high ground."

It was bad enough to listen to the old man at mealtime, but to be caught and held captive with him in a rainstorm was almost more than a man could stand.

Might be better to just get wet and risk drowning in a run for the bunkhouse, thought Jake. *Soaking for the sake of solitude and sanity isn't so bad.*

Jake and Tom made a break for the bunkhouse and quickly learned the rain was as cold as it was wet. It left nothing dry, not even the imagination. And, what little wind there was brought a chill. The result was both dampened skin and spirit.

Morning was not far away. But, the rain would do its best to hold off the approaching daylight.

The sounds of rainfall striking the bunkhouse roof gave way to splashing sounds as water met a thirsty earth. Small rivers ran rushing away toward bigger streams. Millions of small droplets captured in one mighty twisting, turning water torrent. Propelling itself toward some distant blending, and a massive mix of Wyoming sweetness and a salty, undrinkable ocean.

Is that not the ultimate fate of all life? Jake thought. *Just how many happy, naive young men end up being bitter, salty old men?*

It is in these rare moments of reflection, he thought, *that we're often caught in the river of our own thoughts. Grasping if only for a moment something more important than cattle and horses, more inspirational than wide-open spaces, snow-covered mountains or grass-covered prairies, it is the inner nature of who we are and what we've become.*

Rainfall cannot wash away the onward advance of age and loneliness. Jake Summers knew as much. Cowboying was a lonely way of life. He also knew it wasn't the number of years that made him feel tired and old. It was the use and abuse his body had absorbed over those years.

Now with a steady rain outside long into the night, a million tiny drops gently picked him up and carried him softly into slumber and swept him toward morning.

CHAPTER 15
WILD STREAMS AND PANIC

The deafening sound of rushing water tore at Sarah's brain creating a sense of panic and fear. The roar grew louder and she could no longer hear her own thoughts. A wall of destruction careened from muddy bank to muddy bank toward her. The stream and banks formed a funnel, which increased the water's strength and speed. She was trapped.

She tried climbing to safety but the bank was too steep. She slid backwards into the rising stream, where the flow was growing stronger and faster.

Totally soaked and covered with mud, Sarah started back across the creek. And in the darkness, she tried climbing the far bank. Then the rushing, twisting wall of water was upon her. It struck her body with a breath-taking jolt. At the last possible moment, she lunged in the darkness for the overhanging branch of a small cottonwood tree and held on tightly.

The water tore at her legs, pulled at her lower body and grabbed at her waist. A boot on her left foot pulled free, and then the second was gone.

The branch gave way and the churning cauldron of water swallowed her. She fought to rise above the fray, briefly coming to the top where she gasped for air. Her struggle to escape the massive wave of potential death was exhausting and she felt herself weakening. Again and again, she struggled to swim her way free only to be sucked down. She disappeared into the churning mix of debris and muddy water.

The surge overwhelmed her and she lost all sense of control and balance. In the wet darkness, Sarah fought for air, but the fast-flowing water refused to yield. And as the initial wall surged past her, she felt her lungs filling with water. Her chest hurt, but she fought back one last time.

Limbs and other debris attacked her body, leaving bruises and bloody welts. She managed to turn so she could ride the torrent on her back with her feet pointed downstream to deflect further debris. It also allowed her to face skyward and fresh air. Now and then she felt something hit her feet and legs before sliding alongside her body, then on past her.

As the water evened out and slowed somewhat, she realized a sense of peace even as the night raged in fury around her. Sarah thought of her father, her long-passed mother and wondered if on this night she would soon join them. Even as the world roared in angry defiance around her, she felt calm.

Sarah let go, letting the river carry her toward the arms of God.

But, the stream had other ideas. She felt a rocky outcropping with her left hand, once then again. The stream turned sharply, literally tossing her onto a rocky bench. Suddenly, she was on solid ground with the still angry stream flowing past her. Somehow she had cheated death again.

Still out of breath, she fought for air and composure. Neither came easy. She was bruised, battered and totally soaked. She collapsed.

Although the raging stream had dumped her free, she still lay within inches of the now slower-moving stream. She needed to get away from the water. But as she sought the safety of higher ground in the blackness of night, the young woman felt the full physical measure of her ordeal.

The darkness made it difficult to cover

unfamiliar terrain on bare feet. The footing was treacherous. She often slipped, fell and sometimes slid back down the bank. It only added to her dirty misery. But after four or five attempts, she managed to climb to a place of relative safety where she could lie down. Every muscle ached and the soreness was overwhelming.

Mentally, she was confused and exhausted. Although she had no apparent broken bones, there were plenty of bruises, scratches and even a nasty cut on her left arm.

Her dirty hair was matted down and contained several sticks, leaves and other assorted debris. Mud clung to her cheeks. Her clothing was torn, dirty and wet.

She heard the rising sound of approaching rain. Once more, lightning began to illuminate an eerie landscape. A violent thunderstorm, which had spawned the flash flood miles away, was moving in her direction. In a matter of minutes, it was raining again. Lightning was quickly followed by thunderous booms that seemed to shake the earth beneath her. The storm quickly moved on, but the night remained black, wet and quiet.

Morning was slow in coming, but finally broke warm and clear around her. The eastern sky was a colorful palette of reds, oranges and yellows. The storm had blown out over the prairie and was gone. Meadowlarks sang their cheerful songs and the land around her came alive.

Sarah was disoriented . . . but thankful to be alive. Life was in reality simple, if not outright precious.

But without her horse and some idea where she was, Sarah realized she was in serious life-threatening trouble. She was in unforgiving land without a horse and no idea of which direction to start walking.

The teacher was learning a hard lesson in humility. For all her bravado and self-confidence, she now found herself alone on a vast prairie where every hill looked the same.

Sarah climbed out of the ravine and looked at the landscape around her. Using her hand to shade her eyes, she managed to determine east from west, then north from south. On the western horizon she could barely make out the rugged tops of a snow-covered mountain range.

Logically she figured Chugwater was south and southwest between her current position and the Laramie Mountains. Yet, she could not know how far. Walking without provisions, a rifle and more importantly her boots would be next to impossible.

Like it or not she needed help. Better yet, she needed a miracle. She also was feeling the nagging pangs of hunger and surprisingly, thirst.

The sun grew hot on her back so she climbed down the embankment and sought a shady place between some rocks and small cottonwood trees. She fought sleep, but it overtook her and she sank deep into its outstretched arms.

Dreams overwhelmed her. She imagined Sunday dinners after church and Aunt Ruby fixing fried chicken, fresh-picked greens, and glasses of cold buttermilk. There was also peach cobbler and fresh-baked bread. Hunger began to gnaw at her.

Just outside the house she could hear children playing drop-the-handkerchief and laughing.

A young man, Jason Neal, was coming up the path. It was the same young attorney who had introduced himself at a Camp Meeting just last Sunday. Her Uncle Lewis sat in a rocking chair on the plank-covered porch smoking his pipe. He said hello and they discussed the weather.

Sarah was wearing a new dress with stiff starched collar, three petticoats and a pair of high button shoes. She winced at the tightness of it all and longed quietly for the free-fitting boots and pants of her Wyoming days.

Despite staying with her "wonderful" aunt and uncle, she often felt a tremendous loneliness and emptiness. She was homesick for home and the young cowhands with whom she'd flirted each day and called "friends." They were brothers in spirit, if not by blood.

Her mind wandered to a sod schoolhouse where for $30 a month she struggled to educate 15 or so students, depending on the season, children ranging from 8 to 16 years. They were the children of homesteaders who covered the prairie like hungry locusts, eating away the vast grasslands with plow and hoe.

The school was about 15 by 20 feet with a roof also made of sod; grass and weeds grew from the top. In winter it was extremely cold and she often worried about frostbite. Straw spread deeply on the dirt floor helped, but fleas also found the warmth inviting.

She found satisfaction and personal pride in teaching. She enjoyed seeing the students learn and grow. Now she wondered if she'd ever look into their smiling, fresh-scrubbed faces again.

The job was rewarding and an honorable profession. "And it pays better than clerking," she had often said. But something was missing. She now questioned her role in life and its meaning.

Will I ever marry? So many times in recent months she had silently asked herself. *I am 20. Will I marry or am I destined to teach forever? Maybe God plans for me to care for my father into his older years? Have I missed my opportunity for true happiness?*

There had been no shortage of suitors. The young attorney who had come to pay his respects was only the latest. However, school administrators frowned on the idea of teachers getting married. They were to remain single and stay that way as long as they taught. It didn't matter. There was no one in Sarah's life as yet who shared her love of the land, the prairie grasses and the wind. She often felt her mind and spirit adrift on the same wind she loved so much.

Single or not, Sarah missed her father terribly. She also missed the "grand freedom" of the Wyoming prairie and horseback riding with her face pressed into the wind. She loved the spaciousness and never-ending vastness before her. Grasses low to the ground, before an unceasing wind. As a

Nebraska teacher, it just wasn't proper to go riding willy-nilly across the prairie on horseback.

Sarah enjoyed such freedom, unbound by the walls and expectations of humankind. There was a pleasure, an enjoyment over every hill. And in the spring, there were singing birds and many, many wildflowers.

She recalled little six-year-old Cassie Huffman, her arms filled with wildflowers and her face beaming with excitement . . . "all for teacher." The schoolhouse was filled with flowers.

She thought of her students, even the "pestering, dreamy-eyed" boys who liked to aggravate her.

There was the dead bull snake left on her desk one morning. Homer Evans and Jennings Webber had been so disappointed when she merely picked it up and tossed it outside. They didn't know their teacher had often played with snakes as a child, even carrying them at times in her pockets as pets.

Even when they left a lizard in her lunch pail, she never flinched.

In her dream-like trance, she recalled how Briggs Miller tried coaxing a skunk into the schoolhouse one morning. He paid the ultimate price for his efforts and was sent home.

Then she heard Anna Price scream. It was a scream of terror and fear. She ran outside. Some older boys were using sticks to poke at an obviously rabid dog. Younger boys backed them up with shouts of encouragement, and nervous laughter. The girls were huddled at a safe, but uncomfortable distance.

Sarah heard the snarl and then saw the foam dripping from the sick dog's mouth. There was a low throaty growl . . . then there was another growl and then a sharp barking sound from a second direction.

Startled, she woke up. It had all seemed so real.

Then not 30 yards away, she stared into the black eyes of a large gray wolf. He lay crouched on his stomach, not sure of his next move. Then she heard a second wolf growling off to her left just across the now shallow stream. At the top edge of the ravine, she saw a third animal moving back and forth, seeking a better vantage point.

There was a sudden snarl, then a rush to judgment!

Chapter 16
Humiliation Before Dying

Rain clouds from the night before were gone. Behind them came a bright, sunny morning and puddles of thick water, mostly mud.

Molly watched the town's morning activities from her hotel window. Horses and riders steered clear of the muddy mess, or as best they could. A group of young boys seemed to find each one. Better yet and to their delight, each puddle seemed wetter and dirtier than the one before.

Molly realized she was smiling. This was much different than the brick-paved streets she'd known in St. Louis.

Then just as quickly she returned to the problems at hand. This momentary lapse of concern for Sarah and her own state of affairs caught Molly by surprise. She felt a sense of guilt for having forgotten her friend even for a moment. She turned from the street with a desire to do something,

211

anything.

First, she had some unfinished business. She started by going to the cemetery where Marcus Dunn had been laid to rest. It was time to pay her respects to the man she had come so far to marry.

The cemetery was laid out along a high bluff once used by Indians as a buffalo jump. Ironically, the town fathers chose a location already closely tied with death. Except for the wind and some noisy birds, the place had a quiet reverence, a somewhat inspirational aura.

"What can I say, Mr. Dunn?" as she stood over his recently covered grave. "I came like I promised."

She leaned forward and touched the wooden cross.

"Did you really commit suicide? I find that hard to believe, and even harder to accept."

Tears began to flow. She didn't understand why. She didn't know what else to say. She wept for an almost husband who would never be. A man she had never met.

"What am I to do now? I can't go back."

She sat alone by his grave for almost two hours and then walked back to the hotel. There was no sense of closure, as yet no ending, and too many unanswered questions. She felt an eerie sense of foreboding, a lonely depressing cloud seemed to envelop her very soul, and no amount of positive thoughts could shake the loneliness that overwhelmed her. She needed a friend, someone like her new friend Sarah.

"Wonder what's happened?" she asked herself. "She should have returned by now."

Sarah had been gone all night.

"She was going to be back by dark," Molly muttered to herself.

Molly was worried her new friend had found trouble . . . or worse . . . trouble had found her. She realized she had no idea which direction Sarah had ridden and didn't know anyone to ask. It was time to go to work.

I've had some experiences that just might be useful. And it's time to use them, she told herself.

Her lower social class experiences in St. Louis *might pay some dividends in Chugwater if used properly.*

She had cleaned boarding house rooms during the day. But, it was her night work in the bars and dives along the river in St. Louis that just might prove most useful now, and she knew it.

Watching her mother ply her wares to men over the years also had been an education in psychology. Working a cowboy bar in the Wyoming Territory couldn't be any worse, and in fact might be a whole lot easier, she figured.

Besides, she needed information and some type of income. The money Marcus Dunn had sent would not last forever. She wanted information pinning Winston and his bunch to the murder of Dunn and others in the area. She also wanted information on Sarah and why she hadn't returned.

The walkway in front of the town's few businesses was covered with well-worn wooden planks. Stepping carefully past and over several warped and splintered edges, she made her way toward the town's only saloon.

Both men and women stared as she walked, head held high. Molly simply ignored them. She knew she was being watched, but she had felt the same penetrating looks in certain respectable St. Louis neighborhoods.

A tinker headed into the General Store to ply his wares gave her a brief tip of his dusty bowler hat. His instinctive effort was the only outward sign her presence was even noticed.

Molly prayed the saloon was cooler than the streets.

Although, she smiled, *it's pretty chilly here on the street.*

Horses tied to hitching rails along her route stood with downcast heads in the noonday heat. Switching tails kept the horseflies at bay, but provided no further relief. They stood quiet with a forlorn assumption that a rider was somewhere nearby.

First resting one hind foot, then the other, then back to the first, most tried to sleep behind half-closed eyes. Only one smallish, bay gelding raised its head in response to her passing, then decided it was easier to imitate the others.

The saloon owner gave her a brief glance as she stepped through the swinging doors. Then quickly took a second look with his eyes falling on her obviously feminine features. Her red hair glowed in the afternoon sunlight, which found its way through the doors behind her.

Respectable women seldom came into the saloon, at least not on purpose. Even fewer looked like Molly. The barkeeper wiped a dirty hand down the back of his greasy black hair, ran his fingers through an equally rough-looking beard, then hurried to greet the red-headed woman walking in his direction.

Three men involved in a game of poker paid little attention. The town drunk, holding tightly to one end of the bar, was too far-gone to care.

Molly was on a mission involving men. And after years of practice in St. Louis, the saloon owner was about to become her first Wyoming subject.

She will bring me more business, he told himself.

Molly was hired immediately. After all, she was young and attractive. And compared to the overweight, rough-edged beauties already working for him, she would be like a wildflower in a barren desert.

Afraid to ask too many questions at first, quietly Molly did as she was told. The barkeeper took a personal interest in her education.

The few men who came and went worked for Winston. And, they couldn't provide answers. Nobody seemed to know who Sarah was much less her whereabouts.

Just before noon, Winston and his entourage made an appearance. He set up court in a back corner of the saloon and demanded a round of drinks for everyone. He put a match to an expensive but foul-smelling cigar and started a game of solitaire.

Meanwhile, a rancher named Nells Goodman was brought roughly into the saloon and thrown on the floor.

"Now . . . what's this?" Winston asked, flicking cigar ashes on the floor.

Scar spoke before the rancher could speak in his own defense.

"This old man's been going round town saying some nasty things about you boss. Just thought he might want to say them to your face, so we gathered him up and brought him along."

"Well now . . . is this true?" he asked the man on the floor in front of him.

"I find this hard to believe and highly disturbing," said Winston as he looked around the room with an amused smirk on his pock-marked face. "What do you say for yourself Mr. Goodman? Is my friend Scar here telling me square?"

"He's a filthy liar!" shouted Goodman from his hands and knees.

"I'm what?" exclaimed Scar as he stepped toward the rancher.

Winston raised his hand and gestured for Scar to hold off.

"Well, that wasn't very nice Nells. I must say it hurts me deeply that you would think ill of me. I mean I made you a very generous offer for your ranch and all. I just don't know what to think. And here you are calling my associate a liar. That just ain't neighborly."

"You son-of-a . . . ," Goodman started.

Before he could finish Scar's right foot caught him in the ribs and sent him sprawling across the floor and into a nearby table. The old man struggled to stand. But Scar kicked him again, then again.

The old man's fight was soon gone.

Winston stood over him with one hand restraining Scar from further attacks.

"Willie . . . go get Mr. Goodman's horse.

"Nells, I tell you what I'm going to do. Some of my boys are going to escort you home. Upon arriving there you will sign some papers turning your ranch and all of your assets over to me. I've waited long enough. Do you understand?"

"You . . . ," Goodman started to speak then thought better of it.

"Now that's better. Don't make me mad. We're simply conducting some business here. Your life for your ranch . . . seems fair to me," Winston explained with a sarcastic smile.

"Hell, I'll even buy you a stage ticket to Cheyenne just to show I hold no hard feelings. Now get out of here. And if you ever set foot in Chugwater again, I'll personally see you planted at Buffalo Jump.

"Get him outta here. And somebody clean this floor."

Molly had witnessed the poor rancher's humiliation and forced removal. She felt contempt bordering on hatred. She silently wondered if Marcus Dunn had gone through the same kind of torture. Not even in the worst of her young days had she watched a human being so torn down and so degraded.

"Red . . . get back to work," the barkeeper yelled out to her. "Take Mr. Winston a beer. He must have a real thirst by now."

Winston watched Molly closely as if really seeing her for the first time. He checked out every feminine detail but said nothing. His men watched as their boss showed signs of liking the young woman before him.

Molly realized he was watching and sought a way out.

"Now what do we have here?" Winston finally asked as he reached out to touch Molly's cheek.

She felt his cold, calloused, cigar-stained fingers as they brushed along her skin. Her mind recoiled and she fought down an urge to slap him.

"Haven't seen you before. But, I like what I see."

"Boss!"

Winston turned his eyes briefly away from Molly and she seized the opportunity for escape. His temper flared. He obviously was upset at the interruption.

"What is it?"

"Boss . . . Goodman tried to get away . . . and he's holed up in the church. He's got Buster Schutze hostage. And he's demanding to see you and nobody else."

Winston's face turned bright red.

"Damn him! Let's go. And who the hell is Buster Schutze?"

Winston approached the church, which by now was surrounded by his own men. Several townspeople also had gathered at a safe distance to watch. But, nobody dared to interfere, not even the town preacher who stood nearby in silence.

"Goodman," Winston shouted. "Come on out and let my man go. It's too hot for this. And, you're being a little unreasonable don't you think? I thought we had a deal."

The rancher shouted back, "You come in alone Winston. Just you and me. We can settle this once and for all. None of your goons."

"Now you know I can't do that. Hell, you might just ambush me. That wouldn't be good for business, now would it?"

There was silence.

Winston turned to Scar.

"Storm the place. Start shooting and keep shooting until he gives up. And, if that doesn't work burn the place down around him."

"What about Buster?" asked the gunman.

"What about him?" Winston asked rhetorically.

"I mean . . . I mean he works for us."

"Hell, shoot them both. Your man was careless to get caught like that. Now he needs to pay for his mistake. Now boys, I've got female business back down the street. Earn your pay and take care of this."

Winston turned away and started back down the street. Behind him, a barrage of gunfire filled the midday air and two men died.

CHAPTER 17
DEAD DOGS AND SPILT BEER

A long, wide street defined the length and breadth of Chugwater. A few dilapidated buildings, long past their prime, lined each side of the street. And behind them sat a few shacks that passed for homes. All were in bad need of paint and repair. Prosperity had been slow in coming, or more likely had already come and gone.

Only Winston's home approached respectability in its appearance, and much to the annoyance of his wife, it was often mistaken for a different kind of house. It sat on a hill at the far end of town, looking down on the main street. Its location conveyed a sense of superiority befitting the attitude and arrogance of its owner.

As Tom rode into town alongside One Eye and Longwell they passed near the house. However, they paid no attention. The street seemed to empty before them. The town's residents scattered at their sight.

Not enough people out to stop a good dog fight, thought Tom as he watched a couple of stray dogs struggle over a few table scraps.

Winston's men were given much more respect than they deserved. And the Box T cowboy half expected someone to shoot them from ambush. He was cautious and watched for anything out-of-the-ordinary.

They paid no attention to the mud puddles still filled with rainwater. All three riders were equally muddy themselves and another splash or two wouldn't matter. And even though it was still morning when they arrived, they headed straight for the town's only saloon.

"Reckon we'll find Winston in his office," One Eye said with a chuckle.

"That means the saloon," he added. "Besides I got me a thirst that needs quenching."

Tom noticed they were being watched at some distance by a few townspeople. "Must be a terrible thing to live in such fear of one man," he mumbled.

He had to remind himself he could be a target when riding with this crew. Winston and his men had taken several lives. People one day would need to stand up against such tyranny. And, they might not be selective in their targets.

Before stepping down from their horses, they spotted a crowd at the opposite end of town near the church. However, thirst overwhelmed curiosity and each man dismounted and tied his horse to an empty and well-worn hitching rail. Longwell was the first up the steps, followed by One Eye.

Only Tom held back, straining to make something of the activities and those that had gathered to watch. He could hear shooting.

"I'm drier 'an bleached out bone and twice as thirsty," Longwell said to nobody in particular as he crossed the plank covered walkway in front of the saloon. "Come on boys."

"Ain't it the truth," echoed One Eye.

Before getting inside, they spotted Winston walking up the middle of the street toward them. His booming voice called out to the town's citizens as if he were a politician running for office.

"Full of himself, ain't he?" noted Longwell with one hand holding the saloon's swinging doors.

Winston's approach was interrupted by a loud, barking dog . . . a young boy's dog.

"Obviously, a good judge of character," mumbled Tom as he watched the dog bark at the ruthless Winston.

A boy of about nine years old struggled to control the dog by holding him around the neck. But, the upset dog was too strong, and he broke the boy's grasp.

Winston never hesitated, nor gave any warning; he merely pulled a pistol from his belt and shot the dog.

"Serves him right," he said loudly over the dog's dying moans. "He might have bitten me."

The boy was devastated. His scream was heard up and down the street. He rushed to the side of his dying friend only to have Winston grab him by the back of his shirt. And with a smile on his face, he simply tossed the boy aside.

"Shut up and get outta my way," he yelled. "Next time keep your mongrel off the street."

The boy got up quickly and confronted the old man.

"You shot my dog! Why'd you shoot my dog?"

The back of Winston's right hand caught the boy across the cheek and sent him sprawling again.

"Shut up, I said," Winston repeated.

With the slap, Tom started back down the steps. *He shouldn't be hitting a kid.*

One Eye grabbed him by the arm

momentarily stopping him.

"Easy boy. No harm done. The kid will get a new mutt by nightfall. Don't try to be no hero."

Now with his tear-stained face covered with dust and mud, the boy laid still . . . his eyes filled with hatred. He waited for Winston and his now laughing men to pass by. Then he crawled to his lifeless friend lying in a pool of blood.

Before following Winston inside, Tom watched the boy get belated help from his family and friends. Tears streamed down his freckled face. Blood, the life flow of a dear friend, now stained his fingers. And in that dark moment innocence was lost.

Inside they quickly delivered Smitty's message and turned to get a "stiff" drink.

"Boys, have one on me. Hell have two. Then oil up them pistols. New cattle might mean trouble . . . especially from their former owners," Winston laughed.

Tom caught his meaning. It was clear enough. *Not only is he taking over everyone's land, he also is stealing their cattle.*

Man that'll shoot a boy's dog is just ugly mean. He ain't right, Tom thought to himself.

The three men picked up their drinks at the bar and then found a table near the front window. Once seated, Tom caught the sweet smell of cheap perfume rising from the mix of mud, beer and tobacco spit. "Perfume . . . my God . . . and up close."

Turning slightly he caught sight of Molly. Suddenly, the naturally talkative Tom Scott was stone, cold silent. Dead dogs, stolen cattle and the time of day were all forgotten.

She's the one on the stage, he finally observed to himself.

Molly, who had just emerged from a back supply room, spotted the three but paid no attention. She stayed busy serving the midday crowd. The entrance of the three dirty cowboys had caught her attention but little else. She had seen them talk to Winston.

Busy became hectic and except for an occasional glance she paid them little mind. She did wonder why the youngest of the three seemed out-of-place.

Then it happened. The gentle ebb and flow of an otherwise quiet late morning was suddenly interrupted.

A poorly positioned spittoon and more poorly aimed tobacco spit had created a hazardous corner around which Molly had navigated all morning. The barkeep's yell of her name, a loaded tray of beers, and a failure to look down, all met at the same precise moment. She slipped and fell.

The sound of breaking glass, metal tray hitting the floor and splashing beer, coupled with Molly's undignified landing all caught the attention of everyone in the room. Tom, however, was the first to offer assistance.

His offer was soundly and profanely rebuked.

Humiliated and embarrassed, Molly got to her feet, tobacco spit mixed with beer covering the back of her dress. The last thing she needed now was more attention brought to herself . . . especially by a half-drunk cowboy.

"Here, let me help," insisted Tom as he began picking up broken glass and her metal tray.

"Just leave me alone," she stated. "And, go. . . ."

"Your hand," he interrupted. "It is bleeding."

The mixture of blood, broken glass and beer made for an unsightly mess.

"I said leave me alone," she repeated. "I can take care of myself. I don't need anyone's help."

"Didn't say you couldn't," Tom said.

He turned away and started back for the front table. Under his breath, he muttered, "Ungrateful!"

One Eye chuckled as Tom returned.

"Maybe I should go help her since she ain't liking you so much," he said.

"Boy, you ain't much of a ladies man," Longwell laughed.

"Shut up," Tom huffed.

The bartender returned with a broom and began the cleanup. Molly found some water and a rag to clean her wound. The dress would have to wait.

The saloon returned to its pre-accident activities. Winston had watched the events with some amusement, but said nothing. New beers were poured and sent to thirsty customers. Molly was told to go cleanup and return.

Really ungrateful, thought Tom as he watched her leave. *I was just trying to help.*

Still, he found himself admiring her spirit.

Next time I get that close I'll do things a little different.

"Until next time," he said out loud to his otherwise quiet companions while offering up a toast.

As Molly cleaned up back in her hotel room she kept thinking of the young cowboy who had tried to help her.

I was a little rough, she thought. *It wasn't his fault I fell. He did try to help. Next time I get that close . . . maybe I'll thank him!*

CHAPTER 18
ROUGH FIRST MEETING

A breeze swept down off the mountains and out over the prairie cooling the early morning air. The chill was born in the snow still clinging to the high mountain peaks. The wind brought a reminder that while the calendar might say early summer, winter still claimed the high country.

Horses milled about in the corrals urged on with an energy born of the morning chill. They sensed sunrise was near.

A lone night bird called out one last song before giving way to a less than timely rooster. And a fresh new day was born, a canvas as yet unblemished. The horizon had begun to lighten ever so slightly as Jake prepared to leave.

After a quick breakfast, he was saddled and headed north. Morning broke clear and cool. Rain clouds from the night before had blown east and were gone. The air smelled fresh and thoroughly washed. It was a good morning.

The sky was a mix of pale blues and purples, gradually giving way to shades of yellows and taupes. There was a scattered mix of puffy while clouds fringed with light and dark grays in the northwestern sky.

Tom had left for Chugwater early with One Eye and Longwell. They would compare notes later.

The sun grew warm on Jake's shoulders as he rode to find Winston's mysterious herd. It gave him time to reflect and ponder. *Two Box T hands up against Winston and his 40 or so hired guns could prove to be tough odds,* he thought to himself. *Still, we need a plan.*

Thompson will bring more hands. But, can they get here in time? he asked himself.

Jake rode along the hilltops where he could get a better view of the surrounding countryside. Somewhere out ahead were the stolen cattle Smitty had said were being pastured.

After riding due north for about an hour, he spotted a horse grazing in the distance. And while not unusual in ranching country, a horse alone still wearing a bridle was out of the ordinary. He decided to check it out and spurred his own horse into a lope.

One of Winston's talented cow hands must

have lost his mount.

Jake discovered Sarah's horse. But after looking in all directions, he saw neither cowhand nor cattle. He returned to the horse hoping to find some clues about its owner.

Why would a shod and bridled horse be out here without a rider? he thought. *And without a saddle. It doesn't add up. Somebody must be in trouble.*

A search of the moist ground enabled Jake to determine the general direction from where the horse had come. He gathered up the reins of the second horse and began following tracks that led northwest.

The growling, snarling sounds of angry wolves reached him well before he saw them. But, he knew the sound. His horse also caught wind of the noises, sensed danger and listened with ears sharply forward. Jake's nervous horse had to be encouraged to move toward the sounds ahead.

Jake figured the wolves were fighting over the carcass of a recent kill. However, curiosity and a horse with no rider forced him to take a look.

Riding slowly with pistol in hand, he came to a small creek and rode along its banks. His eyes scanned the horizon and creek bed as he searched. The horse's tracks were easy to follow. They also led toward the ominous sounds ahead.

If the rider was left afoot without a weapon and perhaps hurt, this may he an ugly find, he warned himself.

Jake half expected to find a mutilated human body being fed upon by hungry wolves. He shivered at the thought.

Then he spotted someone hiding behind some large boulders along the rocky creek bank. The person appeared only long enough to throw a few well-aimed rocks before ducking for cover. It was only a matter of time before the hungry wolves would rush in for the kill.

A male and female of gray color spaced evenly apart crouched on the far side of the stream ready to attack. A third had already crossed the stream. Only the trapped person's shouts and accuracy at throwing rocks had kept them at bay. However, a fourth nearly black young male had moved around and above. This animal had moved into position where he might leap from above while the other wolves held the person's attention.

The wolf pack had followed the flash flood hoping to find drown or injured prey. They had so far found nothing. Finding a live human had come as a surprise. They were unsure how to proceed, but their hunger prevented them from moving on to easier prey.

Jake quickly dismounted, drew his rifle from its scabbard and took careful aim at the wolf high on the rock. The animal rose to attack as the bullet shattered its skull. It fell in a blackened blur, just missing Sarah.

The three remaining and now startled wolves turned and withdrew as Jake suddenly appeared on top of the outcropping. He fired a second and a third shot in their direction. A yelp of pain and he realized that at least one of the shots had found its intended target.

Standing on top of the rocky outcrop, Jake shouted.

"Hey down there!"

With every worn and tired muscle in her body aching, Sarah tensed and looked around and up. She immediately spotted Jake.

"What the . . . ?"

Jake suddenly realized the person hiding along the creek was a woman.

With the terrible ordeal at an end, the exhausted Sarah managed to lift one hand for a weak wave but said nothing.

"You okay," Jake shouted.

She struggled to stand but her legs would not respond. Under her breath, she cursed her situation and once more criticized herself for getting into such a mess.

"I need help!" she called out weakly. "I need help."

She realized this stranger, good or bad, was her best, and maybe only, hope for assistance. The chances of anyone else stumbling upon her out on this vast stretch of prairie were slim and none.

"Sit still," Jake called out. "I'm coming."

As Jake found an opening in the rocky creek bank to ride down, Sarah remembered where she had seen this guy. *My God, he's the one from yesterday. He's the guy who kept circling our ranch, one of Winston's men.*

While the morning air was warming, the mood quickly chilled with Jake's approach. This man had saved her life but Sarah felt uncertain and uneasy. For some reason, he made her feel nervous, anxious. She kept watching him closely.

The cure may be worse than the disease, she thought to herself.

This man had something to do directly or indirectly with her father's disappearance. She was sure of it.

"Hello," said Jake with a smile. "That was close! You okay? What happened?"

"I'm fine," Sarah said tersely. "I just need my horse back if you don't mind and I'll be on my way."

Sarah struggled to stand then walked barefoot in Jake's direction. First, she had to step around the large carcass of the black wolf. He lay crumpled with his tongue resting over a set of sharp and once dangerous teeth. She shuddered at his ugly, bloody appearance, then caught her breath and stepped away.

"You okay?" Jake repeated as he dismounted. "How did the water catch you? Anything broken? You sure you're okay? Let me help you!"

Sarah thought, *must be hard of hearing.*

She said nothing.

Jake offered his canteen for a drink of water. She accepted without comment, suddenly realizing just how thirsty she was. She was also hungry but held back any comments.

Sarah's face was muddy, her hair wild and uncombed, and her clothing was torn and still wet. Still, it was easy to tell she was a woman, and quite possibly under all the grime and mud she might even be attractive, Jake figured.

However, she's being more than a little aloof to the point of being downright ungrateful.

Jake decided Sarah was okay physically.

He took a few moments to clean an ugly wound on her left arm before wrapping it with some clean cloth from his saddlebag. Sarah watched closely, observing every detail but said nothing.

"You're one lucky lady," he pointed out. "More than one hand has been washed into hell by a flash flood. Yes, I'd say you are real lucky."

"Thanks, I know all that. I'm glad you came along. But now I need to get going. Please point the way to Chugwater? I'll be on my way."

Jake knew better than to tease someone who had nearly drown, then attacked by wolves. But this lady was not at all grateful, or even the least bit appreciative. Like a mischievous schoolboy, he couldn't stop himself.

"I'm curious . . . you picked an interesting time and place to go swimming . . . and with your clothes on?" he pointed out with a sly grin. "Or was it time for a bath?"

Sarah could feel her muddy face warming to red from both embarrassment and anger.

Who is this smart-mouthed cowboy? she asked herself.

"Just give me my horse," she said sternly. "I've put up with enough. Point me toward

Chugwater . . . if you know."

"Chugwater? Looks like to me, you've chugged enough water," he laughed as he took her arm and helped her. "You also have some nasty pets."

Now she was angry, along with bruised and battered.

"Listen, you came along at just the right time. I thank you for that. I was in a real fix. But, for a knight on horseback, you sure are rude," she fired back.

"For someone who looks like a double-drowned rat, you sure are hateful," Jake muttered to himself,

"What did you say?" she asked.

"I said 'must have lost her hat in the rainfall'."

She only glared back.

Once mounted she gave him a brief "thank you", then rode bareback southwest. Within an hour she could see the buildings that made up Chugwater. She had not seen the stranger since leaving the creek bed, but she suspected he was behind her following.

Jake kept his distance, but managed to keep her in sight until he felt she'd safely made town. He then turned back to his assigned duties for the day.

He was impressed with her ability to ride without a saddle. She obviously was someone who had spent considerable time riding and knew her way around horses.

"Interesting!" was all he could say.

CHAPTER 19
DEATH BEFORE DYING

The midday sun warmed Jake's back and the cool breeze he had enjoyed all morning gave way to afternoon heat. The young cowboy didn't notice. He rode slowly, soaking up the land around him, the prairie grasses, the blue sky and the feel of the wind against his face. It was a good feeling, one of familiarity. He was comfortable here. There was an understanding in the simplicity of it all. In God's grand mix everything had a place, everything worked.

"This is what life's all about, old pard," he told his horse. "It doesn't get much better than a day like this."

Thinking about the young woman he'd met earlier, he continued, "Someday I'm going to find me a wife who loves this land like I do. Maybe we could settle down out here and raise us some young'uns and some cattle. Maybe that place along the Sweetwater Thompson has been talking about."

A sudden gust of wind nearly tore the hat from his head and he remembered the task at hand.

It was too late for a normal spring roundup, even if Winston said so. Any respectable hand would know that. The Box T and most other ranches had already completed their spring roundups and were preparing for the fall. Most herds had already been driven to Chadron or Ogallala.

Some ranch owners didn't always follow the normal seasonal patterns of gather, brand and ship. But, this didn't add up. Jake thought of Tom in town with Winston's men. After following the woman, he had been tempted to stay in town and do some digging of his own. However, not listening to Smitty on his first day of work might jeopardize their mission and put them both in danger. He decided to ride.

Didn't even get her name, he reminded himself.

Pulling his hat down tight, he kicked his horse into a nice, easy lope. They covered several miles with ease. Only a few meadowlarks rose to challenge their approach.

After about two hours, he pulled up suddenly. Off to his right at some distance, he could hear a loud commotion and gunfire. It was a mix of laughter, pain and childish play. Some men were shouting and whooping it up, even firing their pistols now and then. The sounds came to Jake long before he saw their source.

Three of Winston's men had roped a gray wolf and were pulling it in three different directions as the same time. They were hollering and laughing.

The inevitable result would be a slow, painful and tortured death for the wolf.

Jake understood the feeling of being pulled in many directions at once. Maybe not from a physical standpoint, but he could relate to the mental agony of the experience. It wasn't the work. He could handle that. It was more the demons of his own mind that now and again tore at him . . . loneliness and uncertainty in this vast, often harsh land.

"Let him go," Jake called out.

His efforts, however, were much too late. Jake realized he couldn't make a difference, not now. But, he had to try. With his right hand resting on his still holstered pistol, he called out once more.

"Let him go boys. You can see the fight is out of him."

And with dangling tongue and tortured

eyes, a free spirit of the prairie was gone, literally torn apart by the world around him. Jake felt a tinge of sadness at the wolf's passing, one more sign of a changing land and times. His crumpled, bloody carcass was left in an undignified pile of fur and bones, hardly befitting his regal role in God's orderly world.

In that world, the wolf might have fought back on even terms. That world, like the seasons, had a sense of order, respect and understanding. *Not this,* thought Jake.

Humans had come and changed the balance of nature, changed the order. The wolf died without understanding those changes, without understanding the new world revolving around him. It was a world changing around Jake as well.

The wolf was simply dead. The political nuances of events leading to his death no longer mattered.

Dead is dead, Jake said to himself.

"Who are you to be giving us orders?" shouted one of the men.

"I'd shut my face if I was you," chimed in a second Winston hand. "We was just having some fun."

"What's it to you?" asked the first man.

Jake turned slowly to face the men. He realized he was outnumbered and outgunned.

"Just seemed a little unfair to me," he noted calmly. "I mean three against one. The varmint wasn't even armed."

The third man, who was moving slowly toward Jake from the side, said, "Oh, he was armed all right. You see those teeth, them fangs?"

The first man, still agitated, said, "This ain't over. You and me will meet again. Now come on boys. Let's go to town and get us a drink."

With that exchange, the three men spurred their horses toward town, leaving Jake with the wolf.

Roping animals other than cattle and horses happened more times than most punchers would admit.

Most hands had a "devil-may-care" attitude about life in general and ranch work in particular. They were happy working, gambling, smoking, story telling, horse racing, and fighting and taking part in certain female-related pursuits in town now and then. Generally, they worked hard.

Throw in a good dose of bravado and you had a "top hand". He was a man who could be counted on when a job needed done. Still, day after day the work could also become overwhelmingly boring. Roping a wolf or some other animal would seem like fun at times like that. It also gave them bragging rights about their roping skills.

"I remember how we once roped us a bear up on the Yellowstone," Jake recalled one old wrangler bragging.

"He just roared and fought us . . . beast to man and back again. Paws flashing with claws laid bare, man he fought us," the man had claimed while shaking his head at the memory.

"You roped a bear?" Jake asked at the time.

"Yup . . . you don't believe me?" the man had responded.

Jake said, "Oh no! I'm sort of curious how you got close enough to a mad bear to put a rope a rope on him. That's all."

"Weren't easy. That's a fact. I'm here to tell you."

The old man had eased back in his chair, knowing he had a full and attentive audience.

"Weren't easy! There were three of us, but old Sam Lawson got the worst of it. Hell, the old man got knocked from his saddle and durn near got killed. Take a look at that bay horse of his sometime. Those scars along his left flank . . . well them are bear claw marks. Nearly opened that horse up like a ripe watermelon. Managed to escape with only a bad scar for his trouble.

"Lawson ran like a scared rabbit. If we hadn't had two other ropes on that bear, he'd more and likely would've caught up to old Sammy," he chuckled at the memory.

"How'd you get free of them ropes?" a man in the back asked.

"That weren't easy either I tell you."

The man turned toward the gent who asked the question. "We counted to three, cut the ropes and hightailed it. Bear didn't know he was loose at first, then couldn't decide which one of us to chase, so he just stood there roaring."

Thompson refused to let his men rope, drag or torture wild animals of any kind. It was a position Jake supported. Still, it was often done and when the men were caught, it meant immediate dismissal.

Winston, unlike Thompson, didn't care. His men often chased antelope, coyotes, wolves, mule deer and even a stray buffalo when they could.

Chasing wild animals for sport was nothing new and Jake realized as much. Still, he didn't like the idea.

A few years earlier up in Montana, Jake and Tom had interrupted gunplay involving six holed-up coyotes trapped in a den along a riverbank. The men were taking turns shooting into the group. Not wanting to kill them at first, the men were wounding for sport so they could hear the whelps of pain.

Jake and Tom had managed to stop them, but not without a confrontation.

They were told to "shut up and stand back if it bothered them so much."

Jake and Tom had each filled a hand with a loaded pistol. Confronted with a serious objection to their play, the men had backed down. And, like the wolf incident, there were threats of "getting even."

After the incident, Tom had said, "We didn't exactly make any new friends did we?"

"We did the right thing," Jake had answered.

With the early afternoon excitement behind him, Jake resumed his search for Winston's cattle. He soon spotted dust from the herd. Then his senses caught the smell of cow manure mixed with dust. Then the smell of burnt hide tore at his nostrils.

Jake managed to get his count and then returned to the bunkhouse just after dark. Supper was long over but Tom had saved him some beans and cold biscuits.

"Learn anything today?" Tom asked in a whisper.

Jake relayed his run-in with Sarah and what had happened. "Didn't even get her name," he chuckled. Then he told about the wolf incident.

Tom told of his own encounter with Molly.

Jake and Tom agreed on one thing. Something big was about to happen. Winston was gathering cattle from his own spreads, plus those he'd acquired by gun and rope. Both men suspected some rustling was involved, but on their first day they had not seen any unexplained brands.

CHAPTER 20
A TIME FOR SHARING

A dry, dusty midday haze had settled over the town as Sarah approached. Although still morning by the clock, many townsfolk had already been gone inside to more shady and cooler pursuits. She made the edge of town unseen except by an old yellow dog that merely glanced at her as she passed.

A six-foot high board fence behind the hotel helped obscure Sarah's approach. She was able to ride in behind the hotel and tie her horse to a picket fence that defined the length and breadth of the hotel's property. She would return the "over due" horse later. That would be relatively easy . . . explaining the lost saddle and rifle would be more difficult.

She entered through an unlocked rear door. Now it was time to clean up and get some much-needed rest. But as she started down the hallway, Molly emerged from her room after her own cleanup.

"Sarah!" she cried out. "Are you all right? What happened? You look terrible."

"I don't feel so hot either," she replied weakly.

Molly took her by the arm and said, "Come inside. Tell me what happened."

Sarah gave a quick and but labored explanation of what had happened and what she had seen.

"You sure are lucky that cow puncher came by when he did," Molly exclaimed.

She went on to tell about her own experiences in town, including the beating and death of Nells Goodman.

"I'll tell you this," Molly added, "I'm surer than ever Winston and his goons are behind the death of Marcus. And, while I hate to say this, after watching what he did to that old man today, I hope your father got away."

Sarah lowered her eyes.

"Yes, I hope so too. But where would he go? There are still too many unanswered questions."

Returning to the saloon, Molly found the place was nearly empty including the front table where the three men had been sitting.

He was just trying to help, she kept repeating to herself. *Nothing more . . . I guess. Maybe I should thank him if he returns. But . . . ,* she hesitated. *He works for Win-*

ston. Why do I care what he thinks?

The harsh realities of her and Sarah's situation came rushing back to her.

Questioning the other women working the saloon about Winston and his men netted nothing new.

One of the older women just mentioned how fat he looked when naked. Another mentioned he had become preoccupied recently with moving cattle, but that wasn't particularly unusual. All agreed he wasn't to be trusted.

Molly learned Winston was gathering a large herd he planned to sell and soon. Some unknown buyer was expected any day. It generally was assumed most of the cattle were from ranches Winston had obtained by brute force.

Witnessing the brutal beating and humiliation of Nells Goodman had convinced Molly that Winston was behind all recent deaths in the area.

Sarah took a long painful look in the mirror and saw herself as Jake had seen her. She looked nothing like the beautiful young teacher that had kept the young men of Nebraska off guard and lined up at her door. Even by tomboy standards, today she looked a mess.

"Give me a good bath, some nice smelling

soap and a clean dress and I can still look good to rude cowboys," she mumbled to herself. "Even if that no account is blind. I'm still a woman and I'll show him someday!"

Sarah slept through the afternoon. She and Molly had made plans to meet for dinner. Both knew it wouldn't be easy standing up to a man like Winston. Two women alone against a ruthless killer and his band of gunmen would be no picnic, if not impossible.

The raspy crow of a solitary rooster from somewhere across town signaled the arrival of sunrise. It was a fact of which Sarah was already well aware. A sleepless night of tossing and turning can have that effect.

Even in the depths of sheer exhaustion the mind can betray the body and deny even the most basic of human needs. Every attempt at sleep met a wall of concern and questions about her father and his fate. Even with the exhaustive ordeal of the previous 24 hours, she could not find peace and comfort behind closed eyes. All attempts failed. And not even a thousand tiny sheep leaping through her mind could bring rest.

Sarah finally gave up and sat by the window. She stared out at the empty street below. Now and then the shadow of some alley cat moving to better hunting grounds could be seen in the lantern light. All else was still.

Then in that hour before dawn, those darkest moments before sunrise, she yawned, then again. And like the flood of the previous night, sleep rushed over her in wave upon wave, devouring her every thought, consuming her mind and soul. She slept as the day unfolded around her.

Sarah woke up about 10 a.m. to the knowledge that morning was nearly gone and she was hungry. She knew Molly was already handing out beers at the saloon, so she ate a late breakfast alone.

The cafe that passed itself off as somewhere to eat shared the building with cockroaches, mice and rats. At this late morning hour, Sarah was convinced the rats outnumbered the customers. She ate a quick, if not satisfying breakfast, then left. Her once-filled coffee cup remained half full.

Since the few townsfolk she knew had provided no worthwhile information on the whereabouts of her father, she debated going straight to Winston. Shocked, yet excited, that she would even consider something so bold, she left the restaurant and headed straight for the saloon.

"I'd better act quickly before I lose my nerve," she mumbled to herself. "He's been telling everyone my father sold out and left town. Well, let him explain all that to me!

"We'll see just what he has to say," she said as she pushed the saloon doors open.

Molly looked up, looked down, and then up again as she suddenly realized Sarah had entered the saloon.

"My gosh! What the . . . ?"

Sarah never acknowledged even seeing Molly as she walked toward Winston's table. Only a few patrons were scattered around the saloon, but the place went quiet as everyone watched the young schoolteacher with clenched fists cross the room.

"Mr. Winston?"

The old man spotted Sarah as she came closer. And with a wave of his hand, his men stepped back to let her approach his table. Befitting his own self-importance and lack of manners he chose not to stand. He merely looked her up and down at her, but said nothing.

"Mr. Winston? I need a minute of your time."

Winston smiled and motioned for her to come still closer.

"Young lady, please have a seat.

"Boys, get this sweet young lady

something cool to drink. She must be thirsty on such a warm morning."

Sarah nervously looked around and offered a polite, "thank you" before sitting down.

"How may I help you?"

"Mr. Winston," as she sought the courage to continue. "I've come about my father."

"Your father."

"Yes, my father. People around town say you bought our ranch and my father left town. I want to know what happened."

Winston leaned back in his chair, glanced toward Scar, and then looked back at Sarah. With a subtle motion of his hand, he urged the gunman to step behind her, effectively blocking any escape.

"Now, now let's start from the beginning young lady. Just who is your father?"

"John Meadows."

Winston's face suddenly turned ashen.

"Meadows? John Meadows?"

"That's right," Sarah continued. "They say you bought us out."

"Well . . . well Miss Meadows. It is Miss isn't it? That's right; I made your father a generous offer. An offer he couldn't refuse. He sold out and left town. I believe he was going to California, or was it Oregon?"

"I don't believe you!"

"Well, it's true. We haven't seen him since. Have we boys?"

"My father would never sell that ranch . . . my mother is buried out there. He would have told me first!"

Sarah was growing angrier by the moment, and she sensed she was losing control of her emotions, and thus any control of the situation.

"Listen, Miss Meadows, and listen good," Winston spoke while pointing his finger at Sarah. "I don't give a tinker's damn about who's buried where. And I care even less if old man Meadows didn't tell his little girl he was selling out. That ranch is mine now!

"Now, I've tried being nice to you."

Sarah stood quickly and pointed her own finger at the red-faced old man.

"You're a liar!" she shouted. "My father would never sell our ranch. And I aim to find out the truth!"

Winston also stood. Failure to make this high-spirited woman back down would cause him to lose the respect and loyalty of his men. There would be talk of how she had bested him. He had to do something and quickly . . . but not here in public.

"Young lady . . . sit down. Let's talk this through."

Sarah was on a roll.

"I'm betting you forced my father off our ranch and stole it from us, just like you did to Marcus Dunn and Nells Goodman. Maybe even killed him as well!"

Winston started around the table while urging some of his men to gather closer.

"Young lady, you are making some pretty serious charges here. I'd be real careful. And I wouldn't go spreading these wild stories around town; things just might get out-of-hand if you get my drift. I mean a young, attractive lady out here all alone. Why, who knows what could happen? Why don't you go back to wherever it was you came from and leave well enough alone?"

"Winston," a defiant Sarah said, shaking her fist at him. "I intend to find out the truth, if it's the last thing I do. And if I stir up this town, then so be it!"

She whirled around to leave and ran headlong into Scar. He grabbed her by the arm and held tight.

"Miss Meadows, I'm trying to run a business here. I can't afford to have you mucking things up . . . not now. Not at all. Now you can calm down and maybe we can negotiate satisfactory answers to your questions. Maybe I can even help you find your old man. Or, I can let Mr. Scar here take you out behind the woodshed for a little old-fashioned arm-twisting. Do you get my drift?"

"Go to hell!"

With that loud and sudden answer, she twisted away from Scar's tight grip, pushed her way past Willie Temple and bolted for the saloon doors. There was no time to say anything to Molly. She had to run.

Sarah burst through the saloon doors nearly knocking down a young cowhand trying to come inside. She untied the first horse along the hitching rail, mounted quickly and kicked the surprised animal into a run for her life.

The horse bolted past an elderly couple out to buy some supplies at the General Store, nearly knocking the old woman down and leaving the old man in a daze. A few chickens of unknown ownership scattered wildly, feathers flying as she rode among them and on down the street.

Sarah turned the horse into an alley behind the General Store and dismounted.

"Need to get my bearings," she said to herself. "What have I done?"

After gaining her composure, she quietly entered the store through an unlocked back door. Sarah worked her way into the main store area without being noticed and immediately began gathering a few basic supplies.

A young boy of perhaps 14 was working behind the counter while the owner was talking with an older couple outside the store about wild riders and unsafe conditions in the street. It was a stroke of luck for Sarah. She was able to quickly gather what she needed along with a rifle and some cartridges without having to explain anything to the storeowner. She made a quick exit out the back, found her "borrowed" horse, and left town unnoticed.

There was no time for thinking, no time for complicated plans. She had confronted Winston. Now he knew she was in town and he would come looking for her. He could ill-afford to have her asking questions and creating problems. She was an unexpected problem that needed solving, a festering boil that needed lancing.

CHAPTER 21
HELP FROM A STRANGER

Morning brought clear skies and cool winds out of the north. Jake had spent much of the night wondering . . . lost in thought about the young woman he'd helped.

Meeting Sarah, even under duress, had caused him to think about his own future. The idea of living the rest of his life alone was not appealing. Something about Sarah's "spirited reaction" to a rough situation made him smile. He felt a strong attraction to her and the feeling was both strange and new.

Who was she?

Jake had more questions than answers. But, their meeting had been more confrontational than conversational, and he regretted being so tough on her. The opportunity to learn more had come and gone.

A breeze caught the edge of his hat and he felt a cold chill from the morning air. He remembered he had a job to do, a serious job that might be life threatening. This was no time for idle thoughts. The Box T hands had a sense of purpose. It was time to bring Thompson and the other Box T hands into the fray.

Tom was sent into town to deliver a new message to Winston. He seized the opportunity to see Molly.

Even if she won't speak, he thought.

"While in town, get word to Thompson," Jake pointed out. "Tell him it's time to come running and bring all the hands we can spare."

Once in town, Tom stopped by the telegraph office long enough to send a message to Thompson that read:

Momma,

Hungry and times a wasting.

Time to bring all the biscuits and papa too!

Love,

Tommy,

A brief stop at the saloon revealed nothing. Neither Molly nor Winston had arrived yet so Tom decided to look around town. Townsfolk scattered at his approach and he could feel their stares. After about an hour, he returned to the saloon.

As he started toward the saloon doors, they suddenly opened and he was forced to step aside. Only his quickness saved him from a broken nose or worse. An angry young woman came rushing past him and down the steps. She mounted a nearby horse and kicked it into a run down the street.

Tom had dodged a full frontal collision with doors and girl only by sidestepping them both at the last possible instant.

"That dang girl," Winston roared. "When did she show up? Take care of her, Scar. We don't need any problems now!" he raged.

Scar motioned to Willie and the two gunmen went out, mounted up and left.

Molly had heard the exchange, and now heard Winston's "take care of her" orders. She was in a panic. How could she warn her friend without drawing attention to herself? She didn't even know where Sarah had gone. Then she spotted Tom entering the saloon.

Sarah had hurried back to the hotel, gathered up a rifle, cartridges and some food. Her only hope was to find any old cowhands still at the ranch or some other ranch still loyal to her father's memory. She needed to find men willing to help her make a stand and retake the ranch from Winston. It was now or never.

Frustrated, she had mistakenly confronted Winston with the hope of forcing his hand.

He had gotten the better of their confrontation when she lost her temper. Now she was on the run. She hadn't meant to confront Winston . . . not that way at least. It had just happened. Circumstances and frustration met opportunity and the battle was enjoined.

Molly was uncertain in her approach. Her trust of men to help was sorely lacking.

Tom was equally uncertain about her intent. Although excited, he wondered immediately why she was coming toward his table.

"I owe you an apology," she began. "I realized later you were only trying to help yesterday. I was very short."

"I noticed," he answered. "But, apology accepted."

As she began to talk more, the young cowboy listened without actually hearing her words. He was lost in the moment. She was actually talking to him. Just what she was saying didn't really matter.

The saloon was virtually empty. Winston was busy with business and paid her no attention. There was no outward pressure for Molly to move on and tend to anything. And, to Tom's total amazement, she sat down.

"So you work for Winston," he heard her

say. "How long have you known him?"

Not sure where she might be headed with these questions and her sudden interest in him and his relation to Winston, Tom measured his response carefully.

"Just a few days," he answered.

Formalities gave way to small talk. Both had their own agendas. They fell into an easy comfortable conversation with Tom carefully avoiding his true employment and reason for being in Chugwater.

Molly kept reminding herself of the real reason for approaching this guy in the first place. The sense of urgency that prompted her approach in the first place returned.

"Tom?"

"Yes."

"I need your help."

She paused and judged his response. He provided little reaction. He said nothing. He merely looked her in the eye and waited for her to continue.

"A good friend of mine is in trouble," Molly said.

"Who is it?" he asked.

"That girl who almost ran over you a few minutes ago . . . ?" There was a pregnant pause. "She made Winston mad, and now he's sent two of his goons to hurt her. That's why she was running."

Tom turned in his chair and took a quick look at Winston and saw he was preoccupied with other duties. He then turned to Molly and asked, "What happened?"

"Well, she got into an argument. That enraged the old man. He sent a couple of men after her. I'm afraid she'll be hurt."

"What could she have said to make the old man so mad?" Tom asked.

"Winston has apparently taken over her father's ranch and he's missing. Winston says he bought the ranch and the old man left the country. Sarah doesn't believe that and neither do I," she said.

"Which ranch are you talking about?" asked Tom. "Seems to me that Winston has gotten his hands on several area ranches lately. Besides, aren't you afraid I'll go tell the old man you've asked me to help your friend?"

"I realize I've taken a great chance . . . but . . . ," she hesitated. "You offered to help me once . . . and well, you're my only hope. I don't have anywhere else to turn."

Tom said nothing, not sure what to say.

After a few moments of silence, she continued. "It was the Meadows Ranch. I think it's north of town."

"Meadows! Are you sure?" Tom asked, suddenly sitting upright in his chair.

"Yes, I think so."

"Your friend . . . what's her name?"

"Her name's Sarah . . . Sarah Meadows."

Tom nearly choked. "Sam!"

Looking around the saloon, he saw nobody was paying any attention to the young couple. Only a couple of old timers had drifted in to escape the heat of the street.

Leaning forward and with a lowered voice, he told her, "Old man Meadows is still alive and safe. That fool friend of yours is going to mess up everything."

"What? Are you sure?" Molly exclaimed. "How would you know that?"

"I can't take time to explain now. But, Winston doesn't have him," Tom said. "His daughter is supposed to be in Nebraska teaching school. What's she doing here? Damn, she may blow the lid off things before me and Jake is ready. I gotta go."

He pushed back from the table and got to his feet.

A confused looking Molly once more asked, "What about Sarah? Who's Jake? Will you help her?"

Tom paused, leaned over the table and quietly said, "I'll try to help your friend but I need to get word to Jake. You see her again tell her to stay in town out of sight. Things are about to blow wide open . . . and . . . well she's got more friends than she knows."

With that said, he left.

Molly sat in a whirl of thoughts. *Old man Meadows alive. Sarah's father okay. Who were these friends Tom mentioned? And, who is Jake? What is about to blow?*

Her thoughts were shattered when the barkeep yelled. "Red . . . you working or daydreaming? Get back to work!"

Chapter 22
Secret Place Shootout

The ride from town went quickly. Sarah had kicked the horse into a run and by the time they reached the ranch he was lathered and breathing hard. She realized confronting Winston had destroyed any thought of discreetly learning about her father. Now she was in danger and indirectly, so was Molly.

Sarah planned to hide in her "secret" spot above the ranch complex until she could develop a plan of action. Before leaving town she had managed to scrape together enough supplies to get by for a few days.

"What a mess I've gotten into," she kept repeating to herself as she rode toward the ranch.

The ride should have given her time to formulate some type of plan. But, try as she might, no plan was forthcoming. Frustration was the result.

In the distance, she caught sight of a

coyote mother with three pups. The female took a quick look in Sarah's direction before leading her family into a mix of sagebrush and silvery lupine.

She was about 20 yards from her destination when a bullet ricocheted off a cottonwood tree behind her. Scrambling from her "borrowed" horse, she pulled her rifle from its scabbard and ran the remaining distance to cover. A second and third shot stirred the dirt at her feet as she ran.

She immediately pulled her rifle into firing position.

From the corner of her eye, she caught sight of someone moving just below and to the right of her position. The man was carrying a rifle. Briefly, ever so briefly, he was caught in the open while changing positions. Sarah didn't take time to ask questions. Her shot caught him in mid-stride and he was dead.

Unsure whether he was her only assailant or not, she decided to wait. The wait wasn't long. A bullet struck only inches from her head. Splinters and shattered pieces of wood showered down around her. Another shot hit a timber behind her with a ripping sound!

The shots were much too close. She huddled in fear for her life. Her assailant knew where she was hiding. She knew it was only a matter of time before the unknown gunman would rush her. Pinned down, she could only wait and pray.

After what seemed like hours, she slowly rose to one knee and peered out at the empty landscape.

Where is he? she thought to herself. *Damn, I hate this waiting.*

Seeing movement in some nearby underbrush, she took a quick shot in that direction. Then she immediately ducked for cover again. If nothing else, Sarah figured her assailant or assailants would know she was still alive and able to shoot back. However, it was of little solace.

After another 30 minutes, she spotted a rider approaching from the southwest. He disappeared into a depression or swale of some type so she waited.

Jake crossed a small creek in search of some stray steers and urged his mount up the opposite bank. Signs of cattle were everywhere. He saw where a few dozen head or so had watered earlier in the day but none were in sight.

As his horse climbed over the edge of the embankment, Sarah squeezed the trigger. However, she misjudged the distance and missed the shot. Her target and his horse disappeared from view.

"Damn! How could I miss him?" she muttered to herself.

The bullet struck with a thud at the hooves of Jake's horse. The horse shied to its left, nearly unseating him as the horse and its rider scrambled back over the creek bank seeking cover. Jake quickly dismounted and grabbed his own rifle. He peered over the edge of the embankment and searched the horizon. He finally decided the shot could only have come from two or three possible areas.

Now there are two men out there, she thought. *Winston's men no doubt.*

Using the creek and its high banks for cover, Jake managed to work closer to the one most logical position. At one point, he thought he saw another person moving in the tall grass but he wasn't sure.

Then he spotted the lifeless form of Willie Temple laying face down. The prairie grass was wet with his blood and a thousand flies had already found him.

Somebody made at least one good shot, thought Jake. *Be careful. Don't get stupid.*

The heat of the afternoon and the burning sun made it difficult to stay hidden. There was no shade from his vantage point and little enough cover. Something had to give and soon.

Then he recognized Scar moving low and silent like a cat about to pounce. Jake didn't know his attacker, but he was sure it wasn't a Winston hand. If Scar was involved, the other man might be some old rancher trying to take revenge.

Too far away, thought Jake. *Gotta try.*

He took careful aim and squeezed the trigger.

Sarah was growing desperate. Exhausted and pinned down by at least two Winston gunmen, the afternoon heat was talking its toll. She kept seeing heat mirages. And, without her canteen, thirst was also becoming a factor. She caught herself weakening and letting her guard down.

"Must stay alert!" she kept telling herself, only to let her mind wander again.

Sarah realized too late that someone had moved in behind her. A shot, a groan and Scar's falling body all came together in one quick, horrible realization that she had narrowly escaped death. In that one brief moment, she gasped for air.

A terrified Sarah looked down at Scar's still twitching body as he fought for one last breath of air. Instinctively, she turned her rifle in his direction just in case he had some fight still left.

His bloodshot eyes stared out at her from a face covered with whiskers and heavily wrinkled from years of exposure to the sun. They were eyes filled with disbelief, hatred and revulsion. Then he was gone.

"Who . . . ?"

She turned back to see Jake. He was standing in front of her with his rifle aimed at her. She started to raise her own rifle but then thought better.

"You!" shouted Jake. "Not you again! You almost killed me out there!"

Sarah found it hard to understand why one Winston hand would shoot another to save her life. She tried asking. But, her attempts were ignored.

Jake wasn't answering questions about the situation, he was asking them. And, he was in no mood for anything else. This woman was getting on his nerves.

Slowly, Sarah told her story to the tall Box T foreman, although she wasn't exactly sure why. There was something in his quiet and confident manner that she found reassuring, almost safe. He had helped her once before, and then let her ride away. Deep down she felt an attraction that bordered on actually liking the cowhand in front of her.

At least he's not being rude like before, she thought, *or at least not yet!*

All the details came spilling out. The words just seemed to come. In talking to him, she found a certain level of comfort, a zone of reassurance. It felt good to share her plight with someone besides Molly, even with this stranger.

"Meadows?" Jake asked with a tone somewhat more subdued than before. "You're not related to old man Meadows?"

"You know my father?" she asked.

Sarah was well aware that if the man in front of her knew about her father then he might have been involved in his disappearance. Her desire to know more was tempered by a degree of caution.

"Keep talking," Jake answered.

For the time being, he figured it best to keep quiet about his involvement with her father.

"What am I going to do with you?" he asked out loud. "I just can't let you start shooting up the country again. Hell . . . you might actually hit me next time."

His decision was bold, but dangerous. He would take her to the ranch compound and lock her up. Word would soon spread that she had shot Willie. Jake figured he might even embellish the story a little.

"Might as well let you take credit for shooting Scar as well," Jake said.

"What do you mean . . . let me take the credit? What are you going to do with me?" she demanded.

"You're my captive," he responded. "Now keep quiet."

"I'm nobody's captive," she answered angrily. Her comfort zone was shattered.

"Mount up lady," ordered Jake. "We're going for a ride."

"Where are we going?" she demanded to know.

"We're going down to the ranch where me and the boys can watch you," said Jake. "And, if I was you . . . well them boys may not be as polite as me, so I'd keep quiet if it was me. You know old Scar and Willie might still have a friend or two down there."

Jake figured locking her up would keep her out of trouble and in a relatively safe place.

Besides Tom and I can keep an eye on her for old man Meadows. She doesn't need to know about Tom and me. She might tell the wrong person, he decided.

Jake was not happy. The girl had almost got him shot and for what? She had some fool notion that she could retake her father's ranch alone.

"What are you going to do with me?"

demanded Sarah. Her determination and defiance had quickly returned.

"Lady . . . you're lucky to be alive. I wouldn't keep pushing my luck if I were you. Now keep quiet and do as you're told."

The root cellar actually had been the original Meadows ranch house thus accounting for its two rooms. The structure had been built into a hillside to make it cooler in summer and easier to heat in winter.

Both rooms had packed dirt floors and a sod roof. Log timbers were used across all four sides. Two windows were in the front with one on each side of the only door.

The front room had been used for cooking and eating. The back room had been used for sleeping. A cloth sheet originally had hung beneath the earthen ceiling to catch any falling dirt. However, it didn't keep out the fleas. Only a few remnants of that original cloth remained, so anyone entering the room usually got hit in the head with falling dirt.

The Meadows Soddy had been abandoned when Sarah was nine years old. It had been used as a root cellar and storage shed since.

A wood frame home, built with lumber hauled down from the mountains, had replaced the sod house. The new house was a whitewashed, six-room structure built about 75 yards north. Two additional rooms were added when Sarah was 14. The house, a barn, outhouse, bunkhouse, cookhouse, two corrals, and the root cellar now made up the entire Meadows ranch complex. There also had been a chicken shed, recently burned.

Sarah knew there was no chance of escape except through the front door. That would mean getting past two of Winston's gunmen. Smitty had been left to stand guard. Winston's foreman had not been happy with having to "nurse maid" Sarah, but had accepted Jake's explanation.

"We'll wait and see what the old man wants to do about her," Smitty said.

Despite her yells, the cellar door had been shut and locked behind her. She was left in the dark room with a smoky old lantern for light and an old cot on which to rest. It was there among old jars of vegetables, rotted potatoes, a broken shovel handle and numerous cobwebs that Sarah found herself a prisoner.

Exhausted from the day's events, she sat on the edge of the cot and cried. She had a mix of ceiling dirt and cobwebs in her hair and her clothes were torn. Tears streaked her dirty face and with each wipe of her hand across her face it became more muddied. Pride gave way to depression and despair.

As Jake headed toward the cookhouse, he spotted Tom returning from town. The two decided to compare notes over a drink of whisky.

"Jake, old friend, looks like the only way you can catch a woman is at gunpoint, or half-drowned," laughed Tom. "What's the likelihood of you rescuing the same woman twice?"

Jake didn't answer. He was lost in his own thoughts.

Finally, he said, "You'll never guess who she is!"

"Sarah Meadows. She's the old man's daughter."

"How'd you know that?" Jake asked.

Then it was Tom's turn to explain about Molly.

"Jake, it looks like if you hadn't come along, I'd been too late," Tom pointed out. "Now what are we going to do?"

"Not sure," answered Jake.

"But, Winston's not going to be happy he's lost Scar and Willie. He may come out here and shoot the girl himself."

With Sarah safe and secure behind a

locked door, Jake and Tom talked at length about their situation. After some time, Jake finally settled into his bunk for some rest . . . but sleep would not come easy.

Sarah Meadows, he kept thinking to himself. *The old man's daughter . . . what's she doing here? She's supposed to be teaching school in Nebraska . . . not out here mucking things up.*

Good grief, thought Jake.

Both men lay silent for several minutes until Tom broke the spell. "Something ailing you Jake?"

Tom had asked the question from a safe distance.

"Nothing," muttered Jake. "Nothing at all."

"Seems to me, something seems to be eating at you my friend," noted a prodding and grinning Tom in the darkness.

"Sometimes," Jake answered. "You should keep your big yap shut and mind your own business."

"Female problems, I suppose?" Tom said with a chuckle. He was making more of a statement than asking an actual question.

"Shut up!" came a voice from the neighboring bunk.

CHAPTER 23
CICADAS, CRICKETS
AND COYOTES

Learning his captive was the daughter of the man he had recently saved from certain death created a sense of urgency. Jake knew he had to watch over the woman even if she didn't know he was watching.

Smitty didn't like the idea of having the woman held captive. He liked the idea of shooting a woman even less. At least until he could talk to Winston, he didn't wish to harm her.

The men assigned to watch her were an unsavory looking lot but otherwise harmless. Only excess liquor might change their disposition, but Smitty had chosen two men he felt he could trust.

Scar and Willie had been sent to deal with her. Now both were dead. Something didn't add up and he was beginning to suspect Jake and Tom were more than drifting punchers.

"She must be one hellava shot," Tom

observed. "She got both of them?"

"That's another can of worms," Jake said. "And quite frankly, I'm getting sick of going fishing."

"What?" a perplexed Tom answered. "What the heck does that mean?"

"I'll explain later," his friend responded with a wave of his hand.

Jake knew if Winston had sent Scar and Willie to take care of Sarah he wouldn't hesitate in ordering Smitty to finish the job. Sarah Meadows was living on borrowed time. Word would soon come from town and she would no longer be a problem.

"Word has it somebody needs all those steers," Jake told Tom. "And that somebody plans to meet Winston in the next few days. They don't need anyone messing things up. And, Sarah Meadows was a threat to do just that. She still is. There are hundreds, if not thousands, of cattle hidden away in the draws and canyons north and west of here. Once Winston makes his deal and moves them out of here, he will be a very rich man, nobody can prove he ever had possession of stolen cattle," Jake explained.

"Somehow we've got to stop him and draw attention to what he's doing."

The day passed uneventfully. Sarah had been fed, but otherwise ignored. There had been no word from Winston on her fate. Rumors circulated about Winston's plans for the cattle. They also spread about Sarah abilities with a rifle.

Jake laid awake deep into the night. The sounds across the hours seemed magnified. Every effort to escape the events of recent days was futile. He was worried. Outside the voices of cicadas, crickets and coyotes rode the wind over the prairie and their words found their way through the bunkhouse walls. They added to the noises already competing in Jake's head for attention.

Several of the men snored, one mumbled something about stealing an apple pie, and still another smacked his lips. The sounds in total were deafening. A sudden clap of thunder and a growing wind outside made Jake forget Sarah Meadows for the moment. There was a rising storm. *Better get some sleep . . . could be a long night.*

Fatigue, like loneliness, began to spread itself over Jake like a cold, wet blanket, at first clinging, then slowly smothering his senses, finally weighing him down. Recent events would not settle. They would not rest . . . each needing its own explanation and place in some broader scheme.

Outside, rain began to fall . . . a cold,

nasty late spring rain . . . born in the craggy cliffs above the timberline and nurtured over deep snow still holding steadfast in the darkened shadows. This was a windy, wet storm sliding down the mountain slopes before rushing out over an unsuspecting prairie.

Jake could hear the horses out in the corral facing the wet onslaught. He thought of Sarah held captive in her earthen prison and wondered if she might be getting wet. Yet, for all his thoughts, he was too physically and mentally worn out to react. He could only listen as the floodgates of hell lashed against the bunkhouse walls and long dead trees shorn of all their massive dignity stood as a wall of defiance.

While others around him were already snoring or sucking on their teeth, oblivious to his own stiff, sore agony, he sought but couldn't find sleep. Sleep could not come soon enough, he thought to himself, and would be all too short when it finally did. Sleep finally came, although reluctantly, surrendering more to exhaustion than restful slumber. Morning would find him worn out, with dry, tired, bloodshot eyes. He felt as if all energy had fled from his body.

Morning was suddenly there. Darkness before dawn's light was black, deep black, like the dark side of a man's soul, or the mud of unspent coffee grounds.

The morning breeze was uneasy . . . tense on a cool, damp wind. But, the uneasiness was not from last night's storm, for it was fast escaping across the prairie. No, there was something else amiss. Two dogs were fighting over a stick, but there was no other activity in the predawn light.

Jake stuffed a couple of cold biscuits into his jacket where they joined beef jerky morsels, hardtack crumbs and lint . . . all left from other black mornings.

He roped his horse, then saddled and mounted quickly and quietly. Others were doing the same. Jake asked about the girl and was told she was okay and being quiet. Satisfied, he rode from the ranch complex. He wanted to get some sense of how and why Winston was intimidating all of his neighbors.

Tom had stayed behind, hoping Smitty would find a need for him to play messenger once more. He needed a reason.

No, I have a reason, he admitted to himself. *What I need is a plausible excuse to ride into town and see the young woman in the saloon. I need to let her know that her friend is okay for now.*

"Smitten are you?" Jake had jokingly

asked his friend in an effort to get even.

Tom had answered no, but in fact he wasn't sure of his feelings. Things were happening so fast and he felt different. Each nerve seemed more awake . . . more alive somehow.

Bad meat will make you sick, but not lightheaded and giddy, he thought.

"You got the love disease," Jake had joked.

"Next thing, you'll be so weak-kneed you won't be able to get on your horse. We had a neighbor once down in Texas . . . got so love sick he stopped eating. Lost so much weight that when his girl sneezed one day it blowed him clear off the porch," Jake laughed. "Better stay off any porches or make sure that girl doesn't have a cold."

Tom could only shake his head, then said, "What about you and the Meadows girl . . . huh? She may be kinda pretty under all that dirt and grime she wears. Besides, her father already likes you. That's half the battle."

Jake didn't respond.

CHAPTER 24
CONFINEMENT AND CONFUSION

Gunfire, the smell of death, the heat and the quickness of it all had merged in Sarah's mind creating a complex and confusing puzzle. The second night of captivity had been long but was made even longer as she stayed awake fighting the demons of her own mind. The events of recent days held sway over her as she sought to free herself of their memory.

In her mind, she struggled to put the pieces of the last few days into perspective, put some degree of understanding to what it all meant. It was a struggle without resolution. More importantly, she was for the first time in her life scared and alone. She felt overwhelmed by a massive loneliness the like of which the vast prairie had never caused.

"Dead! I was almost dead," she kept repeating to herself. She shuddered at the thought.

Just how the man with the scarred face had managed to circle in behind her was unclear. What was clear was that for the second time in recent days, the same tall stranger had showed up to help her. This was the same stranger at whom only moments earlier she had been shooting.

Who is he? she kept asking. *He must work for Winston . . . so why did he kill another of Winston's hired gunman? It doesn't add up.*

Sarah checked every possible means of escape without success, not that she had any viable plan if she'd been successful. She was beside herself with the futility of her efforts.

"Why does this stuff always happen to me?" she kept asking.

She was well aware that Winston had sent his men to kill her. She was not sure why the stranger called Summers had not finished the job.

Maybe he has other notions, she thought with disdain.

Then she remembered.

"Summers!"

During her meeting in town with Elsie Gardner, the old woman had said a man named "Jake Summers" had suddenly showed up out of nowhere to help her. "Just like he did for me . . . twice. Who is this guy and why does he work for Winston?"

In the outside room, she heard voices . . . sometimes-loud voices. A knock on the door sent a brief shock of fear through her body. As the door opened she found Tom Scott standing there with a plate of food. Behind him she could see several greasy, dirty cowhands and misfits watching. They became silent as the door fully opened.

"Here is some food, Ms. Meadows," Tom said.

The door was left partially open to avoid arousing comment from the others and to avoid scaring Sarah anymore.

She said nothing.

"Hope you ain't real hungry," he added with a slight grin. "Nothing real edible . . . except maybe them beans."

"I'm not hungry!" Sarah answered curtly.

Then in a low whisper, he said, "Molly sent me."

"What? What did you say?" she whispered.

"Keep your voice down. This is tough enough," answered Tom.

The two guards were visiting with each other in hushed tones, occasionally glancing through the open door. Neither liked playing "nurse maid" to a wild-eyed young woman, especially one who had shot their friends Scar and Willie. However, it beat nursing cows all day and getting saddle-sore to boot.

Tom looked around then said, "Your friend Molly in town. She asked me to look after you. Looks like I almost got here too late."

"Molly?"

"Yeah," said Tom. "She cornered me at the saloon. Said you were in trouble. Winston finds out I'm here to help you and we'll both be in trouble."

Sarah whispered, "Get me out of here!"

"This is the safest place for you right now. We are developing a plan so sit tight and trust us."

"Who is we?" Sarah asked.

"Better not say right now," Tom noted. "You might let it slip, and then we'd all be in a heap of trouble. I'll be back in touch."

He turned and left as she opened her mouth to speak.

Sarah wasn't ready for him to leave. She had questions, lots of questions and too few answers.

Once he'd left, Sarah was forced to wait and see what might happen next. A couple bites of beans and she realized just how hungry she really was.

From behind her closed door, she listened and learned. She heard mention of a railroad, Chinese workers, hungry soldiers, reservation Indians and steaks on the hoof.

She learned Winston was trying to deal with some big time railroad contractor to supply beef for his construction crews. There was a need for beef to feed the workers. Someone also mentioned something about the U.S. Calvary needing beef to feed Indians being held on reservations.

"So that's it," she muttered to herself.

She also learned that the railroad's representative would arrive any day to close the deal on 1,000 head or more of grass-grazed cattle. Cattle rustled for the most part from neighboring ranches.

"If I can get word to Molly's friend, then maybe, just maybe, he can round up some help before it's too late. We've got to stop this," she mumbled to herself.

There was one major problem. She didn't know of anyone to ask. Four years had brought more change than she had dared imagine. Even the countryside had a different look, more people and even fences. New issues had replaced the familiar memories and pleasant days of her youth.

Life is moving too fast, she told herself.

Tom never returned.

Some of the others, she repeated. *Who? I wish someone would tell me what's going on.*

Was the stranger who locked me up involved? He must be, she continued. Otherwise why didn't he just shoot me himself? Winston had probably put a price on my head. It just doesn't make sense.

Confused and exhausted, Sarah lay down and waited. Nightfall swept over the ranch and brought darkness to her locked room.

The root cellar had not been used much since Sarah's leaving for Nebraska four years earlier. What vegetables and other foodstuffs had been placed in the dark, musty, earthen tomb had long since decayed and rotted. The scent of their natural progression toward dust was overwhelming.

Sarah gasped for fresh air each time the door opened.

Despite the smells and overall condition of her prison, she did have fond memories of the "old days" and how this place had been home. She also remembered when the room actually smelled of fresh onions and new potatoes.

Those had been hard but good days. She hated tending garden, fighting a never-ending battle with weeds and insects, but now after time away the memories didn't seem all that bad.

Much to her father's chagrin, Sarah had preferred riding horses to handling a hoe.

Meadows could only shake his head at her poor attempts at canning and storing vegetables for winter use.

"Girl, you'd better learn soon," her father had often told her. "Or, we'll starve come winter."

The sod home-turned-root cellar had been a good one. Vegetables stored there seldom had frozen, not even their potatoes and carrots. Even during the worst blizzards and below zero temperatures they had food.

There had also been stormy times. There had been many nights when the home-turned-cellar had provided shelter from raging winds and lightning outside. Yes, there were good memories here as well.

However, she thought to herself, this isn't one of them.

CHAPTER 25
MEETING OF OLD FRIENDS

The demons of the night chased away the sandman in Molly's dreams. She tossed and turned all night. Sleep was rare and came born of exhaustion.

Two nights had passed and still Sarah had not returned. Molly feared the worst.

Every sound seemed magnified, somehow foreign, and strange in this vast and unforgiving land. Common and familiar noises became threatening echoes. Shadows danced along the walls of her room taunting her, magnifying her loneliness and unsettled future.

Suppose the cowboy told Winston . . . surely not.

She had placed the fate of her good friend in the hands of a young cowboy she had only recently met. And, he was someone who actively worked for the man trying to kill her friend.

"I may have only sealed her fate," Molly

whispered in the night.

"What a fool I am," she said out loud.

Sick with worry and knowing it would be futile to ride out in search of Sarah, she finally got up and sat worrying through the night.

Morning came and Sarah had not returned or sent word. That only increased her concern.

Molly decided she would learn more in the saloon than in her room, so she dressed and headed for work. As she crossed the street she spotted John William Legress as he stepped down from the stagecoach. She hurried on by without paying him much attention except to think, *what a large man*!

At six feet, eight inches and almost 350 pounds, he was extremely big. Throw in his rugged and rough demeanor and he was even more imposing. He was almost scary.

As the primary cattle buyer for the Kansas City and Denver Railroad Construction Company, it was his job to provide beef, and lots of it, for hungry construction crews. Thus, he came to Chugwater at the invitation of Winston about cattle and lots of them. They had done business before and each knew what to expect from the other.

As far as Legress was concerned, brands didn't matter much. After all they were only skin deep. Once removed, one steer carcass looked pretty much like another. He had purchased stolen cattle before at bargain prices, usually pocketing the difference in price himself.

However, he didn't like bloodshed. "Bad for the company image," he would often say.

He wasn't the only buyer interested in Winston's ill-gotten cattle. The U.S. Army also had sent word they would send a representative to negotiate for large quantities of beef.

Today, it was Legress who came with money to spend. And, he found Winston to be a receptive audience.

By the time Legress entered the saloon, news of his presence and his reason for being in town had arrived well ahead of him. Molly could only watch. If the two men suspected she was eavesdropping, they never said anything.

Molly tried to learn what she could about Sarah. There had been a gunfight. That much she knew. That fact was being discussed all over town.

Details were sketchy. However, one thing was clear. Scar and Willie were dead. There was no word on Sarah except that she had killed at least one of them, probably both.

There also were rumors that Sarah had

been killed by one of Winston's henchmen . . . somebody named Summers.

"Big John," shouted Winston as Legress
filled the saloon doors, his massive frame
momentarily blocking all light from the
street. "Welcome! Welcome!"

Winston had been filled with rage upon
learning Scar and Willie Temple were dead.
And he vowed, "That Meadows girl will pay
a painful price for her interference. Just you
wait." But, now he had business to conduct,
and his mood changed.

His spirits were bolstered by the arrival of
Legress and the prospect of making some
serious money.

"Winston, you old dog. How you been?"
Legress smiled as he shook Winston's right
hand. "Looks like you got things in good
shape around here."

Then seeing Molly for the first time, he
continued, "mighty fine shape."

"John sit down, sit down. What's your
pleasure?"

"Well, since you ask . . ." as he again
glanced toward Molly.

"Bring my friend a whiskey," he shouted
to the barkeeper. "Some of the good stuff.
Not that rot gut crap you serve everyone
else. And, bring a beer chaser."

Legress looked across the table at Winston.

"Hear tell you've got a sweet little operation here bouts. Maybe even a few cattle to sell," he grinned.

"Got me about a thousand prime, grass-fed steers and heifers just waiting for the right buyer to come along. You interested?"

"Maybe . . . if the price is right."

"Price!" roared Winston.

"Hell two old friends like us aren't going to let money stand in the way of a deal. We'll settle the details later. Let's eat us a couple beefsteaks and talk old times. You must be hungry."

The afternoon progressed with the two men reminiscing about the good old days and better days ahead. Both agreed to go look at the herd at some point but neither of them was in a rush. Until then, it was to be a day of beers and poker.

Legress had other plans for the evening, again turning his attention toward Molly, who was carrying a tray of beer-filled glasses toward Winston and his guest. She was intent on learning all she could about Sarah's fate and the role (if any) this new stranger friend of hers might play.

She had not heard anything from the young cowhand to whom she had entrusted

Sarah's fate. *No news was indeed good news to a degree,* she kept telling herself. *Sounds like she's at least alive. But where?*

As she started to set the tray on the table, Winston suddenly reached out and grabbed her by the wrist. The tray, not quite on the table yet, bounced the last inch or so, spilling beer across the table.

"Ain't you friends with that Meadows girl?" he shouted. "I've seen you two talking. And didn't you two hit town on the same stagecoach?"

Frightened, Molly hesitated in responding. She tried pulling away from him but his grip only grew stronger.

"Yes, I know Sarah Meadows," she finally said.

Legress, sweating from the early summer heat, turned to Winston and said, "Perhaps you might consider including this young lady as part of our deal."

"Later. You can have her later," Winston said. "Young lady . . . just how much do you know? Too much I'd bet."

He then turned to one of his henchmen and said, "Take her out to the Meadows Ranch and put her with the other one. Keep them locked up and quiet until I get out there!"

Molly knew it would be useless to fight.

Winston controlled the town. She could not expect anyone to step forward to help her. She was a stranger in town working in the saloon. She was expendable and helpless.

With her hands tied, she was put on a horse and led from town with only a few people seeing her. The ride was rough and the man assigned the job of taking her was less than enthused with his assignment. He had wanted to stay in the saloon drinking beer. Taking Molly for a hot ride to the Meadows ranch was not to his liking.

Once they arrived, she was taken to a nondescript building near the bunkhouse. She noticed it was built into the side of a hill with only one apparent entrance and exit.

Sarah heard voices. Then she heard the voice of a woman. The door opened and Molly was literally shoved into the dimly lit room.

"Molly!" exclaimed Sarah. "My God, what's happened?"

The door was slammed shut and the two were quickly alone.

Molly's eyes at first had trouble adjusting to the darkness after being out in the bright sunshine. However, her nose caught a mixture of lantern smoke mixed with the rotting decay of the cellar's contents.

Then she realized Sarah was there. The

two embraced each other.

"What happened to you?" asked Molly. "I've really been worried."

"What happened to me? What happened to you? Why did they bring you here?" Sarah asked.

Molly quickly explained the day's events and how Winston had finally realized her relationship with Sarah.

Molly was scared. She had to admit as much. Even though she was sharing this darkened hole in the ground with her friend, she was frightened at the uncertainty. The day's events were as surprising as they were terrifying.

Now in this dark, black earthen cellar, she felt confined, entombed with an uncertain future. She felt an overwhelming sense of dread. She fought through an urge to cry.

"Tell me about you," Molly said quietly. "They say in town you killed two or three men. Is that true?"

Sarah explained what had happened providing details of how Jake had once more appeared from nowhere to help her.

"Seems like you've got a cowboy for a guardian angel," said Molly, grinning for the first time and temporarily putting her own fears aside.

Sarah blushed at the thought of the tall,

blue-eyed cowhand being her guardian angel. "If he was my angel, why did he lock me in here? Tell me that!"

Molly said, "Better than being dead. Maybe he's actually trying to help you. Tom said you had friends you didn't know about."

"Tom is it?" smiled Sarah. "Must be the young cowboy who stopped by to see if I was okay. He mentioned your name."

Now it was Molly's turn to blush.

"Seems to me we've both been helped by men working for that no-account Winston. Doesn't make much sense. We need to remember that," Sarah added. "Now we've got more important fish to fry . . . like staying alive."

They spent the rest of the day comparing notes and rehashing recent events. But, deep-down Sarah knew that if the chance for escape came up she had to be ready. She also knew it would be harder with Molly alongside, but she would have to try anyway.

CHAPTER 26
DIFFERENT VALUES,
DEADLY MIX

Dawn broke clear and crisp especially for early summer, but Jake and Tom found the cool morning air invigorating. Both knew the task they had undertaken was fraught with danger. To have their mission discovered or to be recognized by a wayward, transient puncher would mean trouble, even death.

The women would be okay for the moment, or at least until Winston had his herd sold. They were being well fed, but desired the smell of fresh air over food. Their earthen cage had a musty, foul smell and after two days of confinement they sought clean air and a good bath. Food could wait.

Each of the men, punchers and gunmen alike, had been eating since before sunrise and gradually working their way out to the corrals to catch their day mounts. There was no sense of urgency like that expected of a normal crew.

With the cool morning air, a few of the horses still had some kick to them. They put on quite a show of bucking and jumping. More than one rider lost his seat along with his dignity.

In most cases, Jake had no such problems. He had been riding the same horse for three years, a tall bay gelding with an hourglass blaze face and three white socks. Jake had called him "Socks" from the first time he roped him out of Thompson's remuda. They bonded almost immediately and had been together ever since. Now this horse grazed peacefully with several others in Elsie Gardner's plush meadow.

Jake's new mount was more prone to flights of skittish early morning behavior and was often unpredictable. But, Jake had his way of winning the animal over and was gradually gaining the animal's favor.

On this morning, the horse spotted Jake approaching and nickered like a yearling colt. Of course, a morning piece of sugar each day helped set the stage for such a greeting. Jake could only smile and stroke the horse's face.

Tom was less particular about which horse he rode but at the Dunn Ranch he'd found a smallish, but extremely quick, sorrel gelding he called "Red". Turns out Tom's horse of choice was proving to be the best working cow horse he'd ever ridden and maybe best in the territory. He wasn't just fast, but very, very quick. When working cattle, Tom's sorrel could cut and chase with the best of them.

"Gotta be on your toes around cattle," Tom often said. "Old Red will jump out from under you, turn on a dime and leave you on the ground counting change."

With both mounts saddled, Jake and Tom joined the other punchers to help move more of Winston's questionable cattle.

Efforts to find out more details concerning these cattle bearing an assortment of brands were met for the most part by blank stares. Information was not forthcoming.

"I just needed work," noted one cowhand. "With so many settlers moving in and fencing everything, the big spreads are disappearing. Ranchers need fewer hands these days."

"I ain't in no position to be questioning nothin'. I just ride and do what I'm told," explained another young wrangler.

Jake understood the man's plight. Things were changing. The open range was giving way to more and more settlers, especially along the rivers and other water sources.

"You're getting too old for this type of

work," Tom often noted.

Jake, who was two years younger than his friend, would simply give him a wave of his hand and move on.

However, Tom was right and Jake knew he was. There were few working punchers over thirty years old. And at twenty-six, Jake understood his days were numbered as a cowhand. It was getting harder and harder to get started each morning. And, Jake found himself falling asleep in his saddle from time to time. Still, he continued to ride for the brand.

Arguments were frequent between legitimate, if a bit shady, cowhands and Winston's hired gunmen had no desire to "punch" cows. They generally drank to excess and resented taking orders from experienced cowpunchers. The combination was a volatile mix.

There were also increasing numbers of arguments between new homesteaders and the major cattle operations. The fights were usually over water rights and the loss of open range.

Jake and Tom were about to find out just how combustible a mix Winston had thrown together.

Charles Nelson and Bruce Randolph were down-on-their-luck hands. Both had worked their way out of Texas and decided to try punching cows in the Wyoming territory. They learned late that a Winston crew was not typical.

Nelson was a quiet loner who had worked around cattle most of his life in the Abilene area.

Randolph was from Georgia by way of Texas and was one of many black cowboys trying their luck in the West after the Civil War.

Neither man had any formal education except in the "School of Punching Cows." Politics and the various shades of right and wrong were a distant consideration. They cared only about doing a job and drawing their wages. Let someone else figure the right and wrong of it all.

Ben Williams and Angus Todd were founding members of Winston's settlement committee. Both were no-account gun hands plain and simple. Both men hated cattle. They liked work even less. The only thing they liked about cows was a rare steak. They spent most of their time sitting horseback and letting others like Nelson and Randolph do the work.

Middle of the night work involved harassment. Gunplay was their specialty. Both men cleaned their pistols over and over again, and then practiced shooting.

They weren't alone. Winston's diverse crew was split almost equally between these two groups. Williams was originally from Mississippi and Todd was from South Texas. They were not especially fond of working alongside Randolph or any other black cowboy. Nor did they wish to work with any "Yankee" cowpuncher.

The attitudes and the associations only percolated for so long before exploding.

Jake and Tom rode right into the middle, just at the point of ignition.

As Randolph and Nelson pushed yearling mavericks out of the various draws, Jake and Tom would turn them toward the main herd. The system was working well until a young bull calf decided to break from the group.

The yearling broke free and headed back over a slight ridge in an effort to circle back toward the brush-filled ravine where the cowhands had found him. Williams and Todd sat their horses near the ridge top and watched the calf make its break. They made no effort to head off his escape although they were in perfect position to do so. That infuriated Randolph, who now chased the calf, trying to rope him.

Williams and Todd only sat and laughed.

"Hey boy. . . . he went that way," Williams shouted. "Go fetch him back."

Randolph pulled up and approached the two gunmen. Soon Nelson joined him.

"What did you say?" the black cowboy asked.

"We said . . . he went that way," Williams sneered. "Go get him!"

"Why in the hell didn't you cut him off?" demanded Randolph. "Now we gotta spend another hour chasing him down again."

Nelson, sensing trouble, began to ease his horse away from the growing confrontation. "Let's go Bruce. We got work to do," he said.

"Boy . . . listen to your buddy. Don't say another word," Williams said. "It ain't healthy. You hear me?"

Randolph was now infuriated.

"You should be working more and talking less . . ."

Williams shot him before he could finish. The cowhand was unarmed, but it made no difference. The young cowboy died before reaching the prairie grass rising to meet his fall.

Nelson shouted, "What the . . . he wasn't even armed!"

Williams said, "You got something you want to say about this? I say he was going for a gun. Ain't that right Angus?

"Yep! He was going for a gun, I saw it."

Nelson said, "I say he wasn't armed."

"He's calling us liars," said Williams. "I don't like that. It implies we're dishonest or something."

Nelson wheeled his horse away from his fallen friend and dug his spurs into its flanks. Witnessing cold-blooded murder was one thing, but now he realized he could be next. No sense provoking anything. But, it was too late.

Both Williams and Todd fired at the retreating Nelson. One shot hit him in the back; a second shot caught him in the shoulder. He died quickly, with no chance to reflect on poor choices and unfilled promises.

When Randolph and Nelson didn't return with the bull, Jake and Tom pulled away from the other cattle and went to investigate.

They topped a grass-covered ridge, reined up and stopped. In the distance, they could see Randolph and Nelson talking to a couple of other riders. They had not been seen. But they were also much too far away to hear anything. They could only watch what appeared to be an argument.

"Wonder what's going on?" Tom asked.

Jake answered, "Appears like Randolph

and Nelson are having a disagreement with Williams and that cur-dog friend of his Angus Todd."

"What do we do?"

Before Jake could answer, the sound of a shot reached them. They watched as Randolph fell from his saddle. Then they watched in disbelief as Nelson was shot.

While death was a natural thing, Jake shivered at the sight of the two men shot in cold blood.

"What do we do?" asked Tom. "Thompson told us to lay low."

"Yes, he did," Jake sighed.

"But sometimes . . . well sometimes you've got to draw a line in the proverbial sand. Sometimes you just need to do what's right . . . not always what's smart. Them Texas boys never did nobody no harm. They were just trying to earn a little money to feed their young'uns. Now they lay dead most likely. If good people don't stand for justice, who will?"

Tom asked, "You got a plan?"

"Well," Jake said. "My dad once said 'do something even if it's wrong. Don't just stand around doing nothing. I figure we should give the situation a little nudge and see where it falls."

"Okay," Tom responded. "But, my friend,

we ain't no Knights of the Round Table and Thompson sure ain't no King Arthur."

"Let's drift that way and see what those hombres do next," Jake answered with his horse already moving out. "Be ready to shoot first and talk later."

They didn't have to wait long. Williams rode over and looked down at the lifeless body of Randolph, spit on the body then did the same with Nelson.

"Let's ride," Williams told Todd. "I got me a thirst."

The two gunmen started to leave their victims lying in the bloodstained grass when they saw Jake and Tom riding toward them.

"Let me handle this," said Williams.

"What's happened here?" shouted Jake as they drew closer.

"What's it to you?" snarled Williams.

"You two hombres should just keep riding!" exclaimed Todd. "And, mind your own business."

Again, it was Jake who responded.

"Well . . . well you see," he spoke in a slow South Texas drawl. "We got us a serious fault of sorts."

Todd said, "Now what would that be?"

"Well, I'm glad you asked," continued Jake, "Cause we don't take kindly to cold-blooded murder. It's a curse I guess."

An angry Williams said, "Mister, we've already warned you . . . keep moving."

"We can't do that," Jake responded. "Because it's especially bothersome when the dead hombres are unarmed cow punchers."

"You son-of-a- . . . !" called Williams as he reached for his holstered pistol.

Jake and Tom were ready.

The smoke from Jake's pistol had already filled the midday air before Williams' cleared leather. Jake's shot caught him dead center between the eyes.

Todd was quicker, but not fast enough.

Tom had ridden into the confrontation fully expecting trouble. His pistol was already in his right hand, only hidden behind his leg. His shot wounded Todd and knocked him from his saddle. Then as Todd clutched his wound with one bloodied hand, he tried pulling a second pistol. Tom's second shot was more accurate.

Jake and Tom checked all four men for signs of life and found none. They buried Winston's two men where they had fallen. Then they moved the bodies of Randolph and Nelson to a hillside facing south toward Texas and overlooking a quiet Wyoming valley. They were buried side by side.

"I feel sick to my stomach," Jake told his

friend. "Wish we could have helped them."

Tom said, "There is nothing we could have done."

Both men returned to their work with heavy hearts. They said nothing about what had happened.

None of the four men would likely be missed. It was the nature of the land and times. Men drifted in, did a job, then with little or no notice moved on.

Later in the evening, word began to drift through camp that some railroad "big shot" was in town meeting with Winston about buying cattle. Nobody noticed Nelson and Randolph were missing. The others figured Williams and Todd had gone to town and gotten drunk.

The men settled into a normal evening routine of smokes, card games and general bragging. Some of the men bragged of their prowess with women, others threatened to go visit Sarah and Molly . . . "to just keep them company." None dared to follow through on such idle talk.

"We've got to do something to slow this process down until Thompson and the boys get here," Jake quietly told Tom. "Once the herds are brought in, let's plan a little diversion. Maybe run a few pounds off them.

"It will take a couple days to gather them

up again," Jake continued. "That will buy us some time."

For the women, it was a long, dark day of waiting and listening. It was a day of general boredom, now bordering on depression and despair. Both had come to realize they were in serious trouble, with little chance of escape or assistance.

Chapter 27
Bad News Gets Worse

Jake hated to leave the ranch again with Sarah and Molly still held captive. Smitty had ordered him and the other men to start moving cattle from various hidden canyons and gather them in one big herd near the Meadows home place.

Tom was to stay behind and help with morning chores and be ready to deliver any messages to Winston in town.

"Bring them together in the big pasture south of the house," Smitty ordered Jake and the others.

Jake sought out Tom before leaving. "Watch over those two," he warned. "They may get us killed yet . . . especially that Meadows girl. Winston can't afford anyone raising questions, legal or otherwise, about land ownership and missing ranchers. Not now. Mind you, he'll take care of those two after the cattle deal is done."

After riding northeast for about two

hours, he came across the first of several box canyons where many of the stolen cattle were being held. In one of the groups, he recognized the familiar Box T brand.

Wonder when Winston got some of our cattle? thought Jake. *Must've happened after Tom and I left. Wonder if Thompson knows yet?*

Jake and a suspect group of other hands spent the day chasing cows, calves and young bulls.

"Don't worry about any brands," Smitty had made a point to say. "We'll sort all that out later. Just do as you're told."

Jake had wondered what Winston was planning. Rustling cattle from neighboring spreads was obviously something he didn't mind doing.

A "settlement committee" of Winston's gun hands often answered objections with a visit. They came and went in the middle of the night. More often than not, those objecting ended up dead or pistol-whipped into agreement.

Old man Meadows was a good example, thought Jake.

Rumor had it a nearby rancher had tried to fight back. He even wounded a couple of Winston hands in the process.

"Old man Larsen tried to shoot it out with

me and some of the boys," Billy Small bragged as they rode. His comments came from behind three weeks or more of facial hair and trail dirt. His teeth, what few he had left after years of barroom brawls, were a sickly yellow and brown. And, each time he spoke an ugly spit drooled from his open mouth.

"We taught him though," he continued. "Set his house on fire with him and his old lady inside. They come a running out coughing and wheezing from the smoke. It was down right funny.

"We put a rope on the old man and drug him around for awhile. It was great!" Small laughed. "His old lady screaming and crying. She was yelling for us to stop. Chester Holt and T. J. Whitaker forced themselves on the old woman. We made the old man watch before T. J. finally shot him dead, then the woman too.

"Hell, Chester even shot their mangy, mongrel dog just for the hell of it. Said he barked too much."

Jake knew there were others. He already knew about the Larsen family, Sam Bentable, William T. Posten, old man Meadows, Marcus Dunn, and a few others. The Box T foreman said nothing. But, he knew something must be done to stop the bloodshed.

Jake didn't consider himself the hero type. He was more the quiet, but strong type, although at six feet, four inches and about 185 pounds he created an imposing presence that just seemed to draw attention. He was to put it simply . . . a reluctant leader. But, he never backed away from any task that needed doing. He could be counted on to do the right thing. Now was one of those times and he knew it.

With the help of the other hands, Jake started a small herd moving southward adding numbers to the group as they went. It was a slow process but by mid-afternoon they had more than 500 head moving at a leisurely pace.

Back in town, Winston was angry, angrier than Legress had ever seen him. Talk of buying and selling cattle gave way to threats of redemption and retaliation.

"I'll hang her for killing two of my best hands," he told Legress. "And, you can have the redhead. If Scar and Willie had done their jobs, we wouldn't have this mess."

Tom learned a cattle buyer with the railroad had made town and was meeting Winston. Time was a wasting. He was sent to tell Winston that the herd would be gathered by morning, but learning Legress was in town he decided the message could wait. Besides, Winston would learn soon enough his herd was ready for selling.

Town seemed more crowded than normal, or maybe it was Tom's imagination. Crowded or not, he sensed a change. Small groups of men and women were standing together talking. Many glanced his way as he rode by, but none scattered as in previous days.

A stop at the telegraph office produced results. There was a message from Thompson.

To Tommy,

Cookies done. Sacking them now. Be there soon. Dad's coming too.

Mother

He shoved the telegram in his pocket and mounted his horse. Then he turned his horse toward the Meadows Ranch and away from town. "Better not interrupt any meetings," he decided.

Meanwhile, Winston was learning for the first time about the demise of two more gunmen, Williams and Todd.

"More bad news boss," Longwell stammered, hating to be the one to share the bad news.

Winston turned to find the old gunman

standing nearby. "What the . . . ? Now what!"

"Boss, well boss, Ben Williams and Angus Todd were found dead this morning. Some of the boys found freshly dug graves up on the ridge above Sand Dog Coulee. They got curious and dug them up. Williams and Todd had been shot."

Winston stood up and looked carefully around the room.

"I've got a bad feeling about all this and it starts with that damn Meadows girl."

"Boss, it couldn't be her. She was locked up," Longwell added.

"Seems like we've got us some do-gooders out here trying to play hero. We need to find out who and soon! None of this so-called bad luck started until we hired those two new hands . . . Summers and Scott. Maybe it's time we had us a talk."

"Boss, that's not all. Two cowhands from Texas were also found buried up there . . . all neat and proper. They also worked for you."

This time before Winston could respond, Legress pushed his chair back from the table and uncoiled his massive frame into a standing position. Both men had planned a trip out to see the cattle, but given the latest news Legress was reluctant to leave town.

"Winston, I take back what I said. Maybe you don't have things under control around here. That can be bad for business."

"See here. See here. Just a bump in our plans. I'll get to the bottom of this. Now, none of this changes our plans in any way. Sit down and have another drink. Give me 24 hours. I'll find who did this. Then we'll go look at them beefsteaks on the hoof. How 'bout it?"

Legress sat down again but pointed a finger at Winston.

"This is sounding a little messy. That's not good . . . not good at all. You've got 24 hours or our deal is off!"

"Consider it done," Winston said with a less than convincing laugh. "Now 'bout that drink. What's your pleasure?"

Outside against the massive mountain range to the west, ominous dark thunderheads were building toward evening. There was a feeling in the air of an early summer storm. A distant rumble of thunder and a flash of lightning against a black mountain of clouds foretold a rough night ahead.

CHAPTER 28
OF STORMS AND STAMPEDES

Dusk came early with a threat of rain. Clouds were building in the western sky with an ominous blackness.

Jake and three others had been assigned night herd duty, which fit into his plans. Tom had not returned from town. The herd finally was ready for Winston to show off to his prospective buyer. A deal could be closed quickly.

The women could only wait and listen, hoping for some word about what might be happening. Even they could sense a storm was building. The air was still and it was growing darker, even in the cellar. They could also hear sounds of distant thunder.

About midnight, lightning began to appear in the distance and the cattle were becoming restless.

Jake, along with another hand, circled the herd in one direction. Two other riders circled from the opposite direction. Admittedly not much of a singer, Jake chose to whistle instead.

"Doesn't much matter," he had often said to his own men. "Just keep reminding them you're there. Besides cows don't much care where you can carry a tune or not. Get them critters settled into a nice, peaceful sleep and the least little noise, lightning or otherwise will unnerve them. They'll be up and running in a split second.

"Best to keep them awake, dead tired on their feet and milling around, avoid any surprises or they'll spook," Jake reminded the other riders.

That was the normal plan.

However, on this night Jake had his own plan. He wanted to bed them down so he tried keeping as quiet as possible.

"You're awfully quiet tonight Jake," noticed Rufus Barnwell as he passed in the darkness, along with a second rider.

"Saving my voice," answered Jake.

"They're plenty edgy," Barnwell added with concern in his voice. "Good night for running!"

"Mighty likely," Jake answered.

Jake reined his horse toward the passing punchers.

"Rufus," he called quietly. "They go to running you stand clear . . . ya hear. Let 'em go."

The old man just waved his hand and then disappeared into the darkness.

The second rider pulled up alongside Jake and hesitated. The man was George Blatz. He had been among those out "searching" for new cattle, and had only joined Winston's henchmen at the Meadows place earlier that day.

"Don't I know you from some place?"

"Ever punched cows up in Montana?" Jake asked.

"Nope," the man answered.

"How about North Texas?"

"Never been down there," the man said. "Yet, I know you from somewhere. I'd bet my life on it."

"Doubt it," Jake said. "But, I'll study on it."

Barnwell called for Blatz to catch up and the man turned his horse away and disappeared into the night.

"It'll come to me," he told Jake as he rode away.

Jake caught his breath and tried to remember. *Who was this guy?*

The idea that he and Tom might soon be recognized worried him. Their lives could be in danger. However, lightning and the sound of distant thunder brought him back to the moment.

Tom was supposed to help Jake start the running. But, Tom had not returned from town yet. Instead, Jake got help from the rising storm.

Lightning, followed immediately by a loud clap of thunder, had brought the herd to its feet. A second bolt of lightning, followed by more thunder, was enough. They herd moved as one.

Jake reined in his horse to watch the running cattle.

There was just one problem!

The cattle were running in the wrong direction. Instead of going back into the foothills toward the mountain range to the west, they were headed straight for the Meadows Ranch buildings where the women were being held.

Jake spurred his horse to a run. He needed to reach the lead steers and turn them. The other three hands also were riding to gain an advantage over the leaders.

Just as the cattle moved, the heavens opened with a cold, pelting, driving rain. In a matter of minutes Jake and the other riders were soaked. He felt a shiver run down his back.

The sound of falling rain mixed with the roar of running cattle made it impossible for the punchers to communicate. Jake only hoped experience would help each man safely avoid the massive wave of running beef.

All four men were trying to turn the mass. And, in that scrambling of man and horseflesh, of screams and shouts, of thunder and lightning, they raced through darkness into hell itself.

Then one went down . . . a man named Morgan. With the puncher's horse lunging and stumbling away from the cattle, horse and rider lost their balance and fell. And with eyes wide in fear, his last scream was lost on the night and a thousand hooves. Death swept over him. The pounding mix of beast and rain drove the cowboy into a shallow grave and he was gone . . . all features lost to God and memory.

The herd was now running full out. After first climbing over a small hill, they plunged onward. Down the far side they came toward the ranch complex. Men inside the ranch buildings heard them coming and realized the problem. Toward them came the onslaught, a massive wave of beef lightly bound by sinew and skin.

Those that could moved to higher ground. Those unable to get out of harm's way sought safety in the ranch buildings.

In the root cellar, Sarah and Molly could only hear the rumble. They felt the earth shake and tremble like an earthquake. Dust poured from every crack and crevice, followed by rivulets of rainwater. There was a smoky mix of haze and dust which made it hard to see and even harder to breathe. There was no escape.

Suddenly, the right front leg of a stampeding 1,600 pound steer plunged through the cellar roof, tearing away some of the ceiling's brick and timber support. The women screamed in terror at the realization that a massive, thrashing steer was about to fall in the small room with them.

Jake saw the steer go down. And, he responded by spurring the flanks of his frightened horse. He wanted and got more effort. Weaving his way through the running cattle, he managed to reach the cellar.

The steer struggled to stand and free itself from the cellar roof. In his flailing about, he tore up a portion of the cellar roof. At any moment he could fall through the roof.

Jake shot the steer. However, the now lifeless body of the steer hung precariously from the cellar roof. He was half in and half out . . . threatening at any moment to continue his plunge into the dark room below.

With the cellar roof damaged, water from the heavy rain found a conduit into the room. The women could only stand aside and view the eerie sight of the dead steer's now lifeless body hanging from the roof. The sight was made even more eerie with each flash of lightning. Water from the rain mixed with the animal's blood and dripped onto the cellar floor.

The rain-soaked women sought better shelter to protect themselves from flying mud, rain and the massive body of the dead steer hanging from the Soddy roof. However, better shelter was not to be found.

At the door, the lock held fast. The sod structure, except for their tiny prison, was all but gone. Even a corner of their ceiling where the steer had broken through was beginning to cave in on them. They knew that in a matter of minutes the dead steer would fall into the room unless something was done. But, help was not coming, at least not yet.

Out in the darkness, several thousand hooves and horns mixed with the still raging thunderstorm to create a loud roar of bellowing cattle and thunder. The remaining cattle slowed only briefly to dodge the dead steer. They continued to run.

Jake looked at the root cellar. From his

vantage point, except for the dead steer, the cellar roof appeared to be reasonably intact, but he knew it wouldn't stay that way for long. The women would be okay for the moment. He turned his attention back to the cattle now scattering in a hundred directions.

"Winston won't be happy with this," he said out loud with a grin.

Tom arrived from town after the carnage and immediately went to check on Sarah and Molly. He broke the lock and found the two terrified women. They were visibly shaken and suffering from shock.

Stepping outside and seeing what remained of their cellar prison, Molly all but fainted.

"How . . . what?" Sarah stammered.

All around them was devastation and destruction. The scene reminded Molly of damage left by tornadoes back in Missouri. Each building had sustained some degree of damage. Bleeding cowboys seeking help mixed with injured cattle wandering aimlessly in a daze. Now and then they heard a rifle shot as some wrangler put an injured steer or cow down and out of its misery.

A lantern hanging just outside the cookhouse was torn from its perch resulting in a small fire, which was quickly extinguished. The approach of another storm and frequent lightning strikes provided the only illumination of the chaotic scene.

"Scott, get them both locked back up," shouted Smitty. "And, I mean now!"

Tom turned to the women and said, "You heard the man. Besides you'll be a damn sight safer under lock and key. Take my word for it."

"I'm not going back in there," Sarah shouted. "Shoot me if you must. But, I'm not going back into that hole."

As she spoke, some men roped the dead steer on the cellar roof and pulled him to the side. No effort was made to repair the roof.

Molly could only tremble. Her hair, face and clothing were soaked and covered with mud. She touched Tom's arm unconsciously and asked, "Are you sure that it's best for us to remain?"

"It's best for now. Trust me on this."

"Will you be okay?" she asked.

"Who are you?" Sarah interrupted. "And, what are we suppose to do for a roof in this storm?"

"I'll talk to with Smitty about your conditions. And well . . . we came over from the

Box T," he started to say.

"Scott," shouted Smitty, "I said get them locked up. Then get over here. We've got cattle to find."

"What's the Box T? And, who are you?"

"We'll talk later. I gotta go," Tom answered. "Now . . . please go back inside."

Sarah and Molly reluctantly went back inside and saw only about half the cellar roof was still intact. They used a smoky kerosene lantern to examine their wet and damaged quarters where only moments earlier they had feared for their lives.

The cattle had trampled around and over this man-made mound of soil, brick and timbers. Considerable mud had fallen in on them with much of it now in their hair and on the floor. They had feared throughout the ordeal that the entire cellar roof along with one or more steers would come in on them. One almost had.

They also learned the fate of their original guards. In stepping outside to see what was happening one of the guards paid the ultimate price. He was seriously injured and would be dead by morning.

The second man had run for better cover but was caught in the open by the main herd. He was dead too.

A second storm arrived with only slightly

less ferocity, but with a greater likelihood of flooding. Inside the earthen cage where Sarah and Molly still were held captive, muddy water and clumps of ceiling began to fall in on them again. It would be a long night!

"Get us out of here," yelled a wet and muddy Sarah. "The ceiling is coming in on us."

A new guard at first ignored them, and then told them to "shut up." He finally sent word to Smitty about the problem.

"So?" said Smitty.

"Let them get wet. Might tone them down a little."

With Smitty's declaration to once more lock them up, thoughts of escaping in all the confusion had been dashed. They had tried to persuade Tom into letting them escape. He refused. Now they were locked up once more among the rotting potatoes and other assorted trash.

"I don't see how things can get much worse," Molly declared.

"Come morning ladies we'll get you out of there," the guard responded to their latest outburst of indignation. "Besides I'm tired of nursing you two."

"Wonder what they've got planned for us?"

"Don't know. But it can't be good," Sarah answered.

Just before dawn the two women were moved to an old oat bin in the barn. Their new prison smelled like rotting oats. Their new home was also full of dust, cobwebs and the smell of raccoon droppings, but it was dry. Nobody slept for the remainder of the night. The women waited and wondered about their fate.

Outside, wranglers and gunmen alike worked side by side in the darkness to find a few horses.

At dawn, a wagon and two surly gunmen, obviously short on sleep from the night's activities, came to get them. All around them, they could see devastation from the night before.

"Where you taking us?" asked Sarah. "I asked, where are you taking us?"

"Shut up!" said one of the men. "You'll know soon enough."

The second man bound their hands and feet tightly with rope. They were shoved into the wagon. And, although the rope was cutting into their skin, the men showed no concern. They climbed aboard and slapped the team into a brisk walk.

After riding for almost an hour in extremely uncomfortable conditions, Sarah started protesting once more.

Just as one of the men turned to say something, he slumped over and fell from the wagon. He was dead before the sound of the rifle shot reached them.

The second man reached for his pistol just as a second shot tore through his chest. He fell across the wagon's bench seat. The reins fell free.

The team of horses, already skittish from recent events and the sudden fall of the first gunman, immediately broke into a run. The women were helpless. They were still tied tightly and lying in the back of a wagon with no driver.

Jake had fired the shots at a great distance even for an experienced marksman. He knew the risk. One slight error and he might have hit one of the women. However, he had not considered the team might bolt in fear. That proved to be an error in judgment. Now, here they were running full out with a bouncing wagon and two helpless women on board.

However, before he could get mounted, Tom had already begun a hasty pursuit. Given the angle of his rescue attempt he caught the runaway team in a matter of moments. The women were quickly untied.

The close rifle shots and the runaway

team was a bit more than Sarah could handle . . . at least quietly. Molly had also been terrified but was very grateful to see Tom ride to the rescue.

A frustrated Sarah exploded in anger. "You might have killed us or got us killed. What's the matter with you?"

"It was Jake. He's a great shot ain't he?" Tom answered with a broad smile. "He knew what he was doing. Besides . . . aren't you being a little ungrateful? Hell lady . . . we should have let Winston's men have you."

Turning to Molly, he asked, "You okay? Seems like your friend could use some manners and at least say thank you."

"I'm good. Thanks for your help. You were great! But, who is this Jake you keep talking about? How come we never see him?"

"He's my best friend . . . my pard," Tom said. "He's up there in the hills keeping an eye on us right now."

"Now what happens to us?" Sarah wanted to know.

"What happens next?" asked Molly.

"Since some of Winston's men could come along any minute, we need to hide you."

Sarah didn't hesitate. She knew just the place.

"There's a place that overlooks the ranch complex. It's where I had my shootout. Only one of Winston's men, the one that locked me up, would know about it. The rest are dead."

Chapter 29
Privy to a Naked Gunman

The sun had climbed past its midday peak by the time Tom got the two women safely tucked away in Sarah's childhood sanctuary.

The air was hot and sticky without movement. Moisture from the storms of the previous night still filled the air, leaving it uncommonly humid. A cloudy haze hung over the prairie like a blanket, keeping the sun from penetrating and drying the landscape.

Neither woman wanted to be exiled for any length of time in this mix of rocks and pine timbers. But for the moment, both agreed hiding out offered the least of all possible evils.

Tom left them food and water. But, as he rode away he held no false illusions that either of them would stay put for very long.

"Especially that Meadows girl," he muttered out loud. "She's down right close to being a nuisance. Still, what choice do we have?"

Sarah was already forming a plan of action . . . and Tom wasn't even out of sight.

"Mr. Tom and his friend may not want our help, but I figure we can lend a hand anyway. Besides, we can't just sit here and do nothing. Can we?"

Molly answered with little enthusiasm, "I suppose not."

"Let's work our way down to the ranch house and see if we can find a rifle or weapon of some kind," Sarah said with a sense of urgency.

"How are we supposed to get down there and back without being seen?" Molly asked. "There are men everywhere."

"Leave that to me. There's a trail I used as a little girl. May be a little rough, but we can make it."

The going was tough and slow. The once-used path was not quite the trail of Sarah's youth. And, they were nearly discovered several times by hands running strays from the brush and rocks.

The years change things, she thought to herself.

As they came up behind the Meadows house, Sarah spotted a cowhand taking a leisurely smoke near a stack of firewood.

Nearby, the man's dappled-gray horse stood tied to an old clothesline post. The animal's eyes were nearly closed; its head down and his tail flopped gently from side to side keeping the flies at bay.

Neither man nor horse showed much desire or interest in returning to work any time soon.

Unknown to Sarah, the man was Ted Nichols, a young gunman from New Mexico who had only recently joined Winston's band of thieves. He had no interest in chasing cows whether Winston's or those of anyone else.

What Sarah did know was the man's rifle was still in its scabbard and on the horse. She left Molly hiding among the charred timbers of the burnt out chicken house while she circled toward the man's horse. She needed a whole lot a luck. Nichols gave her just that.

Seeking the conveniences of the ranch privy, he threw caution to the wind and left his hiding place alongside the woodpile. It was the same woodpile behind which Sarah now moved into hiding.

Once the man disappeared inside the outhouse, she bolted for his horse where she quickly pulled his rifle from its scabbard. Ammunition was another matter.

Extra cartridges were in the man's gun belt . . . now behind the door with the moon-shaped cutout.

Then to Molly's shock and amazement she watched Sarah open the outhouse door and point the rifle at the man doing his business inside.

"What the hell?" he recoiled in both fear and embarrassment.

"No need to stand up!" shouted Sarah. "Just pull off those britches and toss me your gun belt."

"The hell you say," Nichols retorted as he tried to stand and reach for his pants at the same time.

"Sit down and do as you're told," Sarah answered, with a thrust of the rifle. "Besides, from what I can see, I've got the bigger gun here. Now do as you're told and be quick doing it."

"Like hell I will," answered the nervous young gunman with his pants still around his ankles.

"Your pants and gun belt . . . or die with them down," she demanded.

Sarah took a quick look around. Time was a wasting. She knew she could be spotted at any moment and her efforts would have been in vain. Still, she had to smile at the man's predicament.

"I'm getting tired of waiting. And my trigger finger is starting to itch a little."

The man gave in, loosened his gun belt and carefully kicked it out the door.

"I want your pants and boots too!"

"Lady, you're crazy!"

Sarah said, "One last time!"

"You're one of those dames Smitty had locked up aren't you?" he shouted as he tossed his pants to her.

Sarah didn't answer the obvious. She slammed the door shut and blocked it with a stick of firewood.

A couple cowhands spotted her as she mounted Nichols horse but at such a distance neither noticed it was a woman rider. They did pull up when they saw her circling the outhouse with a lariat rope.

Nichols was yelling for help, but nobody could hear him . . . not yet!

Sarah looped one end of the rope over the saddle horn. Then with a shout and a slap on the horse's rump, she urged the animal into a run toward Molly's hiding place.

It was Molly who got a clear and amusing view of the outhouse toppling over and its half-naked occupant yelling for Sarah to stop. At that point, she dropped the rope and reached for Molly's outstretched right arm. With a quick pull, her friend was astride the running horse.

As other cowhands rode up, the young man's shrieks of embarrassment fell on deaf ears. The two women who were escaping didn't matter. These were cowhands . . . not gunmen . . . and most never liked locking the women up in the first place.

They did find the man's situation funny, and it wasn't long before other riders joined the group and their laughter reached a fever pitch. The young man was not well-liked and now red-faced, half-naked and unarmed, he became the object of considerable laughter and crude jokes.

Sarah and Molly took no detours enroute back to their hideout. Now well-armed and with the horse hidden, they settled in for a long afternoon.

Both women became lost in their own thoughts. Only the wind, the rustling grasses and some noisy birds broke the silence. The wind had blown the morning haze away and the sun was bright and hot against a clear blue sky. Now and then high puffy clouds blocked the sun and cast shadows over their hiding place.

The women could gaze down on the ranch complex and out over miles and miles of rolling grassland beyond. Sarah's mind wandered to other times, happier times.

Now with her father missing and assumed dead, she was torn by indecision.

"Molly . . . was I wrong in taking on Winston? Trying to learn more about my father? Maybe I should just go back to Nebraska and take up teaching again? Everyone says my father is dead. Maybe he is."

"Not Tom," said Molly.

"Speaking of that friend of yours . . . Tom . . . he's really helped us," Sarah said. "Wonder why?"

Then she turned and looked at her friend, who despite the mud and grime on her face appeared to be blushing.

"I don't . . . I don't know," Molly answered.

Sarah could only smile. "Guess I know why. Wait a minute . . . what did you mean . . . 'not Tom'?"

Molly shook her head.

"Tom says your father is alive. With all the excitement of last night and today, I forgot to tell you. Tom says he's alive and Winston doesn't have him."

"What! Are you sure? If it were only true," Sarah exclaimed. "What else did he say?"

"He also said you have more friends than you know. That's all he said."

Sarah's mind was in a whirlwind. "Father alive. Where? How? Winston doesn't have him. He's somewhere safe. Friends I don't know. My gosh, what's going on? Molly, how could you not tell me sooner?"

"I'm so sorry . . . but with everything that's happened . . . I am so sorry."

"Forget it. Now we've got to hang on and see this thing through."

A meadowlark called out its simple song nearby and Sarah watched as a hawk rode the windy currents overhead. Her thoughts had become focused and sharp . . . indecision gave way to determination. She chastised herself for even the brief thought of quitting. Life now had purpose, and she gladly accepted the challenge.

Sarah and Molly watched as the afternoon slipped away. Riders moved small groups of cattle toward a larger herd held somewhere beyond their line of sight.

For the first time in several days, the wind touching her face and rustling through her hair seemed softer, cleaner. The clouds overhead were a pure white and the sky a deep blue color.

Even the Indian paintbrush blooming across the valley floor was a rich red color. And the scarlet gilia and its dark red color seemed more intense. It was as if they were being seen for the first time, although they had always been there, even in her youth.

"Yes, things are about to change," Sarah said quietly to herself. "Things seem much clearer now."

CHAPTER 30
CLEANUP AND REGATHERING

A small stream, which the night before had been filled with a torrent of water, flowed away from the ranch toward the Platte River. Jake rode slowly, carefully. He found a couple of drowned cows. Their carcasses were already bloating. They would soon be a fresh meal for coyotes, buzzards and thousands of noisy flies.

Tom joined him at the junction of two streams known as the Medicine Hat and Buffalo.

"Get the women squared away? Jake asked.

"They're up where you and that Meadows girl had your shootout. Should be safe up there."

"Listen Tom, we may have trouble."

"What's up?"

"Remember George Blatz, that drunken drifter Thompson fired about three years ago? He was only with us a couple weeks.

Got into it with old Elmer Tackett over a card game."

"Kinda," Tom answered. "What about him?"

"Ran into him last night before the stampede. He thinks he knows me but hasn't figured it out yet."

"That's not good. Not good at all," Tom answered. "If he . . ."

"Yes, I know!" Jake said. "So watch your back."

The cattle were being gathered quicker than Jake expected. Once past the ranch complex most had not run far. Surprisingly, they were being found easily.

Too easily, thought Jake.

The Box T hands had hoped it would take a week or so to gather the herd again. Now it seemed it would only take a day or two and Winston would have enough cattle to sell.

"Now what are we going to do?" Tom asked.

"Winston will be back in business in a few days."

Jake didn't answer.

The trail of the main herd was easy to follow. Most of the cattle were found mingling in a small canyon about two miles from the ranch headquarters. Smaller groups had broken off each side and would be more difficult to gather up. Still, Winston would soon have plenty of cattle to show a prospective buyer.

Several badly injured steers were found. A few were shot to ease their suffering. Others were found limping from minor injuries.

Smitty ordered several men to bring the main herd back to the holding area. He figured a few strays would work their way back into the herd over time. Other crews were sent to find strays.

Jake and Tom both worked slowly, not wanting to fix something they wanted to keep broken.

The sun was hot on their backs and it was an unusually humid. Where they found dead animals, the heat and humidity was already hastening the decomposition process. Flies covered the rapidly bloating carcasses. The stench was rising and would only get worse.

By mid-afternoon the main herd had been collected and returned to the original holding area near the ranch complex. The sound of bawling cattle only grew louder as the herd continued to grow in size.

It was estimated another 100 or so strays were still hidden in the draws and coulees nearby. Jake figured it would only take another day or two to gather even those animals.

Much too soon, he noted.

While Jake and Tom helped move a group of 20 steers toward the assembly point, the shadows of late afternoon were growing long. The long, wet night followed by a full day in the saddle had left both men tired and weary.

"Need a good night's sleep," Jake mumbled to himself and his horse. "Not likely anytime soon, I suppose."

Meanwhile, Tom circled south on the pretext of checking on a group of strays he claimed to have seen earlier in the day. Instead, he sought the two women. He found them tucked safely where he had left them earlier. After unloading some food and water, he helped prepare a shelter for the night ahead.

"What's happening?" asked an anxious Sarah.

"Gathering cattle from the stampede mostly," Tom explained. "And, it's going much too fast. Me and Jake may need to run them again!"

A perplexed Sarah said, "I don't understand."

"What do you mean?" asked Molly.

"Did you two have something to do with starting that stampede last night?"

"Well . . . not exactly," Tom replied.

"The storm actually did all the work. Jake just encouraged them a little . . . except . . . well they was suppose to run the other direction, back toward the mountains."

"What the . . . ?" asked an incredulous Sarah.

"Why were you trying to start a stampede?" Molly interrupted.

"We were trying to scatter them and buy some time until the Box T boys to get here."

"We don't understand!"

"Don't even try," said Tom. "Things are pretty complicated. But it will be crystal clear real soon! You two just lay low for a day or two."

Sarah touched his arm and asked, "What about my father? Molly says you told her he's okay."

"He's fine. But that's all I can say right now."

"But, how . . . ! Where's he at? Can I see him?"

Tom turned his back and raised his hand to signal he was done talking.

As he started to mount his horse Molly went to him and asked if he was okay.

"Doing fine," he responded. "I appreciate you asking. Thanks. How 'bout you two?"

"We are okay. Just bored and wondering

what might happen next."

"Like I said, things are about to blow wide open. Just be patient. Trust us. Lay low . . . okay?"

Sarah stepped toward them and said, "We can't hide out up here forever. What can we do to help?"

"Stop worrying. Jake's got a plan."

"Tell us about your friend . . . Jake is it? That wouldn't be the Jake Summers who rescued Elsie Gardner a few days back? Have we met him? Do we know him? He wouldn't be that tall puncher who locked me up would he? And, who are the Box T boys?

"Jake's a good one. But you ask too many questions. I gotta go before I'm missed. You'll be okay here."

As he turned his horse toward the ranch complex, he glanced at Molly and said, "Good night!"

Then under a star-filled sky, he rode toward a rising moon and disappeared.

Jake unsaddled his horse, wiped him down and gave him some oats before turning him into the main horse corral. He glanced at the moon rising over the prairie beyond the ranch house, and then up at the place where he knew the women were hiding.

As he rolled a smoke and leaned against

the corral fence, he watched Tom ride into the barnyard. Together they took care of Tom's horse and started toward the bunkhouse together.

"Anything new with Blatz?" asked Tom.

"Haven't seen him today," Jake answered. "And nobody's said anything. Not yet. You get the women squared away?"

"They're settled. But that Meadows girl won't sit for long."

Nobody paid any attention as they entered the bunkhouse. The men were gathered in two basic groups . . . legitimate cowhands and gun hands. They joined the punchers who were swapping stories and relating experiences on unbroken horses. The scene could have been repeated on any ranch from Texas to Montana.

Across the smoke-filled room, Winston's hired guns were split between two tables playing poker and drinking whiskey. It was at one of the tables that Jake spotted Blatz, who was winning big and drinking more. He was drunk.

"Summers!" Blatz called out upon seeing him enter the room.

Jake looked at Blatz.

"I know I'd seen you before. Now I remember where," said the drunken gun hand while still seated at the table.

Few of the others bothered to even look in his direction. Blatz had a reputation for being boisterous and constantly challenging someone.

Jake looked around the room. Nobody was listening so he tried ignoring his antagonist by turning away.

"Stop right there Summers," Blatz called out. "You've got some explaining to do."

"You dealing or talking?" asked Lester Adams from across the table.

"You've got all our money, so start dealing," said Billy Thomas.

Blatz turned back to those at the table in front of him. "I'll deal all right. But I know that guy and . . ."

Jake interrupted.

"You got something to say to me get it said, or else shut up!"

Blatz pushed back from the table but didn't stand.

Now the room was quiet. All eyes were on Jake and Blatz.

Tom moved to one side with one hand on his pistol ready to back his friend if it came to gunplay. Blatz glanced in his direction, weighing his odds. The tension was thick.

"Like I said, start talking or keep your drunken mouth shut," Jake challenged.

Now on the defensive, Blatz knew he was

backed into a corner. His reputation was at stake. Summers had to die. His fellow gunmen sat quiet, letting things play out. Each respected Jake for making a stand against one of their own, although most felt it foolhardy.

Blatz put his hands out away from his gun and stood, carefully watching Jake for any sign of gunplay. In moving his hands away from his body, he created a more serious problem. As he stood an Ace of Spades and two Queens fell from his sleeve and gently floated toward the floor in front of him. All eyes in the room grew large at the sight.

"Why you cheating . . . !" shouted Adams pulling his pistol and standing.

"You're a cheating, lying thief," young Billy Thomas called out. "No wonder you've got all our money!"

"Now boys, it ain't what it seems!" Blatz said weakly, realizing he was in trouble.

"You're a liar!" Adams retorted.

Blatz backed away from the table and stumbled over a chair, nearly falling.

"I hate a cheater," continued Adams.

"Me too," echoed Thomas, who by now also was standing.

"Boys," Blatz pleaded. "You don't understand. Let me tell you about Summers and Scott."

"Like hell. Cards up your sleeve tell me plenty," Thomas shouted.

Men in the bunkhouse cleared away from the gunfight they knew was coming. Jake and Tom were among those trying to get out of the way. Both Box T hands kept quiet.

Blatz realized he was out of options and reached for his pistol.

Adams shot first.

The wounded Blatz fell to one knee and fired wildly into the ceiling before Adam's second shot struck him in the chest.

As he died, Blatz mumbled, "Thom . . . Thomp . . . Summers no good."

Smitty burst into the room with an air of self-importance, demanding to know what was going on as gunsmoke mixed with tobacco smoke and filled the bunkhouse with a thick haze.

"Blatz was cheating at cards and we caught him," Adams explained. "Then he pulled his gun and we shot him. Ain't that right boys?"

There was a murmur of agreement from around the room.

"That's a fact boss," said Thomas.

"He was also rambling something about Summers there."

"What's the deal Summers?" Smitty asked, while taking a step in his direction.

"Personal matter boss," Jake answered. "This drunk has been saying some unkind things about me and my pard, Tom Scott."

"The hell you say?" said Smitty.

"Couldn't let him go on without calling him out for it," Jake explained. "Adams there did me a favor."

"Wasn't intentional," Adams mumbled.

"Something's not right here," Smitty observed. "Once Winston gets his cattle sold you and me . . . and your buddy there . . . are going to set some things straight. You understand Summers?"

As everyone returned to previous activities, Smitty ordered some of the men to take care of Blatz's body.

"That was a close one," Jake said quietly to Tom. "Thompson and the boys better get here real soon."

The once clear night had given way to cloud cover hiding the stars and moon. The night was pitch black, and strangely quiet around the ranch buildings.

The women had heard the gunfire, but in the darkness they could not make out any details. They were left with the howl of a lonely coyote on a nearby ridge. Both shuddered and returned to their makeshift shelter for the night, neither able to sleep, but both thankful to be out from under

Winston's control.

Each took turns trying to sleep, resting softly on the wings of night birds keeping watch over them.

CHAPTER 31
REDEMPTION AT LAST

Winston heard about the stampede and was again enraged. He had planned to take Legress to the ranch and finalize their sale. Now he would need to stall a few days and buy some time for the cattle to be gathered again.

Legress was not a patient man. He told Winston he was leaving town and would return only when Winston had his act together. That only made Winston angrier.

"Somebody is going to pay for this," he muttered to himself. "I have to do everything myself. Get my horse and rifle," he shouted to anyone within earshot. "I'm going to get to the bottom of this."

One Eye rode a black gelding hard out from town to warn Smitty and the others that Winston was on his way. The horse was exhausted, well-lathered and breathing hard as the gunman slid from the saddle in front of Winston's foreman.

"He's coming. And, he's mad as hell!" shouted One Eye.

"Who?" asked Smitty. "Who's coming?"

"Winston! And, he's out for blood!"

For all the gunplay and hard times Molly had experienced in her 17 years she had never actually seen anyone shot and killed before. So she sat and watched in horror as Winston rode into the ranch complex and shot Smitty dead. There was no warning, no discussion, just two quick shots and the man was dead.

"Son-of-a-bitch was suppose to watch after things out here," he roared. "Get rid of the body. Then get those cattle back together," he shouted to everyone within the sound of his booming voice.

Then speaking to nobody in particular, he shouted, "Anybody got different ideas? And where are those women?"

The bullet from Sarah's rifle hit Winston's saddle horn, catching the still-mounted rider totally by surprise. Had she used that particular rifle before, no doubt Winston would have died never knowing his assassin. Instead, he dismounted before Sarah could adjust. He then used his frightened horse as a shield to find cover behind the ranch house.

Jake and Tom had just returned 10 steers to the main herd and were headed for the ranch complex when they heard the shots.

"Sounds like pistol shots followed by rifle shots," observed Jake. "Tell me you didn't leave a rifle with that fool girl."

"No . . . of course not," Tom answered.

"That Meadows girl is shooting again. I'll bet money on it," Jake said. "Let's ride that way. Be careful though. She'll shoot at anything that moves."

Tom could only smile. "Gets under your skin does she?" he asked his friend.

"You gotta be kidding," Jake responded as they rode side-by-side. Then after a moment, he added, "She does have some grit, just like her father."

Once Winston and his men determined the general direction from where the shots had come, gunfire rained. Sarah found it difficult to return fire.

"You sure you didn't leave her a rifle?" Jake asked again. "She's damn determined to get herself killed . . . and take that girlfriend of yours with her."

They found a spot overlooking the ranch complex and where they could see Winston's men firing toward Sarah and Molly's hiding place.

"Might as well join the fun," Jake said.

"Guess our work here is about done anyway. Let's take some heat off the ladies."

As the two men began firing, Winston and his men were caught in a deadly crossfire. One of Winston's men was shot outright. A second was seriously wounded.

Quickly everyone realized a second front had been engaged. Now with fewer shots in her direction, Sarah found more opportunities to return fire.

After almost an hour of sporadic shooting, there was suddenly another round of gunfire coming from up along the high ridge where Sarah and Molly were hiding. Someone else was helping . . . but who?

"What the . . . ?" Jake shouted to Tom.

"Beats me," he answered. "But, it looks like we've got some help."

"Maybe it's Thompson and the boys," said Jake. "They should have been here by now."

Sarah and Molly wondered much the same thing as rifles opened up a deadly barrage of gunfire into the ranch complex. Some of Winston's men were already scrambling to find horses and escape.

With the gunfire came casualties on both sides, but the advantage was clearly with those on the ridge. After a time the gunfire began to subside until only sporadic shots were being hurled in both directions.

"You ladies okay?" came a voice from behind Sarah.

She whirled and quickly raised her rifle ready to fire.

Molly screamed.

"Don't shoot! Don't shoot!" Charlie Richards shouted as he dove for cover. "We're here to help."

"Who are you? And, who is we?" Sarah demanded while still holding her rifle at the ready.

"We are from the Box T and several other ranches east of here . . . over near Eagle River," Richards explained while still hiding. "Our boss, Mr. Thompson, and old man Meadows brought us."

"Meadows! My father?" Sarah exclaimed upon hearing the name. "I was told he was dead," she said as she slowly lowered her rifle.

Richards, now more confident he wouldn't be shot, eased from his hiding place. "Why is the messenger always the one who gets shot? He's not dead. Jake found him up on Laramie Mesa all shot up. He's been mending with us."

"Where is he?" Sarah asked as she started to stand.

A shot from the still unsecured ranch house tore splinters from a nearby branch and sent them all back into protective cover.

Box T wranglers and those from the other spreads were already moving down the ridge to clean up things and root out any remaining gunmen. Only Winston remained missing.

Jake and Tom recognized who was providing support and had their spirits buoyed for the first time in days.

"There's old Dan Sims and Trace Johnson," shouted Tom.

"It's Thompson and the boys all right," Jake said. "Let's go join them."

After another few minutes of careful maneuvering and circling, things were brought under control . . . except for finding Winston. Some of his men had also escaped.

Thompson joined Jake and Tom, who quickly brought him up-to-date on what they had seen and heard.

"Men, start searching the buildings one by one. Be careful! The big boss of all this is still missing and he won't hesitate to shoot you dead . . . especially if he's cornered."

Meanwhile on the ridge, Charlie Richards finally was able to start explaining things. Then over his shoulder Sarah spotted John Meadows coming toward her. She never heard Charlie's last few words of explanation. She ran to embrace her father.

Molly, realizing the importance of the moment, could only smile. The air was emotionally charged.

"I'm okay. I'm okay," Meadows kept saying.

"I don't believe this is real!" Sarah exclaimed. "They told me you were dead. Then they said you were alive but hurt. I didn't know what to believe or whom."

"I almost was dead," Meadows explained. "Winston had his goons shoot me in the back. Thank goodness for the young cowboy who found me and saved my life."

Sarah said, "I'd like to thank him myself."

"You'll get your chance. He works for my good friend Thompson down there," Meadows said as he gestured toward the ranch complex.

Together they started walking down the ridge toward the ranch house.

Spotting Thompson, Meadows called out, "Got everything under control Bill? Is it safe?"

"Almost. We are still searching for Winston. Most of his gunmen are dead, captured or running."

"Good," Meadows answered. "Bill, I want you to meet Sarah Alicia Meadows, my daughter, and this is her friend, Molly Collins."

"Delighted," said Thompson as he touched the brim of his hat. "Just delighted."

At that moment, Tom Scott came around the corner of the ranch house and started walking toward the assembled group.

"There! That man!" pointed Sarah. "Don't let your men shoot him. He's been helping us."

Thompson and Meadows looked quickly at the approaching Box T wrangler and they both smiled. "That's Tom Scott, young lady," said Thompson. "He works for me."

Sarah and Molly, hearing the news, looked at each other and started laughing. As Tom drew closer, Molly hurried to greet him.

Thompson noticed the greeting and said, "Looks like Tom's found a new friend."

Everybody laughed. Then Sarah turned her attention back to her father. "I still can't believe it. You are actually alive. And, you look great!"

Jake, Charlie Richards and a couple of other Box T hands were still searching the area for Winston and any of his men that might still be hanging around. It was Jake who saw the old man first.

Moving into a grain room inside the barn,

Winston fired twice at Jake, missing both times.

The shots sent Thompson, Meadows and the others into the ranch house for cover.

Jake shouted at Winston to give himself up.

The response was a gruff, "Go to hell!"

"Some of them are still in the barn," Meadows called out.

Thompson stepped toward the front door to join the fray, but Meadows stopped him.

"Bill . . . I appreciate all you've done. More than I can ever repay. But, I need to finish this myself."

"I understand," Thompson said as he stepped aside.

Meadows called out, "You boys cover the front. I'll go around back of the barn. There's a door back there. You girls stay put."

With that he was out the door, motioning for Tom to follow him. They quickly and quietly circled behind the barn and got a good vantage point behind an old wagon frame. Meadows then learned his strong-willed daughter had followed against his wishes.

"What the . . . ?" he exclaimed. "If you aren't going to listen to me, at least stay low and out of sight."

Winston bolted from the back door and was clear of any protection when he spotted Meadows and realized his mistake. He turned white with fear.

However, it didn't stop him from trying to shoot his way clear. Meadows shot a split second faster and much more accurate. His nemesis, the terror of the territory, was dead.

As Meadows, Sarah and Tom approached Winston's lifeless body, Jake emerged from the barn.

CHAPTER 32
NURSED BACK TO HEALTH

The bullet from Sarah's rifle tore aside the skin in Jake's shoulder and exploded through muscle and tissue before lodging in his back. He never heard the sound, and ever so briefly felt the pain before collapsing. Her shot just missed his heart.

A split second later, Sarah's father grabbed the rifle barrel and pulled it downward. Her second shot ricocheted off the ground before hitting the barn.

Tom ran to help his friend, who was lying near death in the barnyard dust. The wetness of his blood creating a crimson mud that attached itself to their boots. Hungry flies wasted little time in finding the man and his exposed wound.

"My God girl," shouted Meadows. "What have you done?"

The old man moved toward the fallen Box T foreman and yelled, "That's Jake Summers. He's been helping us!"

"But . . . ," Sarah replied weakly. "I didn't . . . he does work for Winston . . . I mean . . . I just reacted."

"Jake and Tom have been working undercover. He's the man who saved my life, for heaven's sake."

The rifle fell from her hands and found a home in the barnyard dust. She stood nearby with a horrid feeling of despair and shock.

"What have I done?" she asked herself. "He also saved my life . . . more than once," she whispered. "What have I done?"

Tom, joined by Thompson, Meadows and a few other Box T hands, were trying to help Jake. He was in a bad way, bleeding badly and he was in a state of shock, unconscious.

"Let's get him to the house," Meadows instructed some of the hands. "Be careful. We've got to stop the bleeding and get that bullet out. Sarah, you and Molly gather up some clean towels and get us some hot water. Also . . . find us a reasonably clean, but sharp knife. I'm sure the house is a mess, but do the best you can."

It took some time, but the bullet came out clean. No vital organs were damaged. However, Jake remained unconscious, drifting in and out of a sleepy, feverish stupor. He had lost a great deal of blood in a short amount of time.

Jake's wound was cleaned. Then Sarah applied some heartleaf arnica to the wound. Her father always kept some dried leaves of the wildflower ground up for medicinal use. She covered the wound and said a brief prayer.

The wild and shot-filled afternoon gave way to a quiet evening followed by a cool nightfall. Most of the men and the two young women couldn't sleep after the excitement of the afternoon.

Meadows, with Thompson's help, filled Sarah and Molly in on all the missing details about Jake and Tom. Meadows made sure his daughter understood how Winston had run him off, shot him and left him to die on the prairie, and that Jake had saved his life. Both women were both amazed and gratified. Sarah felt worse than ever about shooting Jake.

Sarah now understood why Jake always seemed close by when she was in trouble. And she understood why he had not shot back each time she had shot at him. She finally could admit she was attracted to the tall, lanky cowboy . . . *just like Molly had said.*

By morning nearly everyone was in a festive mood. Jake had survived the night and had shown positive signs of recovery, although still unconscious.

Thompson instructed Tom and six other Box T cowhands, along with cowhands from several other spreads, to start the process of sorting the cattle stolen from the various ranches. The remaining hands were sent home under the direction of Charlie Richards.

Thompson stayed behind to help Meadows get situated. The house was a mess and the ranch complex was in disrepair. There was much work to be done. Few of the old hands were still around to get it done. That meant hiring men to work.

Winston's gun hands had been shot, captured or fled the country. A few were believed to be hiding in the nearby mountains.

Guilt and concern defined Sarah's demeanor toward the young foreman. For more than three days, she stayed with him day and night. She made sure he received proper care. She regularly changed the bandages and dressing on the wound and kept him clean and shaved.

Along with caring for their patient, Sarah and Molly managed to retrieve their things from the hotel and moved them into the Meadows home. Molly quit her job tending tables in town, and instead, helped Sarah clean up the Meadows home.

Tom managed to spend most of his limited free time getting to know Molly better and checking on his friend. He worried about Jake's remaining unconscious for so long a time.

Finally, on the third afternoon, Jake's fever broke. He woke extremely weak, hungry, hurting and restless. It was also one of the rare times Sarah was not in the room with him. She had insisted Molly go stay with him for a few minutes while she prepared some clean bandages.

It was Molly who found him awake.

As he forced open tired eyes and looked around the room, Jake realized he was in the Meadows main house. There were bullet holes in the bedroom walls, remnants of an earlier shootout.

While in obvious pain, Jake was anxious to get out of bed. Common sense told him better. Still, he tried. With some painful effort he managed to sit up on the side of the bed. He searched the room with his eyes for his pants, shirt and boots. It was at that moment that Molly entered the room with a pitcher of fresh, spring water.

"Get back in that bed," she admonished him with a good-natured laugh. "You had us worried sick."

"I'm alive I think," Jake mumbled. "Who shot me? Don't answer that. I can guess! It was that fool Meadows girl wasn't it?

"Don't bother answering," he continued. "The look on your face is enough. She has been trying to kill me since I got here."

"You're healing. That's all that counts now," Molly answered. "You're going to be okay, thanks to Sarah."

"Sarah?" he asked while finding it hurt his chest to breathe, much less talk.

"Yes, Sarah," Molly continued. "She has stayed with you day and night. She's changed your bandages regularly. Why she even gave you a bath once," grinned Molly. "You were a mess!"

"A bath! You can't be serious," said Jake. "Good grief, she must be real proud. Must be worried sick I'll live."

"Hardly," said a matter-of-fact Molly. "Once she found out who you are and well . . . how you and Tom tried to help us . . . and how you saved her father's life . . . well . . . she feels real bad. In fact, like I said she's the one who has been nursing you . . . more than me," explained Molly while handing Jake his pants.

"If you say so," Jake said weakly as he tried to stand.

"It's the truth!" said Molly.

"Just find me my shirt and I'm out of here," he responded with a gasp. "That girl . . . she's trouble."

Despite his extremely weak condition and tremendous pain, he managed to get dressed with help from Molly. He slowly made his way out of the house and down across the yard toward the bunkhouse, barns and corrals. All were deserted.

Thompson and Meadows had all the punchers still out sorting the stolen cattle by brand, so they could be returned to their rightful owners. Those with obviously altered brands were being held together for later sorting.

Other hands had been sent to track down a few of Winston's old gang still believed to be in the area.

Get me away from that wild-eyed girl, he thought to himself. Although he knew it would be impossible to saddle his horse much less get mounted, it felt good to be outside in the fresh air, if only smelling the familiar scents of horse manure and corral dirt.

Sarah spotted him struggling to reach the bunkhouse and it was her first clue that her patient was out of his sick bed and gone.

"Molly!" she shouted. "How did . . . ? Why

didn't you stop him?"

"He left one very determined step at a time," explained Molly. "Said he had to get out of here."

"Why? He's not near well enough yet!" stammered Sarah as she gazed at Jake moving closer to the out buildings. She took a couple steps after him, but stopped.

Molly could only grin and said, "Well . . . well he actually said he was afraid you might shoot again. He didn't want to take that chance."

Sarah didn't respond. She wasn't amused. She just stared off into the distance, deep in her own thoughts and emotions.

Weakened from the exertion of just getting dressed and walking across the barnyard, Jake collapsed into a painful heap on his bunk and fell asleep.

CHAPTER 33
TIME FOR UNCOMMON VALOR

The sudden and urgent barking of a dog, followed by a woman's scream, woke Jake with a start. It was dark outside but he had no idea of the time. The ranch hands had not returned to the bunkhouse that evening, choosing instead to remain out close to their work.

The two women were likely alone in the house. Even the cook, Manuel, had gone to feed the hands. Thompson and Meadows most likely would have stayed with the hands or gone into town.

Jake knew something was wrong . . . very wrong!

There was a pistol shot, then the painful whelp from the dog, followed by silence.

Despite the agonizing pain in his chest and difficulty breathing, Jake got to his feet and found his own pistol.

The night was clear and the rising moon seemed huge as it hung on the horizon. It cast long shadows and Jake used them as he worked his way slowly and carefully toward the house. It was quiet, too quiet.

Behind the house, he found four horses tied loosely to a clothesline post. If someone had been left to watch the horses, he had for the moment abandoned his post. Boredom, or perhaps the need to relieve himself, had forced him to leave. That enabled Jake to approach the house from behind.

He could see the dog's lifeless body lying in a pool of its own dark blood. The dog was just one of several living at the ranch, belonging to nobody in particular. Now the wetness of his blood was shining in the moonlight. Jake thought, *he wasn't much of a mutt. But, he could sure cause havoc among the horses by nipping at their heels and barking. He had been kicked more than once and had the scars to prove it.*

So long ole boy, thought Jake. *You deserved better.*

After struggling to climb the back steps one soft step at a time, he was able to reach the back door without being seen. However, the urge to rush, the urge to see and know what was happening was overwhelming. The exertion had taken its toll. His breathing was deep and labored.

Gotta get a grip, he thought.

He was sure the thoughts in his head, and the pounding of his heart could be heard by those inside the house.

Jake peered through a window partially covered by an old green curtain. Inside he could see Molly and Sarah seated next to each other along one side of the old kitchen table.

Also, seated at the table was Chester Holt. A pistol lay on the table within easy reach of his big right hand. However, that hand was currently busy stuffing handfuls of bread and beans into his unshaved face.

As he talked and laughed, half-chewed breadcrumbs and beans fell back from where they'd come and onto the table and floor. He didn't care. A bottle of whiskey was in his left hand. From time to time, he tried to wash his food down between bites.

T. J. Whitaker sat at the opposite end of the table. He was more enamored with his own whiskey bottle and Molly's red hair, which he kept stroking and twisting in his fingers. Her efforts to make him stop only encouraged him. He kept talking to her while gradually sliding his chair in her direction.

A third man, One Eye Lumpkin, stood in the shadows near the back door. He said nothing and only stared at the women like a hungry dog that hadn't seen meat for some time.

That's three, thought Jake. *Four horses . . . where's the fourth guy?*

A cough, followed by cursing, and suddenly Jake realized the fourth man was behind him and moving in his direction across the open back yard.

"T. J. . . . that you?" The man called out to Jake, who was partially hidden in the dark shadows of the back porch.

"T. J.?" The man repeated as he started up the steps.

"You ain't T. J.," he exclaimed just as Jake's pistol butt crushed the side of his face. He fell backward unconscious never knowing who hit him.

In striking the blow, Jake felt some stitches pull free from his own wound. The pain made him want to cry out, but he fought down the urge.

He tried dragging the body from view of those who might look outside, but the exertion took its toll. Blood had begun to stain the front of his shirt.

Worn out, out-of-breath, and in more pain than he had ever known, Jake realized he would need to move quickly while he still had energy left. He fought the urge to pass out and climbed back up the steps to the porch.

With the ruffians inside drinking and eating their fill, it would only be a matter of time before they turned their full attention to the women.

Surprise, Jake thought. *I've got one chance to surprise them. Maybe get off two . . . maybe three shots before they can get me.*

Jake waited for an opening and the minutes were agonizing. He fought to stay awake, alert.

Then it happened.

The opening came so quickly it almost caught Jake napping.

Holt turned and motioned for Lumpkin to get him another bottle stored in a nearby pantry. As Lumpkin moved away from his post at the back door, Whitaker stood up to stretch. In doing so, he moved away from Molly just long enough. In that split second, all the planets in heaven moved into alignment.

Jake burst through the kitchen door with his pistol blazing!

Lumpkin was the first to fall dead. Whitaker was shot in the leg but managed to pull his pistol and fire at Jake, missing his head by inches.

Holt, frozen for only a moment, turned

back to the table and reached for his own gun but it was gone. Sarah had not hesitated in that frozen moment in time. She also had been waiting for an opening of some kind. Jake had given her just enough distraction. She fired at Holt but in the confusion only hit him in the left arm. A second shot missed altogether.

Molly dove for cover under the kitchen table.

Whitaker fired a second, and then a third shot at Jake, who moved left and felt himself falling. It wasn't an attempt to avoid being shot as much as it was from the pain and loss of outright energy. Still, he was able to return fire. And, this time his shot hit Whitaker in the head, killing him instantly.

A wounded Holt dove behind the kitchen table and found Lumpkin's lifeless body and his unpulled pistol. Now armed, he turned to see Molly's frightened face staring at him from under the table. He put the pistol barrel against her head and shouted, "Hold your fire or the redhead dies!"

Sarah, who was coming around the table, stopped short, realizing her friend was in mortal danger.

Jake had struggled to his feet and was approaching from the opposite end of the table. He also stopped.

"Drop them shooters," shouted Holt, "Or, I blow her brains out."

Sarah and Jake looked at each other, then carefully laid their guns on the table.

Holt struggled to his feet never taking the gun from Molly's head. Then, using the hand on his wounded left arm, he grabbed Molly by the hair and pulled her from under the table.

He ordered Jake and Sarah to hold their hands high. Then he pulled his pistol away from Molly's head long enough to motion Jake and Sarah to stand against the far wall.

The outlaw never actually saw the gun that killed him. It was a small, never-used, silver-plated derringer worn for protection in Molly's garter. The gunman only saw a flash as its deadly bullet burst free from its tiny barrel and exploded into his chest.

With a look of surprise and shock, he died never expecting this beautiful and frightened young woman to be a threat.

In the years of working the barrooms and saloons of St. Louis, Molly had learned from her mother to always be prepared, and this time it saved her life.

CHAPTER 34
WHERE A GOOD WIND BLOWS

A smell of strong black coffee and fried bacon filled the Meadows house, while outside birds welcomed the early summer day with songs. The long deep shadows of early morning gradually gave way to a cloudless, sun filled sky. It would be warm and without rain. Three such mornings had passed since the kitchen gunfight.

Horses nickered and churned up dust in the corrals while a few chickens searched for something to eat. Two cow dogs waited patiently for their day's orders while lying under an abandoned wagon bed. One old cat sought a place to nap in the barn loft after a long night of hunting.

Old man Meadows was in the mood to celebrate the return of daughter, ranch and cattle, not necessarily in that order.

"What we need is a party," Meadows said over breakfast coffee. "I want everyone to share in Sarah's return and that of my own.

We also need to show our appreciation to everyone who came to help us . . . William Thompson and especially that young cowhand, Jake Summers and his friend Tom."

"Let's," chimed in Sarah. "Molly and I can plan everything. We can have everything ready by Saturday before Mr. Thompson and his men go home."

"What have you got planned?" Molly asked. "You realize it's already Wednesday right?"

Sarah only smiled.

Saturday morning arrived quickly, and Sarah and Molly felt things were ready. There was a positive excitement in the air. The Meadows family didn't have many close friends so it was easy to contact everyone who might attend such an event. Most were eager to attend, if only to cast aside the black cloud Winston had brought to Chugwater.

Just past noon a solitary rider topped a low rise east of the ranch and turned his horse down a long, grassy ridge into the valley. He was still several hundred yards from the house. His well-bred horse kicked up dust, which clung to its black coat.

The man wore a wide brim, black hat, a black vest and a heavily starched white shirt.

He also wore tall black riding boots, riding gloves and small English spurs. He rode with his back straight as if tied to a wide board.

As the man urged his horse into a small creek, which flowed near the house, a wrangler who had been asked to help with party preparations spotted him and started shouting for Meadows to come outside.

"What's all the ruckus?" the old man asked as he stepped onto the porch followed closely by Thompson.

"Stranger coming in," the wrangler pointed out.

Meadows turned in the direction of the man's motioning hand. The early afternoon sun was above and behind the rider, making it difficult to clearly see his features. Even when Meadows used his right hand to shade his eyes, he could not make out the man's identity.

"Ever see him before?" he asked Thompson.

"Can't say I have," the Box T owner answered. "It's really hard to see him. But, that's a fine-looking horse."

As the rider started up the creek bank, it was obvious to both men that he didn't ride like any Wyoming cowhand they knew.

"Wonder what he wants?" Meadows asked.

"Maybe he's selling something," Thompson answered.

"Guess we're gonna find out," answered Meadows.

Jake and Tom left activity at the horse corrals and walked toward the approaching rider. The stranger ignored them and set his sights on the two men standing on the front porch. And although Jake's wound had not fully healed and he often felt pain, each day he managed to get up and get around without much help, so he had no problem getting close to the house.

Two other hands also had drifted in close just in case there was trouble. Each man, including Jake and Tom, was armed and alert. However, as the man drew closer it was evident he was not armed, not even a rifle scabbard.

"What kind of greenhorn rides around Wyoming without wearing a gun?" Tom asked Jake, while not really expecting an answer.

The rider pulled up in front of the porch but made no effort to dismount.

"Gentlemen, I'm seeking Mr. John Meadows of Wyoming," the stranger stated with a high-pitched whine in his voice.

"I'm Meadows! Who are you? What do you want?"

"Sir, it's my pleasure to finally make your acquaintance. My name is Jason Kelly Neal. I'm a good friend of your beautiful daughter, Sarah Alicia."

"The hell you say!"

"Yes, sir! I've come from Nebraska to see Miss Sarah and to ask you a serious question that will impact all our lives."

After some hesitation, Meadows spoke. "Well . . . well get off your horse and come inside. You must be tired and thirsty."

"Yes sir, I am."

"So you claim to know my daughter, do you?"

Tom glanced at Jake as the men entered the house. Maybe it was his imagination, but it appeared his good friend had grown very pale, if not all out ashen. Neither man said anything, but it was obvious nobody had counted on any friend of Sarah's to just show up.

Jake stood for a moment with downcast eyes, and then spoke to one of the wranglers nearby.

"Take the man's horse, wipe him down, water him and feed him some oats."

Meadows was heard saying, "Come inside young man. I want to know how you know my daughter."

"Sir, I'm a lawyer. I'm originally from Boston, but I moved to Buffalo County, Nebraska, where I met Sarah Alicia. I'm starting a law practice there. I think Sarah Alicia is a wonderful woman and I want to marry her."

Meadows nearly dropped his coffee cup.

Thompson, in mid-swallow, suddenly coughed and fought to get his breath.

Plates were heard breaking in the kitchen as someone who had been eavesdropping lost their balance.

Regaining his composure, Meadows asked, "My daughter . . . is she expecting to see you here?"

"Oh, no! I wanted to surprise her."

"Young man, I think you've done that. You've surprised us all."

Before he could respond, Sarah and Molly entered the room. Upon seeing Neal, Sarah gasped as if she'd seen a ghost.

"Jason, what are you doing here?"

"Sarah Alicia!"

"How? Why?"

"My dear, I told mother I would come out here and surprise you. Haven't you missed me?"

"Why . . . I mean we've been so busy. So much has happened."

"I have just now asked your father for your hand in marriage."

"You did what?"

"Sarah!" Molly gasped.

"Father . . . did he really?"

Meadows could only nod yes.

"And . . . and what did you say?" Sarah asked with a look of shock on her face.

"I haven't."

Then turning to his newly arrived guest, Meadows said, "Young man, let's get you settled and we'll talk later. There's a party tonight and we have much to do. "Sarah would you please show your friend to the bunkhouse. We have no extra room here in the house."

Molly was still reeling from the news that Sarah's friend from Nebraska had come to propose marriage.

Jake and Tom could only watch as Sarah walked with Neal to the bunkhouse. Neither man said anything.

"Jason, why did you come?"

"I came for you. I thought you would be glad to see me. This isn't quite the reception I expected."

"Of course, I'm glad to see you. Except . . . I," her voice trailing off.

"Except what?"

"Well, things change. Situations change."

"Listen, I know my coming has been a shock. But, once things settle down it will be just like old times. Just you and me and all our plans."

Sarah looked past her surprising friend and saw Jake giving out instructions to a couple of hands, his left arm still in a sling.

"Maybe . . . maybe," her thoughts drifting off. "I'll come back and see you later."

She stepped outside and started for the house while watching Jake, who failed to return her glance.

Music floated on the night air and was carried across the ranch complex. Laughter had finally returned. Chairs and tables had been shoved back allowing room for everyone to visit and dance. Ranchers, their families, some townspeople and cowhands all mingled in a relaxed atmosphere.

Due to the shortage of women in the area, a few of the cowboys wore red bandanas on their arm indicating that for the moment he would play the female role while dancing.

Thompson stood talking to Meadows as they smoked expensive cigars and talked cattle prices and the future. Thompson was losing a good hand in Tom Scott, and Meadows was gaining a good new foreman. Both men were happy.

Neal was making small talk with some

women from town while waiting for Sarah. They giggled at his attempts at funny stories and were in awe that he was an Eastern-educated lawyer.

Molly had gathered Tom and was attempting to teach him some dance steps.

Sarah entered the room with all the pomp and grace befitting any beautiful young woman. Every man turned and in his own subtle way acknowledged her entrance. She wore a dress of lace and cotton, elegant, as it was simple. Her hair was pulled up and around her neck she wore a pearl necklace once owned by her mother.

Meadows was at first speechless. It was hard to believe this was the same *"cowgirl"* he had sent to his sister four years ago. *Ruby did a job,* he sighed to himself. *She looks just like her mother.*

Thompson turned to his new friend and said, "You have a beautiful daughter. You must be proud."

Meadows never heard him finish as he stepped toward his daughter.

Molly, however, had other ideas. She quickly grabbed Sarah's attention. Even she had never really seen her friend so clean and so nicely dressed. "Well, don't you clean up good?" she laughed.

Then they heard Neal's booming voice

rising above the music. Everyone turned to look.

"Many of you have kindly filled me in on events of recent days. I am only sorry I did not arrive sooner to help, although I do have an aversion to gun play. As some of you know by now, I am a good friend of Sarah Alicia. And, it's only right I think, with all of her family and friends present, that I ask Sarah to marry me."

Those standing near Sarah stepped back providing her both space and air. She was aghast. Her face was white as a ghost. She looked at her father who looked back with his hands and arms spread wide in astonishment.

Jake, who had been standing near the front door, turned and went outside. He sought the cool night air, his emotions in a sudden turmoil.

"Mr. Neal, you presume too much," Sarah finally spoke with a determined focus. "You might have asked me first. You might also have waited for my father to answer your request, a request you only made just this afternoon."

"Yes!" Molly said quietly as she squeezed Tom's hand. "Tell him! Tell him good!"

"Sarah Alicia!" Neal called out. "I thought . . ."

"You thought wrong," Sarah interrupted. "You are a good friend. But I told you things had changed. I intend to be a rancher's wife, out here where the land is big and wide, where the wind blows good and free. I could never be a prim and proper lawyer's wife. I know that now and I am sorry."

"Listen!" shouted Neal. "I came all this way. I can't believe you would choose this God-forsaken land and cowpunchers over me. I will . . ."

Thompson stepped forward and was followed by Trace Johnson and several other men.

"Will what?" Thompson asked. "I suggest you get on that fine horse of yours right now and ride. This isn't Boston or even Denver and you ain't welcome anymore."

With that final exchange the men ushered Neal out the back way and sent him on his way. The guests cheered.

"Where is he?" Sarah asked Molly.

"Outside on the porch."

Sarah moved past her guests toward the front door.

"She doesn't have a gun hid somewhere does she?" Tom asked Molly playfully.

She only gave him a wave of the back side

of her hand.

Outside on the porch, Jake stood alone listening to the music, the talk and the renewed laughter. He was healing. Yes, there was still some pain now and then but he could ride again. It soon would be time to head for home.

The pangs of loneliness, which had overcome him so often, had returned. He could also hear the mournful cry of a coyote on a distant hill and it made him shiver. He had allowed himself to consider future options. Now he felt hollow, sad and empty.

Jake heard the front door open and he turned to see a beautiful young lady walking in his direction. The moonlight created a shine on her soft brown hair and she had a touch of blush on her cheeks. Her brown eyes sparkled in the lantern light. She was smiling.

My gosh, she's beautiful, thought Jake unable to turn his eyes away. *Without all the mud and a rifle in her hands . . . she's pretty.*

He stood unable, unwilling to destroy the moment. She moved toward him, never lowering her eyes. Like two strangers unsure of the moment, and with tension rising, she stopped.

They looked at each other for what seemed like ages. In a sense, they were seeing each other for the first time. It was Sarah who broke the silence.

"Care to dance?"

"But, I thought . . . ?" he started to answer.

She gently took his hand and moved closer.

Soon 300 first calf heifers would be headed for a new ranch home along the North Laramie River. And, just as soon, the Box T would need a new foreman. But, tonight a gentle summer wind lifted a cowboy's loneliness and carried it far away across a sea of grass. And, a schoolteacher and a cowboy danced.

ABOUT THE AUTHOR

Phil Mills, Jr. was born and raised on a farm near Auxvasse, Missouri, and worked more than 16 years as a magazine and newspaper editor. His grandfather ranched in the Judith Basin and Chesnut Valley Region of Montana during the days of Charles Russell. It's from those roots that he developed his great love of the American West.

Mills currently lives in Georgia with his wife, Linda. They have two grown daughters and three grandchildren. He is a member of the Western Writers of America, Western History Association, Montana Historical Society, Custer Battlefield Historical & Museum Association, and Western Music Association. Mills was a 2010 Western Writers of America (WWA) Spur Award Finalist for Best Western Audiobook.